CHRONICLES OF V

Forever Stars

TASCHE LAINE

SKYE BLUE PRESS

Cover Design by 100 Covers, 100covers.com

ISBN-13: 978-1-955674-58-4 (hardcover)

ISBN-13: 978-1-955674-59-1 (paperback)

ISBN-13: 978-1-955674-60-7 (ebook)

Library of Congress Control Number: 2025902832

Printed in the United States of America

First Edition 2025

Skye Blue Press

Vancouver, WA

https://skyebluepress.com

CONTENTS

"Grief, I've learned, is really just love. It's all the love you want to give, but cannot. All that unspent love gathers up in the corners of your eyes, the lump in your throat, and in that hollow part of your chest. Grief is just love with no place to go."

— JAMIE ANDERSON

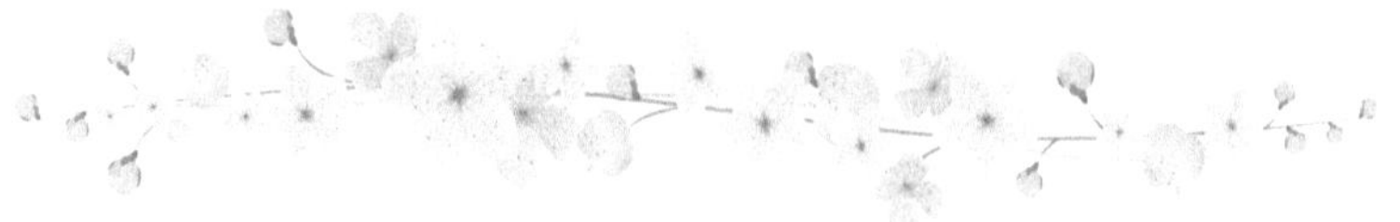

PROLOGUE

*"We understand death only after
it has placed its hands on someone we love."*
–Anne L. de Stael

I sat in the front row of the crowded gymnasium at Sierra High School, the scene transformed into a kaleidoscope of colors. Rows of white plastic folding chairs covered the gym floor, each one occupied. The bleachers were packed, and more people lined the walls—standing room only. Many wore sunglasses, perhaps to hide their tears.

My gaze dropped to my pale yellow sundress—the one my mom and I had selected for sunnier times. Yet here I was, wearing it at a funeral. My first funeral. My mom's funeral. She had insisted on color for her own farewell—a rebel to the end.

My grandmother gave me a memorial program, her hand gently squeezing my knee. I took it without meeting her eyes, my attention caught by the dates, and the dash, printed below my mother's name. That dash—her dash. The small, thin line that represented her time here on this Earth, a mere twenty-one days shy of her birthday. She almost made it to forty-two.

Celebration of Life
Hannah Iris (Kelly) Jiménez
September 4, 1976–August 14, 2018

Lifting my eyes, I blinked three times to try to clear my head and focus on Dr. Fitzgibbon's words. My high school principal was speaking at my mother's funeral. This couldn't possibly be real.

"It is difficult to convey the depth of feeling and loss felt by our Sierra family regarding the passing of Mrs. Hannah Jiménez. During the course of her twenty-year teaching career at Sierra High School, she inspired thousands of students both inside and outside of the classroom. Incredibly smart, Mrs. Jiménez also possessed a magnetic personality and sense of humor that could draw anyone into her world. Mrs. J, as the kids called her, was very popular with students, staff, and parents—that never changed.

"When she was first diagnosed with stage four cancer, she vowed to fight with everything she had, and during her battle she won over an entire legion of people both inside and outside Sierra. Throughout her very public battle with cancer, Hannah Jiménez spread a message of love and hope, for her husband and children, and also for her Sierra family, her UC—Irvine Cancer Center family, and the vast network of people who were inspired by her battle against this terrible disease. Ultimately, Mrs. Hannah Jiménez was much, much more than someone who fought valiantly against cancer."

I shifted uncomfortably as my dad walked to the podium. He shook hands with Dr. Fitzgibbon, then adjusted the microphone for his height. At six-foot-five, and as a History teacher at Sierra, he could command any room. His voice rang out clear and surprisingly strong in his moment of grief.

"As many of you know, Hannah and I met right here twenty years ago, during our first year of teaching," he said, his eyes briefly meeting mine, offering a sad smile. "From the moment I saw that feisty redhead," he continued, prompting a soft ripple of laughter, "I knew she'd be the love of my life. And what an incredible journey we've shared. Hannah spent two decades teaching in this very school. It only felt right to gather here, in the place where we met, fell in love, and pored ourselves into our careers and our students—where we thrived."

A sudden outburst of sobs broke from behind me. I resisted the urge to turn and stare, keeping my focus on my father, who looked both formidable and deeply vulnerable.

He continued, his voice thick with emotion, "I cannot begin to express what your support has meant to the kids and me over these past three years. Your kindness, friendship, and prayers have lifted us through Hannah's courageous battle with illness and her final days. Thank you for joining us to celebrate a life truly well lived and a woman deeply loved. As Hannah often said, we send you all 'mountains of love.'"

He stepped down, making way for Mrs. Nichols, Mom's best friend. As he settled beside me, I couldn't bring myself to look at him, focusing instead on taking slow, deep breaths—for him, for my little brother, Scotty, beside me, and for my grandmother.

Mrs. Nichols took the stage, her voice strong and sure. "Hannah lived fiercely and loved deeply. She leaves behind a legacy that inspires us all. To live courageously, to embrace life with zeal—this is what she taught us. I love you, Hannah. You will live on in my heart forever, and in the hearts of your students, colleagues, friends, and family, as well as the countless lives you touched. You did not go gentle into that good night. No, you fought the bravest fight, and you lived. Rest in peace, my friend. I will always love you. And because I know you wouldn't want it any other way"—her voice broke slightly—"fuck cancer!"

Her last words startled a laugh and cheers from many, especially the students. It was so quintessentially Mom, challenging everyone around her to be the best version of themselves. I had to give her credit, even in death. That was the only time I'd ever heard Mrs. Nichols swear.

As the ceremony continued with music, a montage of photos, and more heartfelt speeches, person after person shared how Mom had touched their lives. Most wore bright colors, contrasting with the few stark blacks of more traditional mourners. Each story added layers to my understanding of the impact my mom had made, not just as a teacher, but as a mentor and a friend. Even after the service, strangers felt compelled to tell me how my mom had impacted their lives. Many of her former students had gone on to become teachers themselves, and they told me how they had been inspired to follow in my mother's footsteps. She had been revered and loved, beyond anything I could have ever known or imagined.

The gym had been packed with over three thousand people that day, yet it felt impossibly small under the weight of her absence and the vibrant legacy she left behind. I missed her more deeply than I thought possible—more than I could imagine one person could miss another. It was an endless abyss of grief and despair.

I

LAST FIRST DAY

"I love you beyond words,
to the stars and infinity—forever."
—Mom (Hannah Jiménez)

It was my last first day—my senior year of high school—and I couldn't be more done with school. It had been two weeks since my mom died. If one more person talked to me about her 'passing on' or said, "She's in a better place," I felt I would implode. As I peered into the darkness of my locker, bracing myself for the day, a soft voice behind me whispered my name. I knew who it was instantly, but I didn't want to talk to her. I didn't want to talk to anyone.

"V?" Emma touched my shoulder.

I sighed heavily as I turned around. "What?"

"Look, I know it doesn't matter what I say. It's not going to be the right thing. But I'm going to talk to you anyway because you're my best friend, and I'm not going to say nothing. So you can try to freeze me out if you want to, but I'm not going anywhere. Got it?"

"Whatever."

"Walk me to class?"

"Okay."

"We have English together again this year. That's pretty cool, right?"

"I guess."

"Hey, I got more than one word out of you. I consider that a personal victory."

I rolled my eyes.

"Did you just smile? Wow, you cracked a smile."

"Nope."

"Not even a little smile?"

"Cut it out, Emma. That might work on my little brother but not me. Let me just be quiet today, okay? Please?"

Emma nodded, and we walked to first period together in silence. When we got to AP English, I let her choose our seats in the second row. I shrugged off my backpack and slid into the seat next to hers, trying to ignore the glances from our classmates.

While Ms. Calloway went over the syllabus, memories pulled me back to the last weeks of Mom's life, when we had set up a hospital bed in our living room. Mom had insisted on discussing her death openly, which none of us wanted at first. But she turned it into a dark game, constantly revising her "death plan."

"Carlos," she'd said to my dad, "you need to have me cremated because I don't want a bunch of worms poking around in my skull and eye sockets. And you have to promise to scatter my ashes in Key West, Florida. That's where Ernest Hemingway found inspiration for many of his novels, you know. It's far more romantic than Ketchum, Idaho, where he died."

Dad had agreed, smiling softly at her whims.

A few days after that, she'd said, "You know how I always say, 'Another year above ground'? Well, the truth is, I don't want to be in the ground—at all. I mean it. Don't put me in a box. Don't visit me at some gravesite where you put flowers at my headstone. That's not me. I'm not there. I won't be there. Promise me, okay? Promise me, Carlos. You have to cremate me and release my ashes outside . . . somewhere in nature. A tropical paradise. But not Florida. Somewhere else. Somewhere we've been together as a family."

THE SHARP SOUND of the bell pierced through my thoughts, snapping me into the present. I blinked, as if I could force the tears back into my body and dry my eyes. I wiped at my face and glanced around. Chairs scraped across the floor as students hurried to leave, no one noticing me. I gathered my books slowly, attempting to shake off the hollow feeling in my chest. Emma was already at the door, chatting with one of her soccer teammates. She glanced at me and waved for me to follow. I trailed behind her, barely registering their voices over the buzzing in my head.

The hallways were a blur—faces, lockers, snippets of conversations swirling around me—but none of it mattered. It felt like walking through a fog, moving but not really there. As the day wore on, each class seemed to meld into the next, the same motions on repeat over and over. Sit, listen (sort of), take notes, stand, leave. I went through the motions like a robot running on autopilot.

At least I had a short schedule. I'd planned it that way. I had maxed out my credits freshman through junior years, which left me with a few Advanced Placement classes this semester. AP English Lit, AP Gov, and AP Statistics. The workload was heavy, but it didn't bother me. In fact, I preferred it that way. The busier I stayed, the less time I had to think.

After Stats, I was a TA for Miss Torres's sophomore English class, my last responsibility of the day. Then my day was over and I could eat lunch at home—alone and quiet. Perfect. The less I had to be around people, the better.

When I walked into Miss Torres's classroom, I was already counting down the minutes till I could leave. Yet, no sooner had I set down my backpack than Miss Torres said, "V, Dr. Sykes wants to see you in her office."

My heart sank. Great. Just what I needed. The counselor's office. And on the first day of school. Couldn't she at least leave me alone on our first day back?

I picked up my backpack and slung it over my shoulder with an audible sigh, resisting the urge to roll my eyes. Miss Torres gave me a sympathetic look, but that only made it worse. I didn't want sympathy. I just wanted to get through the day without anyone looking at me like I might break at any minute.

"Thanks," I muttered, my voice flat.

The walk to the office felt longer than usual. My feet dragged, like the weight of the day had finally caught up to me. Outside Dr. Sykes's door, I hesitated. I wasn't in the mood for one of her "check-ins" or whatever this was. Taking a deep breath, I knocked lightly.

Before I could lower my hand, her voice came through the door. "Come in, V."

Dr. Sykes sat behind her desk, wearing the same kind, slightly-too-knowing expression she always did. Her office was warm—framed quotes on the walls, a big comfy chair in the corner. It looked like the kind of place that wanted you to feel safe, but today it felt like a trap. I closed the door behind me and perched on the edge of the big chair, not allowing myself to relax or sink into it. I needed to maintain control.

"How are you doing today?" she asked, folding her hands on the desk.

I shrugged. "Fine."

She didn't push it. Instead, she reached into a drawer and pulled out a small flyer, sliding it across the desk toward me. I picked it up, my stomach churning when I saw the bold letters at the top:

Waves of Hope: Teen Grief Journey
A grief support group for teens who have lost a parent to cancer.

I stared at the flyer, a lump forming in my throat. My hands were cold, the edges of the paper sharp under my fingertips. I didn't want this. I didn't want to talk about any of it. Not with strangers. Not with anyone.

Dr. Sykes spoke softly. "I think this could be really helpful for you, V."

"Uh . . ." I blinked, my mind racing for an excuse. "I don't know."

She leaned forward, her tone gentle but firm. "V?"

I shook my head, feeling heat rise to my cheeks. "You don't waste any time, do you?" I tried to sound casual, but the sarcasm didn't come out right. It sounded bitter. Too raw.

Dr. Sykes sighed, her gaze never leaving mine. "I know this is hard—"

"No, it's fine," I cut her off, forcing myself to look at the flyer again. My chest tightened, frustration brimming in my eyes. "Really. Thanks. I'll think about it."

"They're meeting after school today," she added, her voice soft but insistent. "Don't think too long, okay?"

"Today?" I blurted. "But—" I paused, incredulous. *Today?*

Was I supposed to drop everything and talk to a bunch of strangers about . . . about her? My hands gripped the edges of the flyer. "Do I have to go?"

"No," Dr. Sykes said, shaking her head. "I can't make you go. But I think it's a good idea."

I couldn't meet her eyes. My heart pounded as anger built up along with something else I couldn't quite name. I didn't want to go. I didn't want to sit in a circle, listening to people talk about their dead parents like it would fix anything. I wanted to be alone. Why couldn't people leave me alone?

"I don't know," I said, folding the flyer into smaller and smaller squares in my lap.

Dr. Sykes didn't push any further. "Just give it some thought, V. You don't have to do this alone."

I stood, tucking the crumpled flyer into my pocket. "Yeah, okay. Thanks."

As I walked out of her office, I let out a long breath, not real-izing until then that I had been holding it in. My backpack felt heavier than usual as I slung it back over my shoulder. The hallway outside was quiet, the faint teacher voices from distant classrooms co-mingling from open doors as I walked past. I reached into my pocket and pulled out the flyer, smoothing it out against my leg. Waves of Hope. I stared at the words until they blurred, a knot tightening in my stomach again.

I didn't want to go. But then, I didn't want to keep feeling this way either. I shoved the flyer back into my pocket, left the school, and walked toward the student parking lot. I couldn't go back to fourth period. I knew Miss Torres would understand. She was cool like that. I didn't need a bunch of curious sopho-mores staring at me.

And I definitely wasn't about to stick around during lunch to tell Emma about Dr. Sykes and her latest *super idea*. I could picture Emma's concerned expression, her head tilted a little to the side as she asked, *"Are you okay?"* Yeah, that conversation wasn't happening. I drove home.

THE HOUSE WAS SILENT—AN eerie, suffocating kind of silence that seemed to creep into the corners, weighing down the air. Even the usual hum of the fridge felt muted, swallowed up by the stillness. Lucky, our scrappy little Yorkie-Pom, greeted me at the door, his wiry tail wagging furiously, a blur of energy in an otherwise frozen world. His soulful eyes locked on mine, full of unspoken questions. I knelt down and scratched behind his ears.

"Hey, buddy," I whispered. Lucky responded with a warm lick on my hand, his breath carrying the faint smell of kibble and dog treats. Somehow, it steadied me, if only for a second.

I wandered into the kitchen, opened the fridge, and stared at its contents as if expecting them to rearrange themselves into something appetizing. Leftovers. A couple of sad apples. An unopened carton of milk. I settled on nachos. Not because I wanted them—just because they were there. Easy. Reliable.

I piled tortilla chips onto a plate, scattering shredded cheese over the top. I watched the cheese melt in the microwave until it bubbled. Good enough. Plate in hand, I made my way to the couch and sank into the cushions. The TV remote was already on the armrest. I flipped it on without looking, and some talk show blared to life, filling the room with cheerful voices that grated against the quiet. They spoke too fast, too loud, about things I couldn't care less about. I let it run anyway, a low buzz to drown out my thoughts.

Lucky hopped up beside me, curling into a tiny ball of fur against my thigh. I ate without tasting, each bite a hollow crunch. The melted cheese had cooled into rubbery clumps. Whatever. It was still food.

When my plate was empty, I slid it onto the coffee table and pulled the flyer out of my pocket. The creases were deep, folding the words into awkward angles, but I smoothed them out enough to read:

"Waves of Hope – Grief Support for Teens.
Meets Tuesdays at 3:30 p.m.
at the Orange Community Center."

Not far. Convenient, I guess.

I stared at the address like it might change into something else. Anything else. But it stayed a support group. Always a support group. I could hear Dad's voice, full of that forced optimism he used whenever he talked about Dr. Sykes. He thought she was some kind of miracle worker, some magical fixer of broken people. But what did I know? Maybe she was.

I folded the flyer back up, my fingers lingering on the edges. Lucky nudged my knee with his nose, as if reminding me that the clock was ticking. Dad didn't have time to deal with me right now—not with Scotty. Not with everything else. He was holding it together, but barely. I didn't need to add to that.

I stood, carried my empty plate to the sink, and rinsed it clean. The water was warm, almost too warm, but I let it run over my hands anyway. It gave me something to focus on. Something real. When I set the plate in the drying rack, I'd made my decision.

I'd go to the stupid group meeting.

2

WAVES OF HOPE

"Her absence is like the sky,
spread over everything."
–C.S. Lewis

Nearly three hours later, I stood outside the community center, squinting against the late afternoon sun. The August heat pressed down on me, the kind that clings to your skin and refuses to let go. Palm trees swayed lazily in the warm breeze, their shadows stretching long across the pavement. I stared at the door like it might spring open and swallow me whole. My hand hovered over the handle, slick with sweat, before I finally forced myself to push it open.

The cool air hit me first, a welcome relief from the ninety-degree furnace outside. The room wasn't what I'd expected—bright, with big windows framing a perfect view of the park, where a couple kids chased each other across the grass and someone jogged beneath the rows of palms. But the chairs? Yep. You guessed it. A circle. Of course.

I was fifteen minutes early, not because I was excited to be there, but because I wanted to avoid walking in late and having everyone turn to stare at me. As I stepped inside, a woman with long black hair pulled into a loose braid approached me, her smile warm but not overbearing. She looked like she belonged there, calm and collected, like she'd seen her fair share of grief and wasn't scared of it.

"You must be Violet," she said, reaching out her hand. "Molly said you might be stopping in today. I'm Kailani, but everyone calls me Kal. I'm the counselor here. Welcome to Waves of Hope."

I hesitated. "Molly?" I asked while awkwardly shaking her hand. Her grip was firm yet gentle.

"We're all on a first-name basis around here. We find it breaks down barriers. I meant your school counselor, Dr. Molly Sykes."

"Oh, right," I said, my voice sounding flat, even to me.

Kal's smile widened. "I'm glad you're here. I know it can be hard to walk into something like this. We're a pretty relaxed group though, and you only have to share what you're comfortable with."

I nodded, not trusting myself to say more. Her calmness made me uncomfortable, like she could see right through the mask I'd been wearing all day. I muttered an excuse about needing to use the restroom and slipped away before she could say anything else. Inside the bathroom, I splashed water on my face and stared at my reflection. My eyes were tired, dark circles lingering underneath. *Do I really want to do this?* I asked myself, but the truth was, I didn't know. It wasn't like I had a better plan.

I scanned the room as I walked to a seat near the door. Posters on the back wall caught my attention.

"When *I* is replaced with *WE*
Even *I*llness becomes *WE*llness.
Together we are stronger!"

"Feelings Are Valid."

"Grief Is Not Linear."

Beneath the posters, a round table held a neatly arranged spread: tea bags, a thermos, a box of tissues, and a plate of store-bought chocolate chip cookies, all laid out on a red-and-white checkered plastic tablecloth. Paper plates and napkins were stacked off to the side, like someone had tried too hard to make it all feel welcoming. I dropped into one of the seven chairs in the circle and pulled out my phone—not because I had anything to do on it, but because it gave my hands something to hold. I glanced at the time. Ten minutes to go before the meeting started. Maybe I could slip out before anyone else arrived.

The door opened, and a girl walked in, her dark curls bouncing as she practically skipped to a seat across from me. She smiled at me. "Hi! I'm Caitlyn. You're new, right?"

"Uh, yeah," I said, looking back to the phone in my hand.

"Caitlyn, nice to see you," Kal said as she took a seat next to her.

Caitlyn beamed.

The door opened again, and a tall guy strolled in, slouching like he'd rather be anywhere else. He didn't look at me, or anyone, as he took a seat.

"Aiden," Kal said with a nod.

He gave a small grunt in response. His hood was pulled low over his face, and he crossed his arms as if daring anyone to talk to him.

The next person to arrive was a girl in an oversized hoodie, her hands shoved into the front pocket. She barely glanced up as she sat two chairs away from me. She immediately pulled a notebook and pen out of her bag, balanced it on her knees, and appeared to be drawing something.

"Hi, Zuri," Kal said.

The girl gave a small nod, her pen never stopping.

A boy came in after her, his shoes squeaking against the linoleum. He was skinny, with a big grin plastered across his face that didn't quite reach his eyes.

"Joon," he said, plopping into the chair next to me. "What's up, everyone? We all grieving today, or what?"

"Joon," Kal said, her tone gentle but firm, "let's save the jokes for later, okay?"

He shrugged, still grinning. "No promises."

The last to arrive was a girl with long, blonde hair that looked like it had been straight-ironed to perfection—not a hair out of place. She sat gracefully, smoothing out the front of her pink floral blouse. Her posture was rigid, her hands folded neatly in her lap.

"Hi, Melody," Kal said.

"Hi," Melody said, her voice cool and polite.

I gripped the edges of my chair, my nachos threatening to come back up as I glanced around at everyone while avoiding eye contact in that awkward, I'm-here-but-let's-pretend-I'm-not way. *This was a bad idea.*

Kal began the meeting. "Aloha, everyone."

"Aloha, Kal," the group murmured back, almost like a ritual.

"Okay," Kal said, "let's start by going around the circle and introducing ourselves. Just your name, who you've lost, and, if you're comfortable, how you're feeling today. Caitlyn, why don't you go first?"

Caitlyn sat up a little straighter. "Sure. Hi, I'm Caitlyn. My dad passed away five months ago—lung cancer. Um, I guess I'm feeling okay today. Better than yesterday, anyway." She smiled at me. "And I'm really glad we have someone new with us."

I nodded but said nothing, unsure how to respond.

Aiden went next. "Aiden," he said flatly. "My mom died a year ago. Brain cancer. Still sucks." He leaned back in his chair, crossing his arms. "I'm feeling annoyed, since you asked."

The room went quiet for a moment, but Kal didn't seem fazed. She gave him a small nod before turning to Zuri.

Zuri glanced up briefly, then looked back down at her notebook. "Zuri," she mumbled. "My dad passed away three months ago. Pancreatic cancer." She shrugged. "I don't know how I feel today."

Her pen scratched softly against the page, and I caught a glimpse of her drawing—what looked like the start of a flower.

"Joon," he said cheerfully when it was his turn. "Dad died six months ago. Colon cancer. Feelings? Hmm. Hungry." He pointed at the cookie table. "Grief snacks are the only thing getting me through, you know?"

Caitlyn rolled her eyes. "Do you have to make jokes about everything?"

"It's called coping," Joon shot back with a smirk.

When it was Melody's turn, she spoke carefully, like she'd rehearsed it. "I'm Melody. I lost my mom seven months ago— ovarian cancer. I'm doing okay, I guess. School keeps me busy."

Finally, it was my turn.

Kal smiled at me gently. "Violet, would you like to share?"

All eyes turned toward me, and for a second, I considered bolting. My heart thudded in my chest, and my hands were sweaty. But then I remembered Dr. Sykes's words, and Dad's tired face, and I forced myself to speak. "My mom. She . . . she died two weeks ago. Breast cancer." I swallowed hard, staring at my knees. "My school counselor made me come. And I prefer to be called V."

"That's really brave of you to share," Kal said, her voice warm. "Thank you, V. We're so sorry for your loss."

The group nodded or murmured their agreement. Even Aiden gave me a slight glance, his expression softer than before.

When the meeting ended, I was the first to stand, ready to leave. But before I could, Zuri appeared at my side, holding out a folded piece of paper.

"For you," she said, her voice barely above a whisper.

I opened it after she walked away. It was a simple drawing of a sunflower, with the words written in small, neat letters.

For the first time all day, my heart didn't ache quite so much. I folded the paper carefully and slid it into my pocket.

3

BACK TO NORMAL?

*"How lucky I am to have something that
makes saying goodbye so hard."*
–A.A. Milne, *Winnie the Pooh*

The house smelled like garlic bread. It hit me the second I walked through the door, warm and familiar, but instead of comforting, it felt off—a cheap imitation of normal. Pretty sure it came from a box in the freezer.

I kicked off my flip-flops, the soles smacking the floor, and dropped my backpack with a heavy thud. From the dining room, I caught the soft hum of Dad's voice, low and patient. When I peeked around the corner, I saw him and Scotty at the table, their heads bent over the open pages of a workbook.

"No, not like that," Dad said, gesturing with the back of his pen. His hand trembled slightly as he pointed at the page. "Here, let me show you—"

"It's four," Scotty groaned, slumping in his chair. "I already know the answer, Dad!"

Dad laughed, leaning back like he was trying to relax, but his shoulders never quite stopped drooping. "Okay, Mr. Smarty Pants. Then why don't you explain it to me?"

Scotty stuck his tongue out, flipping his pencil over to furiously erase whatever he'd written. His blond curls bounced with every exaggerated move, and for half a second, it felt like everything was normal—like Mom might walk in at any moment, holding the mail or talking on her phone.

But she wouldn't.

It had only been two weeks. Grandma and Aunt Jen had practically taken shifts, filling the house with casseroles, cleaning supplies, and tight-lipped reassurances. Aunt Jen had planned to stay longer, but Dad sent her back to North Carolina on Sunday. With school starting this week, he said it'd be easier to adjust to our new normal without a house full of people taking care of us.

I stayed at the edge of the wall, watching them. Dad looked .. . tired. He wasn't the type to wear his feelings on his face, but I could see it anyway: the way his laugh didn't quite reach his eyes, the slump of his shoulders, the dark circles under his eyes that hadn't faded since the funeral.

Scotty, on the other hand, seemed fine. Or maybe nine-year-olds just bounce back faster. He fidgeted constantly, tapping his pencil against the workbook or swinging his legs under the table. He kept moving, like he was trying to outrun the silence that always seemed to settle over us these days.

"Hey, V," Dad said when he finally noticed me standing there. He straightened up, forcing a smile that looked more like an apology. "How was your meeting?"

I shrugged, walking in and sitting across from him. "It was fine."

He waited, hopeful, like he thought I might say more, but I didn't. I wasn't ready to talk about sitting in that circle, listening to strangers spill their hearts out.

"You should've seen your brother earlier," Dad said, shifting the subject. "He figured out a trick to multiply by nines on his fingers. He'll have his times tables memorized in no time."

"Uh-huh," Scotty chimed in proudly. "I can do it faster than Dad!"

"Faster than me, sure," Dad said with a small chuckle. "But the bar's not that high, li'l man."

I forced a smile, though it felt paper-thin. Dad was trying so hard to act normal, like if he kept things light, we'd all just forget. Forget how empty the house felt without Mom in it. Forget the quiet that settled over dinner, or the way her shoes still sat by the front door, untouched. I'd walked past them every day, telling myself I'd move them tomorrow. But I never did.

"It's spaghetti tonight," Dad added, his voice softer. "Scotty's choice. Garlic bread, too."

I nodded, not trusting myself to speak.

"I'm gonna go upstairs," I said finally, pushing my chair back and standing.

"Okay," Dad said, his eyes following me as I turned to leave. "Dinner will be ready in ten minutes."

I could feel him watching me as I walked away, like he wanted to say something else but didn't know how.

ONCE IN MY ROOM, I shut my door and let out a long breath. It felt too quiet, so I put in my earbuds and listened to a random playlist on Spotify. Music usually helped calm me, but right now it didn't do much.

The group meeting had messed with my head. It wasn't just the stories everyone shared about their dead parents or the strange knot of emotions I'd felt listening to them. It was the way they'd looked at me—like they all understood something about me that I didn't even understand about myself.

I curled into myself—a ball on my bed, staring at the wall. Memories of Mom washed over me—her final days with us replaying in my mind.

IT WAS NEARLY MIDNIGHT, and the house was quiet. The only sound was the soft, steady hum of the oxygen machine in the corner. Our living room had been transformed. The couch had been shoved against the far wall to make room for the hospice bed, and the coffee table was pushed back against the fireplace. It looked like a hospital room now, even though Mom had tried to make it cozy. A beautiful patchwork quilt her students had made was draped over her, but it didn't hide how thin she'd gotten.

I sat cross-legged on the floor beside her, leaning back against the coffee table. My body ached from sitting in the same spot for so long. My knees felt stiff, my back sore from the hard wood pressing against it. I shifted, trying to get comfortable, but nothing worked. The hardwood floor was cold beneath me, sending a dull ache through my legs. Even through my pajama bottoms, I could feel the chill sinking into my skin. I wrapped my arms around my knees, curling into myself, but the tension didn't ease. It felt like I'd been sitting there for hours, days— waiting, even though I knew there was nothing to wait for.

Mom's breathing was shallow, each rise and fall of her chest barely visible under the blankets. Her skin was pale. *She needs sunlight, vitamin D*, I thought.

The hospice nurse slipped into the dark room and turned on a lamp. "Good evening, V. I'm here now. All set for the night shift. I even brought a good book to read." She smiled too wide, too cheerful. "You should go on up to bed. Don't worry, sweetie. Your mama's in good hands."

A KNOCK at the door jarred me back into the present. My eyes flew open just as Scotty cracked the door open and peeked in. "V, Dad sent me up here to tell you dinner's ready."

"Okay, thanks," I said, uncurling my body and sitting up. "I'll be right down."

Scotty shrugged and walked away, leaving the door wide open.

4

EMMA'S NEW CAR

*"When you're happy, you enjoy the music.
But, when you're sad, you understand the lyrics."*
–Frank Ocean

At last, it was Friday. The first week of my senior year was almost over, and I felt every single minute of it like it was dragging me down. During English, Emma leaned over and slipped a folded piece of notebook paper onto my desk.

I raised an eyebrow and mouthed, "A note? Seriously?"

She shrugged, a sly smile tugging at the corners of her mouth. "Just read it," she whispered before spinning back around, suddenly very interested in Ms. Calloway's lecture.

I hesitated for a second, then unfolded the note.

Hey, so, I want to be respectful and give you space and all . . . but I haven't seen you all week except in English. Are you, like, actively dodging me or just passively ghosting? Haha. Anyway, let's hang out tonight. You know, just Netflix and junk food and celebrate getting through the week. Please? I miss you. Xoxo! E

The word "miss" hit me hard, but I didn't let it show. I wanted to tell her I missed her, too—that I missed everything the way it was before . . . but the words wouldn't come. Ever since Mom died, I'd shut out everyone who cared about me, even Emma.

I turned the note over and wrote, "Sounds like a plan." Then I drew a smiley face. I handed the note back and watched her read it.

Emma beamed at me, her whole face lighting up in that way only she could manage—like a walking burst of sunshine in our dreary high school classroom. She gave me a quick thumbs-up before turning back to face the front, her lustrous black ponytail bouncing as she scribbled something in her notebook. I knew she'd be planning our junk food lineup already, probably debating between sour gummy worms or her favorite pint of chocolate chip cookie dough ice cream. Or both!

Ms. Calloway's words blurred into the background as my gaze floated to the window. Outside, the sky was pale blue, the kind of morning that made it hard to sit still. My thoughts kept pulling me back to Emma's note, the way she'd written, *'I miss you.'* There was more weight behind those words. I knew she meant it, the same way I knew I'd been avoiding her on purpose. Not because I didn't want to see her, but because being around her felt like holding a mirror to my own grief. She knew me too well— saw straight through me—and I couldn't risk cracking under her gaze.

But tonight? Tonight, I could try. Maybe for a few hours, I could pretend things were okay again.

The bell rang. Books shuffled. The usual hum of students rushing for the door filled the room. I stuffed my notebook into my bag and slung it over my shoulder, trying not to linger.

"Hey, V," Emma said, catching me before I could escape.

I turned back, finding her already by my side. She grinned, holding her bag loosely at her hip. "You better not bail on me tonight. I already told my mom you're coming over, and she's going to order pizza."

I smirked despite myself. "Wouldn't dream of bailing. Pizza and junk food? Sold."

"Good." She nudged my arm lightly as we stepped out into the hallway, the noise of lockers slamming and voices shouting over each other making the air feel heavier. "And if you don't show, I'm coming to your house. Pajamas, ice cream, and all."

I almost laughed at that, the image of Emma standing on my porch in her flannel PJs flashing through my mind. "Noted."

Her grin softened, and she looked at me like she wanted to say more, but the crowd carried us in opposite directions. "See you tonight, V!" she called over her shoulder, disappearing into the flow of students.

"See you tonight," I murmured under my breath, though she was already gone.

For the first time all week, the weight on my chest lifted a little. Maybe tonight wouldn't fix everything, but it might be a start.

✦ ✦ ✦ ✦ ✦

It was a perfect late-summer afternoon, where the heat had mellowed enough to make being outside pleasant. The sunlight cast a golden glow over Emma's neighborhood, the kind that made everything look softer and more alive. I pulled into her driveway, parking next to a silver car I didn't recognize. *Whose car is that?* I wondered, just as Emma came bursting through the front door.

"Isn't it gorgeous? What do you think?" she called out, practically bouncing down the steps.

"What do I think of what?" I asked, getting out of my car, completely confused.

Emma didn't answer—she just darted over to the silver RAV4, throwing her arms out like she was showing off a prize.

"My new car!" she squealed, her voice going up an octave as she beamed at me.

I froze, my jaw dropping. "Emma," I said slowly, my voice rising. "Wait—this is seriously yours?"

She stood up straighter, her grin somehow getting even bigger. "Yup!" she said, bouncing on her toes. "Can you believe it? Mom and I picked it up after school today!"

I walked closer, eyeing the car. Up close, it looked even shinier, the kind of clean that screamed fresh off the lot—even if it wasn't. "It's gorgeous," I said, lightly running my hand over the hood. "But how the heck did you pull this off?"

Emma shrugged, still grinning like she couldn't believe it herself. "Well, it's not brand new—it's a 2015—but it's in amazing condition. Mom, Abuela, and I pooled our savings together to get it. It's, like, the first big thing I've ever owned."

I could hear the pride in her voice, mixed with a hint of disbelief, like she wasn't sure it was real yet.

"That's huge," I said sincerely, looking over at her. "I'm so happy for you, Emma. This car suits you."

Her face lit up even more, and she stepped aside, gesturing

toward the car like a game show host showing off a prize. "Wanna see the inside?"

"Absolutely," I said, already reaching for the passenger-side door.

We climbed in, and the faint smell of new leather hit me, even though the car wasn't brand new. The dashboard was spotless, the seats smooth, and a little sunflower air freshener dangled from the rearview mirror, spinning lazily in the breeze.

"Okay, tell me you didn't add that," I said, pointing to it.

Emma grinned and rolled her eyes. "Obviously. Gotta put my touch on it, right?"

I laughed, running my hands over the smooth seat. "This is seriously amazing. It feels . . . I don't know, like a big deal."

"It *is* a big deal," Emma said, sliding the key into the ignition. The engine purred softly to life, and she gave me a quick, triumphant look. "I told my mom it's perfect for senior year."

We sat there for a moment, the car idling quietly, as sunlight filtered through the windshield. The air felt easy, warm. One of those rare moments where everything clicked, and nothing else mattered but right here, right now.

"So," Emma said, turning to me with a mischievous glint in her eye. "Wanna go for a ride?"

"Of course!" I buckled up and sat back, happy for my best friend.

THE LOW HUM of the engine filled the silence as Emma's car glided along the neighborhood streets. She had the windows cracked just enough to let in the warm late-summer air, and Taylor Swift's voice played softly through the speakers. After a few minutes, Emma reached over and fiddled with the stereo, turning the volume down.

"You've barely talked to me all week," she said, breaking the quiet. Her hands stayed steady on the wheel, but her voice had that familiar edge, like she was trying to sound casual but wasn't. "You never told me how the grief group went."

"It's not a grief group," I muttered, crossing my arms. "It's a 'support group.'"

"Okay, fine," she said, glancing over at me with a knowing look. "Support group. How was it?"

I stared out the window, watching the golden sunlight filter through the trees. How was I supposed to explain sitting in that circle of strangers? The way my throat had closed up when someone mentioned their mom, or how it felt even harder to talk about mine?

"It was . . . fine," I said finally, the words stiff and unconvincing.

Emma sighed, glancing at me quickly before returning her focus to the road. "I get it, you know. If you don't want to talk about it, I mean. But I'm here when you're ready."

Her voice was steady, calm. Emma never pushed too hard—she'd just wait, patient and loyal, like she always did. That somehow made my throat tighten even more.

I nodded, swallowing hard. "Thanks."

For a while, we didn't say anything, the car filling with quiet music and the soft whoosh of the wind. It wasn't awkward, though—it felt easier now, like I could finally breathe.

"So," I said, glancing at her with a wry grin. "How's your summer crush doing, now that he's a big college man? He's at MIT, right? Impressive."

Emma's cheeks turned pink. "Miles? He's good."

I snorted. "That's all I get? Who knew all that flirting I had you do with your soccer team's stat keeper last year would land you a boyfriend! This is the thanks I get for playing Cupid? Spill."

"Whatever." She grinned, shaking her head. "He's so sweet. Did you know he wrote me a poem after our first kiss?"

I blinked. "No way. Can I see it?"

Emma hesitated. "Well . . ."

"Oh, come on, Emma. Please?"

"Um, I have it saved in my phone . . . but I'm driving, so—"

"No prob. Unless you changed it, I still know your password." I swiped her phone from the center console.

"V, seriously?" she huffed, reaching for it with one hand before thinking better of it. "You're the worst."

"Yeah, yeah. Just tell me where to find it."

With an eye-roll, she did. A few taps later, I had it:

> *Your Kiss*
> *Our lips meet—*
> *warm, soft, unhurried.*
> *Lingering.*
> *My pulse jumps.*
> *Your lips part,*
> *our tongues brush—*
> *I need more.*
> *Your mouth moves against mine,*
> *slow, searching—*
> *sending a charge through me.*
> *Soft. Sweet.*
> *But also something deeper,*
> *like a spark catching fire.*
> *It's electric,*
> *pulling me in,*
> *a promise of something I can't even name—*
> *but I want it.*

Didn't see it coming.
Didn't know a kiss
could steal my breath like this.
Wow.

I stared at the screen. "Wow, Emma. You're dating a poet! This is amazing."

Her smile lit up her face. "Yeah, he is pretty amazing."

I hesitated, setting her phone back down. "So . . . how's it been? With him being so far away?"

The question hung there for a second. Emma's smile faltered slightly, and her fingers tightened on the wheel. "It's fine," she said quickly. "We text all the time, and he calls when he can. I mean, it's only been two weeks, but so far, so good."

I nodded, but something in her voice made me pause. She was saying all the right things, but I wondered.

"You know," I said carefully, "long distance is . . . hard. Like, really hard."

Emma glanced at me, frowning. "You think I don't know that?"

"I'm not saying you don't," I said, holding up my hands. "I'm just saying, it's easy at first, when you're both making the effort. But after a while—"

Her frown deepened, and I could see her jaw tighten. "After a while, what? You think he's going to forget about me?"

"No," I said quickly. "I just mean . . . it's complicated. When you're not in the same place anymore, it's easy to feel disconnected. Like you're on totally different planets."

Emma didn't respond right away. She stared straight ahead, her expression unreadable.

I exhaled. "I'm not trying to be a jerk," I added softly. "I just don't want you to get hurt."

Emma let out a slow breath, shaking her head. "You sound

like my mom," she said. But her voice wasn't angry—it was quieter, like she was still figuring out what to say next.

"Maybe your mom's right." I shrugged. "This isn't like last year, when you saw him all the time at your soccer games. He's living in this whole other world now. He's meeting new people, doing new things . . ."

Her grip on the wheel tightened, and I winced, realizing I'd said too much.

"Sorry," I said quickly. "I just don't want you to be the only one trying."

The words hung in the air, awkward. Emma's gaze flicked to me, and her expression softened—a little.

"You're being a total downer right now," she said after a long pause.

"Sorry. I just—"

"I know." Her voice was quieter now. "I know you're just looking out for me. And I appreciate it. I do. But I want to try. I want to believe it can work."

I sighed, looking out the window. "I just don't want you to get hurt."

Emma smiled faintly, her shoulders relaxing as she reached for the volume knob. "I know. But maybe it'll be okay. Maybe we'll be okay."

"Maybe," I said softly.

She glanced at me with a teasing grin. "You sound like an old lady, you know. So what's next? You gonna tell me to adopt a dozen cats and call it a day?"

I laughed, leaning back in my seat. "Don't knock it. My cats would have their own Instagram."

"Oh, obviously." Emma laughed with me. "It'd go viral in, like, a week."

For the first time in what felt like forever, the laughter between us felt easy.

EMMA PARKED her car in the driveway, cutting the engine as the last streaks of sunset faded into a warm purple glow. "Okay, seriously," I said, stretching my legs as I got out. "You're already driving like you've had this car for years."

Emma smirked, twirling the keys on her finger. "What can I say? I was born to drive a RAV4."

The smell of pizza hit me the second Emma opened the door, warm and garlicky. "Finally," I said, heading for the kitchen.

"Mom! We're back!" Emma called as she dropped her keys on the table by the door.

"In here," Rosa called. She was at the counter, wiping her hands on a dish towel as she smiled at us. "I left the pizza out for you girls. There's 7UP on the counter."

"Thanks, Rosa," I said, grabbing a plate and immediately helping myself to a slice.

"Seriously, Mom, you're the best," Emma added, grabbing her own slice. "And not just because of the pizza."

Rosa rolled her eyes, clearly amused. "All right, girls. Just make sure you clean up after yourselves, okay? I've got an early meeting tomorrow."

"How early?" Emma asked, already halfway through her slice.

"Six-thirty." Rosa made a face. "Manager stuff." She leaned down to kiss Emma on the top of her head, then gave me a quick pat on the shoulder. "Good night, girls. Don't stay up all night, and keep the noise down. Abuela's already in bed."

"Sure thing!" Emma called after her mom as she disappeared down the hall.

We carried the pizza box, our plates, and two glasses of 7UP into the living room. Emma flopped onto the couch, grabbing the remote. "Okay," she said, scrolling through Netflix. "What are we watching?"

"Something good," I said, plopping down beside her and tucking my legs under me.

Emma snorted. "Your idea of good is, like, rewatching episodes of *Veronica Mars* for the tenth time."

"First of all, it's a classic," I said, pointing at her. "Second of all, what are you suggesting? A Taylor Swift documentary?"

Her jaw dropped. "Don't you dare slander *Miss Americana* in this house."

I rolled my eyes as she kept scrolling. After a few minutes, we finally landed on a murder mystery comedy that seemed cheesy enough to be fun.

As the movie started, we dug into the pizza, the room filling with the sounds of dramatic music and over-the-top dialogue.

"Okay, but tell me you wouldn't make an amazing detective," Emma said, pointing at the screen with a greasy finger.

I smirked. "What, solving suburban crimes? Sure. I'd totally crack the case of the missing pizza slice."

Emma laughed, throwing a napkin at me. "Whatever. You'd still rock the leather jacket."

"Obviously," I said, pretending to flip an imaginary collar.

By the time the movie ended, we were sprawled out on the couch, the pizza box nearly empty and our drinks long gone. Emma groaned, flipping onto her stomach and letting her arm dangle off the side.

"That was so dumb," she said into the pillow.

"Yeah, but the good kind of dumb," I said, stretching my legs out and yawning.

Emma rolled over to look at me, her hair a complete mess. "I'm glad you came over," she said softly.

I smiled. "Me, too."

For the first time in weeks, things felt easy—like maybe the weight I'd been carrying wasn't so heavy anymore.

Emma sat up suddenly, grabbing the remote. "Okay, round two. My pick this time."

"Not happening," I said, grabbing a pillow and whacking her with it. "We're watching something that's *actually* good."

Emma laughed, dodging the next swing. "Like what, *Kiss Kiss Bang Bang*? You and your noir detective shows."

"I'll take that over your rom-com nonsense any day," I said, laughing as she tackled me with the pillow.

The rest of the night passed in a blur of bad movies, jokes, and the kind of comfort that only comes from spending time with your best friend.

5

THE FIRST WITHOUT HER

*"There are no goodbyes for us.
Wherever you are, you will always be in my heart."*
–Gah

I got home around noon on Saturday, groggy from staying up way too late at Emma's. We'd watched bad movies, eaten too much pizza, and laughed until our stomachs hurt—the kind of night that almost made me forget what weekend it was.

Labor Day.

Mom's birthday was Tuesday.

The first of many holidays without her.

Dad had decided we should spend the day at Mom's favorite beach—a way to be together, to honor her, to pretend, just for a little while, that we weren't completely falling apart. Even Lucky got to come, his little paws kicking up sand as he ran circles around us.

But none of us were really here for the sun or the waves.

Dad had brought a letter.

Mom had written it before she died, leaving him with specific instructions to read it out loud to us on the first holiday after she was gone. Since her birthday fell on a school day, today was the day.

We set up our towels, unpacked the cooler, tried to make it feel like a normal beach day. But there was this . . . weight, pressing down on all of us. Like the tide had pulled back a little too far, leaving the air thick and heavy, like something was about to crash down.

Dad reached into his pocket and pulled out the letter. His hands shook slightly as he unfolded the paper, smoothing it over his knee. Then he cleared his throat and began to read.

My Darling Family,

I know this is hard for you—celebrating your first holiday without me. But don't be sad, because I am with you, always. I'm in your hearts, I'm watching over you, I'm in the sunshine, I'm in the breeze, I'm in the roses, I'm in your morning coffee, I'm in your favorite things.

I am everywhere and all around you, all at once, because there is no box that can hold my love. There is no coffin, no container, no walls that can keep me in. I am free.

And I want to be free to love you, to be with you for all eternity.

So scatter my ashes somewhere beautiful.

Somewhere peaceful. A place you love, a place that brings you joy—go there together as a family.

That is my dying wish.

Husband of mine, you need to take the kids somewhere nice. You need to go on a vacation. A tropical paradise. A beautiful beach. You know the one. Aloha!

I love you to the stars and infinity—forever.

Give each other extra hugs and kisses for me.

Love, Mom/Hannah

The wind picked up as Dad finished reading, lifting the edges of the letter, making it flutter like it wanted to escape. Like it didn't belong in this moment, like it belonged somewhere lighter.

Scotty sniffled, his shoulders shaking. Then he let out a small, choked sob. "How can she be in all those places, but I can't see her?" His voice wobbled, thick with tears. "I want to see her. I miss Mommy."

I looked down, kicking at the sand, my throat burning. How was I supposed to comfort him when I felt the exact same way?

I wanted to scream. I wanted to cry. I wanted to see my mom, too.

But I stood there, clenching my fists, my fingernails digging into my palms.

Dad wasn't much better. His eyes were red, his grip on the letter too tight, like if he let go, he'd lose another piece of her.

This wasn't comforting.

It wasn't healing.

It made everything feel more real. *Too real.*

She was gone. She was really, truly, *completely* gone.

And where did we go from here?

Because right now, we were all just lost.

WE DIDN'T STAY at the beach much longer. After Dad read the letter, it felt like there wasn't anything left to say. We packed up in silence, the waves crashing behind us, the weight of Mom's words settling over us like the sand that clung to our feet—everywhere, impossible to shake.

The car ride home was quiet, except for the occasional sniffle from Scotty in the back seat. Lucky curled up beside him, resting his head on Scotty's leg like he knew something was wrong.

I stared out the window, watching the coastline blur past and thinking about Mom's letter. *You know the one,* she'd written, like Dad would instantly have an answer. But did he? Did any of us? Because right now, we weren't the kind of family that planned vacations. We were the kind that barely made it through the day.

Halfway home, Dad pulled into the drive-thru at our usual ice cream place. "Chocolate swirl, Scotty?" he asked, his voice forced-light.

Scotty nodded, rubbing his eyes with his palms.

Dad glanced at me. "Sundae with hot fudge?"

I shrugged. "Sure."

It was such a *Dad* thing to do, trying to make things feel normal when they weren't. Ice cream couldn't fix today. It couldn't make Mom's absence less real. But I ate it anyway, letting the cold numb my tongue.

When we got home, I went straight to my room, kicking off my flip-flops and collapsing onto my bed. My phone buzzed.

EMMA

Hey. Just checking in.

I stared at the screen, debating. Emma wouldn't push, but I knew if I didn't answer, she'd keep waiting.

Hey. I'm okay. Just tired.

A few seconds later, another buzz.

Yeah, today was probably a lot. Wanna come over? We can just chill. No talking if you don't want.

I hesitated, fingers hovering over the keyboard. I should stay home. Spend time with Scotty. Be a good daughter. A good sister.

But the truth was, I didn't want to be in this house right now, where Mom's absence pressed in from every corner.

Be there in 10.

I grabbed my bag and headed downstairs. Dad was at the kitchen table, staring at Mom's letter, his elbows resting on the wood, his hands in his hair. He didn't even notice me at first.

"I'm going to Emma's for a bit," I said.

He looked up, blinking like he was pulling himself out of a fog. "Oh. Okay. Text me when you get there."

I nodded, hesitating. I wanted to say something, maybe, *"Are you okay?"* but the answer felt too obvious.

Instead, I said, "See you later," and walked out the door.

BY THE TIME I got home, the house was dark except for the dim glow from the kitchen. The air inside felt still, heavy, like it had been holding its breath since I left.

I set my bag down by the door and walked toward the light, already knowing who I'd find.

Dad was at the table, the letter spread out in front of him. He wasn't reading it, though—just staring at it, his fingers loosely gripping a half-empty cup of coffee.

"You're gonna be up all night if you keep drinking that," I said, my voice quiet.

Dad glanced up, surprised, like he hadn't heard me come in. "Probably," he admitted, but he took another sip anyway.

I hesitated, then pulled out a chair and sat across from him. The letter sat between us, the paper slightly crinkled at the edges.

"She really thought of everything, huh?" I said, tucking my hair behind my ears.

Dad exhaled a small laugh. "She always did." He rubbed a hand over his face, looking exhausted. "I keep thinking about what she said. About taking you and Scotty somewhere. Scattering her ashes." He shook his head. "I don't even know where to start."

I swallowed, my throat tight. *You know the one,* Mom had written. But did he? Did any of us?

After a moment, I said, "Do you think she meant Hawaii?"

Dad huffed out a breath, something between a laugh and a sigh. "Yeah, I guess so. She always wanted to go back there."

I nodded. "I guess it's kinda nice, that she wanted it to be somewhere we'd enjoy."

Dad looked at me then, really looked at me, like he was checking to see if I was okay. I wasn't. Not really. But I was here. And maybe that was enough for now.

"She would've loved today," he said finally. "The beach, all of us together . . . Lucky stealing Scotty's sandwich."

I let out a small laugh at that, picturing Scotty's dramatic outrage as Lucky had made off with half his PB&J. It was a brief moment of normal in a day that felt anything but.

Dad leaned back in his chair, rubbing a hand over his jaw. "I know today was hard. And I know the letter didn't make it easier."

I glanced at him, surprised he'd said it out loud.

He sighed. "I just—I don't know. I thought maybe it would help. Maybe hearing her words would . . . I don't know. Make us feel like she was still here, somehow."

I looked down at the letter, the familiar curve of Mom's handwriting. "I think it did," I said quietly. "And it didn't."

Dad nodded, like he understood exactly what I meant.

We sat there for a while, the silence stretching between us, not uncomfortable but not easy either. Just *there.*

After a moment, he reached for the letter, folding it carefully before tucking it back into its envelope. "You should get some sleep," he said. "Long weekend ahead."

"Yeah," I said, pushing back my chair. But before I left, I hesitated.

"Night, Dad."

He gave me a small, tired smile. "Night, kiddo."

I went upstairs, closing the door behind me. And for the first time since Mom died, I felt a little less lost.

THE NEXT MORNING, I woke up to the smell of pancakes. For half a second, still groggy with sleep, I thought Mom was in the kitchen, flipping them like she always did on weekends, humming along to whatever song was stuck in her head.

But then I opened my eyes. And remembered.

The house was too quiet. Mom wasn't humming.

I pulled on sweats and padded downstairs, my feet cold against the hardwood. In the kitchen, Dad stood at the stove, spatula in hand, a plate stacked with pancakes next to him. Scotty sat at the table, swinging his legs under his chair as he drowned his plate in syrup.

"Hey, you're up," Dad said, flipping another pancake. "Hungry?"

I shrugged, pulling out a chair. "Yeah. Sure."

Dad slid a pancake onto my plate, and I stared at it for a second before picking up my fork. It looked right—golden-brown, fluffy—but it wasn't quite the same. Mom had always made pancakes from scratch, adding cinnamon or vanilla to the batter, making us guess the secret ingredient. Dad had gone for the boxed mix.

It was fine. It was still breakfast. But it wasn't hers.

"So," Dad said after a moment, sitting down with his own plate. "What's the plan for today?"

Scotty perked up. "Can we go to the park? Lucky needs to run!"

Dad nodded. "Sounds like a plan." Then he glanced at me. "V?"

I poked at my pancake with my fork. "Yeah, sure."

We spent the late morning at the park, watching Lucky go absolutely feral. Scotty laughed as Lucky zoomed in circles, his little legs kicking up dirt, his tongue flopping out of his mouth like he was having the time of his life.

It was . . . nice. Almost normal.

When we got back, I crashed on the couch while Scotty flipped on the TV. He scrolled for a bit before settling on an old cartoon we used to watch together on Saturday mornings. I used to love watching cartoons, back when Mom would tease us about watching the same episodes over and over.

Now, it felt different. Quieter. Not as festive.

I must've dozed off at some point because the next thing I knew, Dad stood over me, my phone in his hand. "Grandma Gwen's on the phone," he said, offering it to me.

I hesitated before taking the phone. "Hey, Grandma."

"Hi, sweetheart," she said, her voice warm but careful, like she wasn't sure how much I could handle. "How are you doing?"

I swallowed. "I'm . . . okay."

A pause. Then, softer, "I know this weekend must be really hard."

I nodded, even though she couldn't see me. "Yeah."

She sighed. "I've been thinking about you, your dad, and Scotty a lot. I know the next couple days are going to be tough. If you ever want to talk—about anything, not just about her—I'm here, okay?"

My throat tightened. "Thanks."

"I mean it," she said gently. "And, V?"

"Yeah?"

"Your mom would be so proud of you."

I bit down on the inside of my cheek, staring at the TV screen, not really seeing it. "Thanks, Grandma."

We hung up not long after, and I sat there, gripping my phone.

She meant well. She really did. But I didn't feel like someone

Mom would be proud of. I felt like someone who was barely keeping it together.

MONDAY FOLLOWED SUNDAY, and it was more of the same. The Labor Day holiday meant no school, but it didn't feel like a break. It just felt like waiting.

I spent most of the day in my room, scrolling through my phone, reading texts over and over without answering. Emma had checked in a few times. So had Aunt Jen. Even Miles—Emma's long-distance boyfriend—had sent a "tell V I'm thinking of her" message.

I didn't know what to say, didn't want to talk, to feel . . . I just wanted to escape.

So I went for a walk.

I drove to a hiking trail nearby and started moving, aimlessly following the winding dirt path. The late afternoon sun filtered through the trees, dappling the ground with golden light, but I barely noticed. My feet crunched over dry leaves and packed earth. My mind buzzed, loud and restless, but I wasn't ready to face it.

I needed to *be* somewhere else.

Footsteps sounded behind me. I ignored them, hoping whoever it was would pass, but instead, a guy—maybe a few years older than me—fell into step beside me.

"Nice day for a hike," he said.

I glanced at him. Messy hair, faded T-shirt, scuffed-up hiking boots. He didn't look like a creep, but I wasn't in the mood for small talk.

I shrugged. "I guess."

"Do you come here a lot?"

"No."

"Cool spot, though. Good place to clear your head."

I stayed silent, hoping he'd get the hint. He didn't.

"What's your thing?" he asked.

"My *what*?"

"Your thing. Everyone's got one."

I shook my head. "Not me."

"Come on, everybody has something."

I sighed. "Nope."

"You play sports?"

"No."

"What are you into?"

"Nothing."

His eyebrows lifted, but he kept his tone light. "What do you do for fun?"

"Nothing."

That made him pause. Then, casually, he said, "What's wrong with you?"

I stopped walking. Turned to him, fists clenched. "My mom died. Cancer."

His expression didn't change. "So?"

Anger flared, hot and instant. My chest tightened, and my hands shook. "What's *wrong* with you?" I snapped. "Do you have *any* compassion? I just lost the only person who ever truly loved me. The only one who really *saw* me. I'll never hear her laugh again, never feel her hugs, never listen to her corny jokes—" My throat closed up. I swallowed hard.

He looked at me. Then he said, quietly, "I know."

Something in his voice stopped me. I frowned. "What's *that* supposed to mean?"

"You think you're the only one who's lost someone?" He gestured at the trail, at the mountains in the distance. "Look around. Everyone walking this path, everyone out in the world, has lost *something*. You're not alone in that."

I clenched my jaw. "That doesn't make it hurt any less."

"No, it doesn't." His voice was calm, steady. "But it does mean you have a choice. You're still here. You woke up today. You put on your shoes, got in your car, and started walking. You might not realize it, but that's something."

I exhaled sharply. "So what? You think if I just go through the motions, one day it won't hurt anymore?"

He shook his head. "No. The pain never really goes away. But you *can't* let it win."

I looked away, focusing on a dry weed poking up through the dirt. I kicked it with the toe of my shoe.

"You're not the only one grieving," he said.

"How would you know?"

"Is your dad around? Do you have any siblings? Extended family?"

I nodded.

"They lost her, too." He paused and let that sink in. Then, in a gentle voice he asked, "If your mom were here right now, what would she say to you?"

I squeezed my eyes shut, but it didn't stop the tears from coming. I wiped them away angrily, my breath shaky.

"She'd say . . ." My voice cracked, barely a whisper. "She'd say, 'Enjoy the sunshine. Dance. Celebrate. Be happy that you're still here. Another day above ground is another day to *live*. Don't take it for granted. Love. Laugh. Do all the things.'"

The words felt like they were tearing out of me. Like I was saying them for the first time. Like maybe, just maybe, I was ready to hear them.

The guy nodded. "Then do that. If you can't do it for yourself, do it for her."

I let out a shaky breath. "It's not that easy."

He half smiled. "Ah, but it is."

I frowned. "What do you know about it?"

He hesitated, then looked out at the trees. When he spoke, his voice was quieter.

"I lost my family," he said.

I blinked. "*What?*"

"My mom. My dad. My two sisters. Car accident. A drunk driver ran a red light." He let out a slow breath. "I was supposed to be in the car that day. But at the last minute, I got called into work."

A cold weight settled in my stomach. I barely managed to whisper, "I'm so sorry."

He nodded once. "It's okay."

"No, it's not. That's terrible."

"Yeah, that's not even the kicker. Here's the irony. My sister had leukemia. They were driving her to the hospital for surgery."

I sucked in a breath. "Oh."

"Yeah," he said, looking out at the horizon. "That one always surprises people." He kicked at a loose rock on the trail. "So yeah . . . you could say cancer killed my family."

After that, we walked two miles in silence, the wind rustling through the trees. I drove home feeling a little less alone.

Tomorrow would be my mom's forty-second birthday. She didn't get to say, "Another year above ground," this time. She won't get to see me graduate from high school, or college, or fall in love, take me wedding dress shopping, start a family . . . all the milestones in life. But I should still do those things. Because I know she would want me to.

I didn't know how I was supposed to get through tomorrow, let alone the rest of my life. Was I supposed to celebrate? Pretend it was just another day? There was no right way to do this. Every option felt wrong.

With a sigh, I rolled over and reached for my nightstand drawer. I hadn't looked at it in a while, but I knew exactly where it was. I pulled out the photo.

It was from two years ago, at the same beach we'd gone to on Saturday. Mom and I stood side by side, feet in the water, arms around each other. She was laughing—really laughing, the kind where her eyes crinkled and her whole face lit up. I looked happy, too, but when I stared at it now, all I could see was before.

I traced the edges of the photo with my thumb, swallowing hard.

Happy birthday, Mom. I love you to the stars and infinity—forever.

I set the photo on my nightstand and turned off the light. Tomorrow was coming whether I was ready or not.

6

THE BIRTHDAY THAT WASN'T

"The reality is that you will grieve forever.
You will not 'get over' the loss of a loved one;
you will learn to live with it."
–Elisabeth Kübler-Ross

6:45 a.m. The worst part was waking up and knowing exactly what day it was.

Mom's birthday.

For a second, before I opened my eyes, I almost expected to hear her voice from the kitchen, singing, "Happy birthday to me," off-key while making herself an ultra-sweet coffee—extra caramel, extra whipped cream, extra *everything.*

But no such luck. The house was quiet.

I rolled onto my side as the glow of the phone on my nightstand caught my eye. A couple unread texts.

EMMA

Thinking about you today. Love you, V.

GRANDMA

Good morning, sweetheart. If you need
anything, I'm here.

I set the phone back down and pulled the covers up, cocooning myself and wanting to just sleep through the day. But I forced myself to get up, get dressed, and go through the motions anyway, knowing the obligation I had to Dad and Scotty. Somehow, everything felt heavier today—like my limbs were weighed down by something invisible, like even breathing took more effort than usual.

By the time I made it to the kitchen, Scotty was already at the table, half asleep over a bowl of Cheerios. Lucky curled up at his feet, his soft snoring filling the silence.

Dad was at the counter, filling his coffee tumbler. His usual morning routine before heading to work—except today, he looked exhausted. Like he hadn't slept much.

"Morning," I mumbled.

Dad glanced up, giving me a small, tired smile. "Morning, V." He hesitated, then said, "You sleep okay?"

I shrugged. "Yeah," I lied.

Scotty didn't say anything, just kept pushing his cereal around with his spoon.

Dad sighed, taking a long sip of coffee before glancing at his watch. "We should probably head out soon."

Neither of us moved right away.

Normally, Mom would have come into the kitchen on her birthday, stretching with a big grin and announcing, "Another year above ground!" like it was some kind of miracle.

Today, she wasn't here to say it.

Scotty suddenly looked up, his face scrunched in frustration. "It's not fair," he said. "She's supposed to be here. She's supposed to say it."

Dad set down his coffee. His face softened. "I know, buddy."

Scotty's lower lip wobbled, and before I could think of something to say—*anything*—Dad knelt down beside him, resting a hand on his back.

"Maybe we say it for her," Dad said gently.

Scotty blinked fast, like he was trying not to cry. Then, barely above a whisper, he said, "Another year above ground."

It was shaky. It wasn't the same. But it was something.

I swallowed the lump in my throat. "Another year above ground," I echoed.

Dad nodded, his voice thick as he repeated it, too.

For a few seconds, we sat with it. The quiet. The missing space where Mom was supposed to be.

Then Dad patted Scotty's back. "Come on, let's get moving. V, I'll see you at school."

I nodded, grabbed my backpack, and followed them out the door.

BEING at school was the worst.

Nobody knew what today was—why would they? It was just another Tuesday to them. But for me, every second felt like a countdown.

I kept my head down through my morning classes, going through the motions, barely registering anything my teachers said. I turned in a half-finished math worksheet. Didn't even pretend to take notes in Government.

At lunch, I left. Grateful for half days and senior privilege.

Dad saw me in the hall as I was heading out, and I thought for a second he might stop me—ask if I was okay. Instead, he just gave me a small nod, like he understood, and let me go.

I drove home with the music off. Noise felt like too much. Silence felt even worse. Nothing felt right. I just wanted the ache in my chest to stop, even for a little while.

As soon as I walked through the door, I collapsed onto the couch, pulling Lucky into my arms. He curled up against me without hesitation, his small, steady breaths grounding me. I buried my face in the pillow, and before I could stop myself, the tears came. Silent at first, then shaking, then everything all at once.

At some point, exhaustion won. I cried myself to sleep.

When I woke up a couple of hours later, my head was heavy, my eyes puffy. I dragged myself to the bathroom, splashed cold water on my face, brushed my hair until it didn't look like a disaster, and left for support group.

7

NO FAIRY TALES HERE

"It is perfectly okay to admit you're not okay."
–Anonymous

Once I got to group, I hung back and tried not to think too hard about why I was here.

Joon asked if I'd seen the latest episode of *Stranger Things*, Caitlyn complimented my tank top, and Melody ranted about her physics test. Normal things. Easy things.

But then Kal, our group leader, called the meeting to order, and suddenly, it wasn't easy anymore.

It was my turn to share.

I inhaled slowly, steadying myself before speaking. "We haven't spread Mom's ashes yet."

Just saying it out loud made my throat tighten, but I pushed through. "She had stage four breast cancer. She was sick off and on for three years. When they diagnosed her, the doctors gave her a year." I twisted a strand of hair around my finger. "She made it to three years. Everyone kept saying she was 'lucky,' that she 'cheated death' and got extra time."

I let out a breath, shaking my head. "But that's not true. She didn't cheat anything. She was the one who got cheated. She didn't even make it to her birthday. Which is today." I swallowed hard. "And . . . she's in an urn in my living room."

The group murmured their condolences, but I barely heard them. The air felt thick, heavy with the weight of words I'd been holding in.

Then Joon spoke up, his tone lighter but edged with something darker. "Have you ever noticed how many main characters in Disney movies are motherless?"

A few people turned to him, surprised by the sudden shift.

"Bambi's mom? Gone. Peter Pan, Mowgli—orphans. Snow White, Ariel, Belle, Jasmine, Pocahontas, even Nemo. All without moms."

Caitlyn chimed in. "You forgot Cinderella! Oh, and Anna and Elsa, too. Their parents were shipwrecked."

Kal tilted her head, intrigued. "Why do you think that is?"

Joon smirked. "Walt Disney hated mothers?"

A ripple of laughter spread through the group.

"Yeah, seriously," Melody added. "And it's not just missing moms. Look at the villains. Evil stepmothers everywhere. And Cruella?"

"She wasn't a stepmom," Aiden said, scowling.

"No, but she was kind of a stepmom to all those dalmatians," Caitlyn teased.

"Oh, you mean the ones she wanted to turn into fur coats?" Joon shot back. More laughter.

Kal raised a hand slightly, signaling the group to settle. "Okay, guys, I think we've gotten a little off track. But it's an interesting observation. What do you all think the absence of mothers in those stories really represents?"

Before I could stop myself, the words tumbled out. "To force the main character to grow up."

The room went silent.

I felt my face heat as everyone turned to look at me, but I kept going. "It's true. I looked it up. It's called a 'narrative device.' Writers kill off the mom to push the hero's journey forward, to make them mature, become independent, whatever." My arms crossed tightly over my chest. "But I call BS. I'm with Peter Pan on this one. I'd rather 'never grow up.' I just want my mom."

Nobody laughed this time.

The words sat there, heavy, until Kal nodded. "Thank you for sharing that, V," she said softly. "That was really powerful."

The room stayed quiet for a long time after that, the energy completely different now.

Then, after what felt like forever, Aiden spoke.

"Death has a name," he said. "It's The Grim Reaper. I've stared into his empty eye sockets where there should be a soul. I just call him Grim. I think I've earned that right."

That's when Zuri finally spoke more than a few words.

She sat two seats away from me, wearing an oversized hoodie that swallowed her small frame. "My dad died three months ago," she said, her voice barely above a whisper. Her hands were folded tightly in her lap, her fingers pale from gripping them too hard. "Pancreatic cancer. He was in hospice for a month before . . ." She trailed off, swallowing hard.

A flicker of recognition sparked. Hospice.

Zuri's hands twisted together as she kept going. "There was this nurse who spent a lot of time with him. She was nice, I guess, but . . . I don't know. She was kind of weird."

Weird?

Kal leaned forward slightly. "Weird how?"

Zuri shifted, clearly uncomfortable. "She was really . . . spiritual. Like, she kept whispering stuff to my dad in another language. Prayers, I think. It made me uncomfortable, but I guess she was just trying to help."

My heart seemed to skip a couple beats. A memory snapped into focus, crystal clear.

Spiritual. Prayers. A nurse who whispered in another language.

I sat up straighter. "Do you remember her name?"

Zuri flinched at my tone, her eyes flashing with surprise. The whole group turned to stare, silence stretching between us, heavy and uncomfortably long.

"Uh ... no," Zuri said finally, frowning. "Why?"

I realized too late how intense I sounded. I forced a shrug, willing myself to appear calm while leaning back and crossing my arms. "Just curious," I mumbled, avoiding Kal's searching gaze.

The conversation moved on, but I wasn't listening anymore.

My mind was stuck on Zuri's words, replaying them over and over like a song I couldn't turn off.

Spiritual. Prayers. A nurse who whispered in another language. My mom's hospice nurse had done that, too.

THAT NIGHT, the three of us stood in front of the fireplace. Mom's urn sat on the mantle, surrounded by framed pictures of her—of us—laughing, hugging, goofing off at the beach.

Scotty held a pink rose. Dad had picked up a small cake from the grocery store—a poor substitute for the one Grandma and I baked last year, but it was something.

Nobody really knew what to do.

Finally, Dad cleared his throat. "Your mom never wanted a big fuss on her birthday, just to be surrounded by the people she loved." He let out a small, sad chuckle. "And cake, a movie, and maybe a glass of wine."

"She always said the same thing," I murmured. "Another year above ground."

Scotty sniffled, staring at the urn. "I wish she was here."

Dad reached for Scotty's hand and squeezed it. "Me, too."

"Wait, I made something for Mommy." Scotty pulled away from Dad and disappeared into the kitchen. He came back seconds later with a piece of paper in his hands. It was a drawing of all of us: me, him, Dad, and Mom. She was in the sky, surrounded by stars.

"Do you like it?" he asked, holding it up proudly.

My throat tightened as I looked at the picture. "Yeah," I said softly. "It's perfect."

"Do you think she's up there? With Thunderbird and the stars, watching over us?"

I glanced at Dad, unsure what to say.

"I think so, li'l man. I also know that a part of her is right here, in your heart, so she can always be with you." He placed his hand over Scotty's heart.

Scotty looked down and placed his hand over Dad's. "Is she in your heart, too?"

"Yes, son. She's in my heart, too."

"And V's?"

"And V's!" Dad said, motioning me over.

I smiled through my tears and hugged my two guys.

We stood there for a while, the three of us holding each other as tight as we could.

Then, without saying anything, Dad grabbed three forks and passed them out.

No plates. Just the three of us standing in the living room, eating bites of cake straight from the box.

Mom would've laughed at that.

After a while, Dad stepped closer to the mantle. He pressed his fingers to the side of the urn, like he was memorizing the feel of it. Then he whispered, "Happy birthday, Hannah."

Scotty sniffled. "Happy birthday, Mommy."

I hesitated, my throat tight. Then, softly, "Happy birthday, Mom."

We didn't stay much longer. Scotty gave the urn a gentle touch before heading upstairs. Dad lingered for a second, staring at Mom's photos. Then, with a sigh, he squeezed my shoulder and followed Scotty to bed.

I stayed behind. Just me and Mom's urn. I traced the rim of the mantle, my eyes landing on a photo of us together, arms wrapped around each other, her face lit up with laughter.

"Happy birthday, Mom," I whispered again.

I didn't know if she could hear me. If she was *everywhere,* like she'd said in her letter. But I hoped so.

8

THE NOTEBOOK

"When someone you love becomes a memory,
that memory becomes a treasure."
–Unknown

As I got ready for bed and brushed my teeth, exhaustion weighed heavy on me. My body was done, but my mind wouldn't quit. The day had been long, draining in a way that went beyond just being tired.

Then it hit me. Like a punch to the gut.

Zuri's story. Her dad's hospice nurse. Mom's hospice nurse.

Could they be the same person?

A chill prickled the back of my neck, sharp and sudden.

I spat out the toothpaste and braced myself on the counter, my reflection staring back at me in the mirror. My pulse had kicked up, and I had no idea why. *So what if it was the same nurse?* Hospice nurses saw tons of patients. It wasn't weird. So why did it feel weird?

Nurse April had been Mom's hospice nurse, but I'd actually met her before that—months earlier, at the hospital, when she took care of Zack's sister, Amanda. She had been kind, cheerful. Always smiling. Always knowing the right thing to say.

At the time, I'd thought it was comforting. But now, thinking back, something about her hadn't felt . . . right.

When she became Mom's nurse, she didn't recognize me. I didn't think much of it then—she met so many patients and families, after all. But now, after what Zuri had said, I couldn't shake the feeling that I was missing something.

I turned away from the mirror and went back to my room. I closed the door and leaned against it, scanning the room for something . . . and then I found the box.

Mom's things. I'd brought it up here after the funeral, telling myself I'd go through it when I was ready. I wasn't ready. I didn't think I'd ever be ready. But something had shifted. I needed to see.

I pulled the box onto my bed and lifted the lid. The familiar scent of Mom's perfume lingered inside, soft and faded. Her favorite green scarf sat on top, folded neatly. Beneath it was a bundle of sympathy cards, some framed photos, and a small leather-bound notebook.

I froze. I'd seen her writing in this before. Late at night, when she thought no one was watching. My hand hovered over it. *This is wrong. This is private.*

But something in my gut told me to look. I hesitated, then picked it up and flipped to the first page.

MOM'S familiar handwriting stared back at me from page one.

Big and loopy, in purple ink. I traced my finger over her name at the top of the page

Hannah Jiménez

I hesitated. Part of me wanted to snap the journal shut, shove it back in the box, and pretend I'd never found it. But my fingers refused to let go. It felt like she was here with me, like her words might be the closest thing I'd ever have to hearing her voice again.

July 20

The last round of chemo didn't work. Dr. Khatri says the cancer's too aggressive. There's nothing more they can do. Now, it's all about pain management and focusing on comfort. And every time I sit down to write an update I think, This one is the hardest. I'm thinking that again right now.

Oh God, this is so hard.

Carlos, the love of my life, has been my rock. He continues to hold my hand through every step of this maddening, saddening, awful journey. And the kids . . . I can't even go there right now.

The hospice nurse started today. April Dawson. She seems early thirties, yet she's calm in a way that feels old, like she's

already seen everything. And she's very cheerful
—too cheerful. She mentioned "peace" and how
it's important to let go. I know she's trying to
make this easier, but I hated hearing it. I'm
not ready to let go.

I frowned. I didn't remember much about April. I'd barely
spent any time around her—I'd mostly kept to myself during
those last few weeks. But reading about her now, something
about the way Mom described her made me uneasy.

I turned the page.

July 27
April was here again today. She stayed
late, sitting with me after Carlos and the kids
went to bed. She talked about how she's seen
patients struggle with pain, with fear, and how
sometimes the kindest thing we can do is "help
them let go."

She didn't say it outright, but it felt like
she was trying to tell me something. Like she
wanted me to . . . I don't even know. Give up?
Agree to something?

I hate how paranoid this is making me
feel. I'm probably just imagining things—after
all, isn't it her job to make me comfortable?
But something about her eyes when she said it

. . . It didn't feel comforting. It felt like she was deciding something about me.

My breath caught, and I closed the journal for a moment, my hand shaking. Deciding something about her? It was ridiculous. Hospice nurses were supposed to help. They were the good guys —the ones who came in when doctors had given up, the ones who stayed when the rest of the world moved on. April must've been trying to reassure her, right?

But I couldn't stop thinking about that one line—"*It felt like she was deciding something about me.*" I took a deep breath and opened the journal again, flipping to the last entry.

August 7

I heard April on the phone today. She was in the kitchen, talking quietly, but I could hear every word. She said, "It's my duty to help them when they're ready." And then she laughed. She actually laughed.

I've been so tired lately. So foggy. I wish I had a brain that worked! Carlos keeps telling me to rest, but it's more than that. It feels like I'm slipping. And every time April comes into the room, I feel like she's watching me.

Maybe I'm overreacting. Maybe it's just the pain, the medication, everything. But if something happens to me, I just want Carlos and

the kids to know . . . how very much I love
them. I just hope I'm wrong.

I slammed the journal shut. The words imprinted in my mind: "*I just hope I'm wrong.*"

Mom's death had never seemed suspicious. It wasn't sudden, wasn't shocking. The cancer had taken her, just like we'd all known it would. No one had asked any questions, not the doctors, not the hospice team, not even Dad.

But now? Now I wasn't so sure. I sat there, clutching the journal, as memories flooded back.

What if Mom had been right? What if something *had* happened to her? What if April had been the one to make it happen?

I sat on the edge of my bed, staring at the journal in my hands. My heart felt like it was beating too fast, too loud, like it was trying to drown out my thoughts.

It didn't make sense. None of it made sense. Mom was sick—she was dying. That's what everyone said, what we all knew. That's what hospice care *was*—helping people die as peacefully as possible.

So why did it feel like the ground had shifted beneath me?

I ran my hand over the journal's cover, feeling the smooth leather under my fingertips. It was warm now, almost like it was alive. Like it was holding a piece of my mom, a piece I didn't know existed until today. *What if my mom had been right?*

The question kept echoing in my head, louder and louder, until I couldn't ignore it anymore. What if Mom's death hadn't just been the cancer?

I stood up abruptly, the journal still clutched in my hands, and began pacing. Music was playing faintly in the background

—acoustic and sad—but I could barely hear it over the noise in my head.

I tried to think back to those last few weeks and remembered April sitting by Mom's bedside, always so calm, her hands resting on her lap. She had this way of tilting her head when she talked, like she was trying to read your mind. And her voice— always soft, always soothing, like she was telling you everything would be okay, even when you knew it wouldn't.

One night, I'd walked in to check on Mom, and April had been adjusting the IV drip. She'd looked up at me with that practiced smile, her voice dripping with sympathy. "She's resting now," she'd said, her hand still on the IV line. "It's good for her to let go of the pain."

I hadn't thought much of it at the time—Mom had been in pain. But now . . . now, the memory made my skin crawl. I sank back onto my bed, letting the journal fall beside me.

I was being ridiculous, wasn't I? People don't just *kill* their patients, especially not hospice nurses. They're there to help, to make things easier for people like Mom. April had been doing her job. That's it.

And yet, I couldn't shake the feeling that Mom's words meant something. She'd heard April say, "It's my duty to help them when they're ready." *What does that even mean?*

If April really had done something—if she'd hurt Mom or pushed her into dying sooner than she needed to—then how could no one have noticed? How could Dad not have seen it? He'd been at her side when she breathed her last. He'd been holding her hand, whispering to her, telling her it was okay to let go. He hadn't seen anything wrong. He hadn't questioned anything.

Maybe that's why this felt so impossible. If Dad hadn't noticed, how could I? But maybe he wasn't looking. Maybe none of us had been.

My eyelids felt heavy as I fought off the exhaustion. I paced some more as a thought took root. If April had done something, there had to be proof—some kind of evidence. Something more than my mom's journal entries.

I thought about the box of Mom's things. It was mostly sentimental stuff, but maybe there was something else in there, something I hadn't noticed before. I pulled the box down from my bed and dumped its contents onto the floor.

The scarf, framed photos, and sympathy cards spilled out in a pile. Then I saw what I was looking for, the medical stuff—papers and pamphlets that had been stuffed in the bottom of the box.

There was a discharge summary from the hospital, detailing when Mom had transitioned to hospice care. A few brochures from the hospice company. A list of medications she'd been prescribed: morphine, lorazepam, haloperidol.

I froze, my eyes scanning the list. Morphine. That was the one April had talked about the most, the one she'd administered near the end. She'd said it was to manage Mom's pain, to keep her comfortable.

But what if it wasn't just that? What if she'd given her too much? What if she'd done it *on purpose*?

I felt sick at the thought. I didn't know much about medicine, but I knew morphine was strong. And if someone gave you too much, well . . .

I picked up the hospice brochure. My hands shook as I flipped through it, looking for anything—names, numbers, a way to contact the people who'd taken care of Mom.

At the back of the brochure, I found a list of the staff members. My heart stopped when I saw April's name: *April Dawson, R.N.* There was even a photo—a small, professional headshot with her wide smile and clear, bright eyes.

I stared at the picture, and for the first time, I realized how much that smile unnerved me.

If Mom had been right—if April had done something to her—then no one else was going to figure it out. Not Dad. Not the hospice company. No one . . . except me.

I glanced at the clock on my phone. 1:12 a.m. I had to get some sleep. All-nighters were bad for my health. I knew that if I kept this up, I'd get sick in no time. And I didn't have time to be sick. I had a new case to solve.

I crawled under the covers and turned off my lamp. "I'm going to find out what happened, Mom." My voice trembled. "I promise."

9

ON THE CASE

"No one ever told me that grief felt so like fear."
–C.S. Lewis

The next morning, I woke up with a start. Did I really believe my mother had been murdered? Was finding her journal just a bad dream?

Sunlight streamed in through my window, making everything feel too bright, too ordinary. But nothing about this felt ordinary. I sat up, scanning my room. The journal was on my nightstand, open to the last page. *"If something happens to me . . ."*

I stared at the words, feeling the weight of them all over again. *It wasn't a dream.*

I had to figure this out. I promised Mom I would right before I fell asleep last night. *But . . . I don't have a clue where to start.*

★ ★ ★ ★ ★

THE SMELL of burnt toast and scrambled eggs hit me as I entered the kitchen. Dad and Scotty sat at the table, their plates half empty and a stack of papers sitting beside Dad's coffee.

"Okay, so what happens if you pour vinegar into baking soda?" Scotty asked, his voice way too energetic for this early in the morning.

"You get a mess in the kitchen," Dad said, not looking up from the paper he was grading.

Scotty groaned. "No, you get *carbon dioxide*! It bubbles up and fizzes, like when you shake a soda can and open it."

"Sounds like you've been reading ahead in science class," Dad said, finally glancing at him with a faint smile. He looked tired—the dark circles under his eyes were a dead giveaway that he'd been up late, probably grading papers or lesson planning.

Scotty grinned, stabbing a piece of scrambled egg with his fork. "We're gonna do the experiment today, and I get to help set it up!"

"Well, don't go blowing up the classroom," Dad said, flipping to the next paper in his stack.

"I'm not gonna blow it up, Dad. It's not that kind of experiment."

"Glad to hear it."

I lingered in the doorway for a second, watching them. Scotty had crumbs on his face and marker smudged on his hand, and Dad looked like he was running on caffeine and sheer willpower. But they both looked . . . normal. Almost like nothing had changed.

Except everything had.

"Morning, V," Dad said, glancing at me over the rim of his coffee cup.

"Morning," I mumbled, moving to the counter. I grabbed a piece of toast from the plate he'd left there, but I didn't bother buttering it. I wasn't hungry, but I knew Dad would give me *that look* if I skipped breakfast again.

"Guess what, V!" Scotty said, turning in his chair to face me. "We're doing a science experiment at school, and I get to measure the vinegar!"

"Cool," I said absently, picking at the edge of my toast.

Scotty frowned. "You're not even listening."

"I said it was cool," I replied, trying to sound more enthusiastic.

"You didn't *mean* it, though."

Dad sighed and ruffled Scotty's hair. "Cut her some slack, bud. It's still early."

Scotty didn't look convinced, but he turned back to his plate, stuffing a piece of egg in his mouth.

"Hey, V," he said through a mouthful of food. "Can you take me to Alex's house after school? Dad's got that teacher meeting thing."

"It's not a meeting; it's curriculum night," Dad corrected, finishing his coffee. "And yeah, I'll be busy. So it's up to you, Violet, but I think Scotty could use a break."

"Yeah, sure," I said, nodding absently.

"Awesome!" Scotty cheered, pumping his fist in the air like he'd just won a championship.

I said nothing more, just took a bite of my toast and chewed, the flavor lost on me. My thoughts returned to the journal, to the words Mom had written. To April.

Dad stood up and grabbed his papers, gathering them into a neat stack. "I've gotta head out early today. The new history teacher's been asking about the classroom tech setup, so I told him I'd walk him through it before first period."

He leaned down and pressed a quick kiss to Scotty's head. "Be good today, buddy. And don't blow up anything that isn't part of the experiment."

Scotty rolled his eyes. "I told you, it's not that kind of experiment."

Dad chuckled and turned to me. "You good, V?"

"Yeah," I said automatically.

He looked at me for a second longer, like he wanted to ask something else, but then he just nodded. "Okay. I'll see you both tonight."

As soon as he was gone, Scotty turned back to me. "So, when we go to Alex's, can we stop for ice cream first? Please?"

I sighed and pushed my plate away. "We'll see."

He groaned, throwing his head back dramatically. "You always say that."

I stood up, grabbing my backpack from the chair. "Because I'm not making any promises. Now finish your breakfast."

AFTER I DROPPED Scotty off at his school, I let my mind wander on the way to mine. I couldn't stop thinking about Dad. The way he looked at me when he asked if I was okay. He didn't know.

He didn't know about Mom's journal, about what she'd written in those last weeks. About how she thought April might have been watching her, deciding something about her. Would he even believe me if I told him?

Dad was practical. Logical. He'd always been the kind of person who needed proof to believe something, and all I had was a journal and a gut feeling. But if I was right—if Mom hadn't died the way we all thought—then I couldn't ignore it.

I gripped the steering wheel tighter as I pulled into Sierra High's student parking. I wasn't ready to tell Dad. Not yet. But I could start figuring this out on my own. And I knew what I needed to do next.

April Dawson. I didn't know much about her, other than what I could remember from those last weeks—her perfectly neat bun, her calm smile, her voice like syrup, thick and sweet. She was everything you'd want a hospice nurse to be on the surface: kind, professional, steady.

But Mom hadn't seen her that way. Not in the end. Her journal had made that clear enough. Mom had noticed things about April, things that didn't feel right. And I couldn't stop thinking about those last entries, the way her handwriting turned shaky as she wrote: *"She watches me so closely, like she's deciding something about me."*

I didn't know what I expected to find, but I knew I had to start somewhere.

THE FIRST THREE periods of the day dragged by in a fog. I barely paid attention to my teachers, my notebook open but mostly blank. I even ignored Emma in English. She knew better than to push it when I was like this.

Finally, fourth period came, and I asked Miss Torres if I could do some research in the library. She said she didn't have anything for me to do today anyway, so it worked out. Being a teacher's aide had its privileges.

The library was empty since everyone was in class. I headed directly for the row of school computers along the far wall and chose the one farthest away. I didn't want anyone peeking over my shoulder, even the librarian. I slid into the chair and pulled up the browser. My fingers hovered over the keyboard for a second before I typed: "April Dawson hospice nurse."

The search results loaded, and I leaned closer to the screen, scanning the first page. The top result was the UC Irvine

Medical Center's website. I clicked on it and scrolled past the generic stock photos of smiling medical staff and happy families. It was all polished, professional, and way too cheerful.

I finally found the staff page and clicked on the section for registered nurses. My stomach twisted when her picture popped up. April Dawson. Her photo was just as I remembered her—unremarkable ash-brown hair swept into a neat bun, soft green eyes, and that same practiced smile. Beneath the picture was a short bio:

"April Dawson, R.N.

With over 10 years of experience in hospice and palliative care, April is dedicated to providing compassionate support and care for patients and their families during life's most difficult transitions."

The words felt clinical and detached, like they were written by someone who'd never actually met her. Nothing about the bio hinted at the strange things Mom had written in her journal. Nothing about it seemed suspicious.

I stared at her picture for a while, wondering what she was hiding under that smile. I decided to do a deeper dive and searched, "April Dawson hospice nurse complaints."

Nothing.

I tried "April Dawson reviews" next, but the only things that came up were glowing testimonials about a hospice care facility she also worked at. No one had written anything specific about her, at least not that I could find.

Growing frustrated, I opened a new tab and searched just her name: "April Dawson."

That turned up a lot of results, but none of them seemed to match her. There were a few generic social media accounts—a Facebook page with no profile picture and no posts, and a LinkedIn profile, but it was the same polished, professional listing I'd already seen.

I tried adding location—"April Dawson California"—but it didn't help. Nothing about her seemed out of the ordinary. No complaints. No controversies. No red flags.

I slumped back in the chair, dropping my hands into my lap. *What did I think I would find? A confession? A list of her crimes?*

This was stupid. I was being stupid. I rubbed my temples, trying to push back the growing frustration. But no matter how much I tried to convince myself I was overreacting, I couldn't shake my suspicions. Mom had been *afraid* of her. That had to mean something.

I stared at the screen, April's photo still pulled up. Her smile seemed different now—less warm, more calculating. Maybe I imagined it. Maybe this was just my grief twisting things in my head. But then I thought about Mom writing that she'd overheard her on the phone: *"It's my duty to help them when they're ready."*

I didn't know what that meant, but it didn't sound like something a nurse should say. I might not have found anything suspicious online, but that didn't mean there wasn't something to find. I just had to keep looking.

As the bell rang, I logged off the computer and grabbed my backpack. Lunchtime. Now I could go home and dig some more.

10

FIELD TRIP TO RIVERSIDE

"You gave me a forever within the numbered days."
–John Green, *The Fault in Our Stars*

When I got home, I grabbed a yogurt out of the fridge and headed upstairs. I still had a couple hours before I needed to pick up Scotty from school and take him to Alex's. I wanted to look through Mom's hospice paperwork again, in case I missed something. I'd already highlighted every mention of April Dawson's name. That too-bright, calm smile of hers was burned into my brain.

She'd been at Amanda's bedside, too. One night, one shift, and then Amanda was gone. Just like my mom.

I opened my laptop and typed "April Dawson nurse" into the browser search, again. Same results as the library computer. Same stupid smiling headshot on the UC Irvine Medical Center website. Same bland bio about her passion for hospice care.

But this time, I noticed something new. A link buried on the third page of results:

"Family Questions Sudden Deaths at Local Hospice."

I clicked it, my heart racing. The article was short, but it was enough. It mentioned a hospice in Riverside where April used to work and a family who'd gone to the media after their loved one died suddenly. No charges had been filed, but it was obvious they thought something was off.

This was it. It had to be.

The article about the Riverside hospice stuck with me like a splinter under the skin. I couldn't leave it alone. If April had a history of sudden patient deaths there, maybe someone remembered her. Someone who could help me prove what she'd done to Mom.

I googled the hospice name—Riverside Serenity Care—and hit the jackpot: an old staff directory buried on an archived page of their website. April Dawson's name was there, listed as a hospice nurse from 2016 to 2017.

I kept digging. The article mentioned a specific family, the Fennons, who'd gone to the media about their grandmother's death. I found a Facebook post from a woman named Trina Fennon. She'd written about how her grandma had been stable, even improving, before she died suddenly during a night shift. The name "Nurse April" wasn't in the post, but I knew. I just knew.

I stared at Trina's Facebook page for a long time before finally sending her a message:

Hi Trina, My name is Violet. I'm really sorry for what happened to your grandma. My mom was also in hospice care, and she died recently. I think we might have had the same nurse. I was wondering if you'd be willing to talk to me about what happened.

I hit send before I could overthink it. Then I stared at my screen, willing her to reply.

An hour passed.

It was time to pick up Scotty.

AFTER DINNER, I excused myself and headed upstairs to my room. I opened my laptop and checked my Facebook messages. There it was.

Trina Fennon: *Hi Violet, I'm sorry for your loss. What do you want to know?*

My fingers shook as I typed back: *Do you remember a nurse named April Dawson?*

There was a long pause. Then her reply came through:

Trina Fennon: *I do. She was the one on duty the night Grandma died. Why?*

After messaging Trina for nearly an hour, I pieced together more of the story. She and her family had noticed weird things about April—how she always seemed to know when a patient was "ready to go," how she spent extra time with patients during her shifts, how she whispered prayers in Spanish before they died.

Trina's family had been suspicious enough to request an autopsy, but the results were inconclusive. No one could prove anything. April left the hospice shortly after the media attention, and the family didn't have the resources to push the case further. I had to take it from there.

THE NEXT MORNING, I skipped third period, ducked out a side door of school near the student lot and drove to Riverside

Serenity Care. I came up with a cover story on the drive. I was an aspiring journalist doing a report for a school project on end-of-life care. It was the kind of lie I thought Veronica Mars would approve of.

The woman at the front desk looked bored when I walked in, which worked in my favor. I told her my "project" was focused on how hospices handle challenging situations, like patient deaths under suspicious circumstances. I dropped April Dawson's name casually, watching her face carefully for a reaction.

Her lips tightened. "I don't know if I can help you with that," she said.

But I wasn't giving up. "I heard there was a case here a couple years ago," I said, leaning on the desk like I belonged there. "A family thought one of their relatives died too soon. I just want to understand what happened. Did Nurse Dawson leave because of that?"

Her gaze flickered. Bingo. "You'll have to talk to administration," she said quickly.

Administration didn't tell me much, but they didn't have to. A few pointed questions confirmed what I suspected: April left the facility under a cloud, and they were all too happy to see her go.

By the time I got home, my head was spinning. April had a pattern—I could see it now. She worked at hospices and oncology wards for a few years, long enough for people to notice the deaths piling up, and then she moved on. Riverside Serenity Care was just one stop on her road to UCI (University of California—Irvine).

I spread everything out on my bed: Trina's messages, printouts of the articles I'd found, notes from my conversation at the hospice. I added it to what I already knew about Mom, about Amanda.

Then I spotted something I'd missed.

It was a detail from Trina's story—how April whispered a prayer in Spanish before her grandma died. Zack had mentioned something similar about Amanda, and I remembered April doing the same thing with Mom.

The prayer wasn't just a coincidence. It was a ritual.

II

NO TURNING BACK

"Grief changes shape, but it never ends."
–Keanu Reeves

Finally, it was Friday. I'd have the weekend to work on the case distraction-free. I took out my notebook and began jotting down my next steps—talking to my mom's oncologist, Dr. Khatri, checking the medical records again, finding a way to confront Nurse April—when Emma slipped into the seat behind me and tapped my shoulder.

"Whatchya doin'?" she asked, craning her neck to peek at my notebook.

I jumped, snapping it shut. "Don't scare me like that, Emma."

She arched an eyebrow. "Since when did you get so jumpy? This is English class, V. We have it together, remember? You've barely talked to me all week, and you ghosted most of my texts. I've been trying to make plans for the weekend. What gives?"

"Nothing," I said, too quickly, the lie sharp on my tongue.

"Come on, it's me. What's going on with you? I mean, besides the obvious."

I scoffed, bitterness leaking out. "What? You mean a grieving daughter, mourning the too-soon death of her mother?"

Emma winced, her gaze avoiding mine. "Ouch."

The guilt hit me, sharp and unwelcome. I rubbed my temples, trying to ease the ache blossoming there. "Forget it, Emma. Sorry, I'm just not dealing with it well right now."

She was silent for a moment, the hum of the classroom filling the space between us. "You know you don't have to do this alone, right?"

I hesitated, fingers tracing the edges of my notebook. "I know. But right now, I just need to be alone. Give me some space this weekend, okay?"

Her face fell, but she nodded, forcing a small smile. "Sure, okay. No problem. But if you need me, I'm just a text away."

I managed a nod, turning back to my notebook, though the words blurred on the page.

BY BREAK, my head was pounding, and my body felt heavy, like I was carrying every sleepless night and unanswered question on my back. I hesitated outside Miss Torres's classroom, gripping my notebook so tightly the edges curled under my fingers.

This is stupid. She's my teacher, not my therapist.

But before I could talk myself out of it, I pushed the door open.

Miss Torres sat at her desk, flipping through a stack of papers with her green gel pen in hand. When she saw me, she smiled, but her eyes narrowed like she could already tell something was off.

"Hey, V," she said, setting the papers aside. "You're early."

I swallowed and nodded, stepping inside. The classroom was quiet, the usual chaos of English class replaced by the steady hum of the overhead lights. I'd always liked this room—it smelled like books and vanilla, and it had been a kind of refuge for me in the past.

"I just—" My voice cracked, and I cleared my throat, trying again. "I just needed to talk to someone."

She nodded like she'd been expecting this. "Okay," she said gently, gesturing to the chair across from her desk. "What's on your mind?"

I sat down, gripping my notebook in my lap. The words I wanted to say tangled in my throat. I could tell her about my mom, how everything felt wrong, how I was unraveling. I could tell her about Nurse April, about the gnawing suspicion that wouldn't let me sleep. I could tell her everything.

Instead, I just said, "I don't know how to do this."

Miss Torres leaned forward, resting her elbows on her desk. "Do what?"

"Keep going. Pretend like I'm okay. Everyone expects me to just be fine. But I'm not." My voice was barely above a whisper.

She was quiet for a long moment, and when she spoke, her voice was softer than I'd ever heard it. "You know I was fifteen when I lost my dad, right?"

I nodded.

She exhaled, twisting a ring on her finger. "People mean well, but they don't get it. They don't know what it's like to wake up every day with that weight on your chest. To feel like the world just keeps moving, and you're stuck in place." She paused. "But you don't have to pretend with me."

Something in me cracked open, just a little. I looked down at my hands, fingers still curled around the notebook. "There's something else, too," I admitted. "Something about my mom's death that doesn't feel right."

Miss Torres didn't rush me, didn't push. She just waited.

And for the first time, I let the words come.

As I left Miss Torres's classroom, I let out a long exhaled breath. My hands weren't shaking anymore. The weight in my chest felt lighter, like I wasn't the only one carrying it now. Telling her had been the right move.

She hadn't looked at me like I was crazy. She'd listened, really listened, nodding along as I explained the uneasy feeling I had about Nurse April—Mom's journal entries, the moments that didn't add up. Her brows had knitted together in concern.

"I don't want you to go looking for something that isn't there, V," she had said carefully. "But I also know that gut feelings usually mean something. If you really think there's more to this, you need to be smart about how you proceed. Be careful."

Be careful.

The words echoed in my head as I made my way down the hall. She hadn't dismissed my concerns, but she also hadn't given me blind encouragement. And honestly? That was what I needed. Someone to hear me out, to take me seriously, but also to remind me that this wasn't a game. But I couldn't stop now. The case must go on.

I dug my phone out of my backpack, my fingers hovering over the screen before I pulled up the hospital's number. My mom's oncologist, Dr. Khatri, had always been kind, patient. If anyone knew whether something had been off with her treatment, it was her.

I took a deep breath and hit call. The line rang twice before a receptionist answered. "Dr. Khatri's office, how may I help you?"

I tightened my grip on my phone. "Hi, um, I was wondering if I could make an appointment with Dr. Khatri. I'm—" I hesitated, my throat suddenly dry. "I'm Violet Jiménez. She was my mom's oncologist."

A pause. Then, a softer tone. "Oh. I'm so sorry for your loss, Violet."

"Thanks." I swallowed. "I have some questions about her treatment."

The receptionist hesitated. "Dr. Khatri is very busy, but I can see when she's available."

"Please. I just need a few minutes of her time."

Another pause. My heart pounded against my ribs. "Let me check her schedule. Hold please."

I held the phone tightly to my ear as I walked to my third period class, hoping she'd come back before the tardy bell rang. And then, the receptionist picked up and said, "The doctor can fit you in for a five-minute consult Monday at 1:00 p.m. Does that work?"

"Yes, thank you." I turned my phone off and slid into class just as the bell rang.

12

GHOSTS, GUILT, AND MY EX-BOYFRIEND

"Grief is the price we pay for love."
–Queen Elizabeth II

I was in my room, going over my notes, when the front door opened and shut. Lucky, curled up at the foot of my bed, perked his ears, then bolted downstairs. A moment later, I heard Dad's voice, followed by Scotty's.

They were home.

I ignored them and refocused on the page in front of me, my pen tapping against the page.

•April: Hospice nurse. Mom's journal suggests she felt uneasy around her.

•Amanda: Zack's sister. Died in hospice almost a year ago. April was the nurse on call that night.

•Trina: Grandmother's death suspicious. April was her hospice nurse.

·Dr. Khatri: Mom's oncologist. There since Mom's diagnosis. Moved her to hospice care. Brought April onto the team.

If anyone knew more about April, it had to be her.

But what would I even ask?

"Hey, Dr. Khatri, do you think the hospice nurse you recommended might have killed my mom?"

Yeah, right. I needed a real plan before Monday.

I flipped back through Mom's journal, scanning for anything else she had written about Dr. Khatri. Most of it was routine—appointment notes, test results, little details about their conversations. But one entry stood out:

Dr. Khatri said April is one of their best nurses. I guess I should trust her judgment, but sometimes I feel like no one is really listening to me. Like they're all just going through the motions, waiting for the end.

A chill ran through me. It wasn't much, but it was enough. Dr. Khatri had known April. Had trusted her. Had *chosen* her. If anyone could tell me more about the way April worked—or whether anything about her had ever seemed off—it would be her.

Still, the thought of talking to Dr. Khatri made my stomach twist. What if I said the wrong thing? What if she didn't believe me?

Or worse—what if she did? What if I opened some kind of Pandora's box that I couldn't close?

But then I thought about Mom. About the way her handwriting had looked in those last few entries—shaky and uneven. The way she had written:

"If something happens to me . . ."

My door slammed open.

I jerked, nearly knocking my notebook off my lap.

"V, Dad wants you downstairs," Scotty announced.

I let out a breath, pressing a hand to my chest. "Geez, Scotty. Ever heard of knocking?"

"He says you have to come down now." His arms were crossed, his face unreadable. "Right now."

"Wow, bossy much?"

Scotty didn't smile. Just stared at me. Something was up.

I sighed and set my notebook aside. "Fine. I'm coming."

He led me down the stairs, and the second we stepped into the kitchen, I saw Dad at the counter, a huge grin on his face.

In front of him? A stack of college brochures and application packets.

I groaned.

UCLA, Stanford, USC, UC Irvine, San Diego State, Cal State Long Beach, Chapman, Cal Poly Pomona—all in California, of course.

"Seriously, Dad? Why are there so many?"

Dad's smile faltered, but only slightly. "I just wanted to get a head start on the process. Deadlines will sneak up before you know it, and I figured—"

"You figured if I just picked a school, everything would magically go back to normal?"

His face tightened. "That's not fair, V."

No, maybe not. But I was too tired to care.

"V, come on. You have to start thinking about your future."

"My future?" I let out a sharp laugh. "I can't even think about tomorrow, and you want me to plan for next year?"

Dad sighed, rubbing his face. Scotty hovered near the fridge, pretending to search for some string cheese while keeping one eye on us like watching a train wreck.

"I get it," Dad said finally, his voice softer. "I know it's hard, but your mom would want you to—"

I slammed my hands on the counter. "Don't. Don't tell me what Mom would want. You don't know."

His face darkened. "Of course, I know. We talked about your future all the time. She wanted you to go to college, V. She wanted you to have a life."

"She wanted to have a life, too," I shot back, my throat burning. "But she didn't get one, did she?"

The words hung between us, too sharp, too cruel. Scotty flinched.

Dad's jaw tightened, his hands clenching into fists at his sides. "I am *trying* to help you," he said, his voice low and controlled.

"Well, you're not," I snapped. "You're just pretending like everything can go back to normal if I fill out some stupid applications. Newsflash, Dad—it won't. Nothing will."

He exhaled, slow and frustrated. "You don't have to decide today. Just . . . *think* about it."

I shook my head. "I can't do this right now."

Then I turned and walked out, leaving him and the brochures behind.

I ran up to my room—to my bed—and buried my face in my hands. My throat burned, but I refused to cry. I couldn't cry. Not yet.

Because the case wasn't over. Because I didn't have time to think about college when Mom deserved justice.

THE NEXT MORNING, I woke up with a new thought. Perhaps not the best thought . . . but these were desperate times.

I stared at my phone for a long time before making the call.

I could just text. Keep it casual. *Hey, how's life in San Francisco? How's Malia? By the way, think your sister might've been murdered?*

Yeah. No.

I took a deep breath and hit call before I could chicken out.

The line rang. And rang.

Then a voice—deeper than I remembered, but still unmistakably Zack's. "Uh . . . hey?"

I swallowed. "Hey. It's . . . me."

A pause. "Yeah. I see that."

Great start. I exhaled, trying to sound casual. "How's San Francisco?"

"It's fine. Different, but fine." His tone was polite but stiff, like he was still deciding if this was a prank call. "Didn't expect to hear from you."

"Yeah, well . . ." I forced a weak laugh. "Guess I just wanted to check in. We haven't talked since—"

"Prom," he finished.

Right. Prom. The disaster of a night when he told me he was leaving, when I found out he was following Malia to San Francisco.

I pushed past it. "So, senior year. How's that going?"

Another pause. "It's . . . going."

He wasn't making this easy. I swallowed hard and forced myself to keep my voice steady. "I know this is out of the blue, but . . . I wanted to ask you something."

"Okay?" He sounded wary.

I hesitated. "It's about my mom."

Another pause. Then, softer, "V . . . I'm really sorry."

The words caught me off guard. Zack hadn't come to her funeral, and we hadn't spoken since before she died. But he had known her—she'd even been his English teacher for a little while, before she got sick again.

"Thanks," I murmured, gripping the phone tighter.

A beat of silence stretched between us. I knew I had to say something next, but my throat felt tight. Finally, I pushed forward. "Actually, I was thinking about Amanda."

A longer pause this time.

"...Why?"

I hesitated. "I've been going through some of my mom's things. And I noticed something."

"What kind of something?" His voice had sharpened, like a defense mechanism kicking in.

"She and Amanda had the same hospice nurse," I said carefully. "April."

Zack went completely silent.

I pressed the phone harder against my ear. "Zack?"

"April," he repeated, like he was turning the name over in his mind. "She wasn't Amanda's nurse."

I frowned. "What do you mean?"

"She wasn't assigned to Amanda's care team. She was only there once. Filled in for a shift." His voice grew tighter. "And that was the night Amanda died."

A cold weight settled in my chest. "Wait," I said slowly. "Amanda wasn't terminal, right? I thought—"

"She wasn't," he cut in. "Her prognosis was good. She was getting better. We thought she had more time. *A lot* more time." His voice cracked. "I gave her my kidney, V. I didn't do that just to lose her a few days later."

I blinked hard, my grip on the phone unsteady.

"Then how did she—?"

"No one knows," Zack said bitterly. "She was fine, and then she was gone. Middle of the night. No warning. The doctors made it sound like her body rejected my kidney and she went into organ failure. But . . ."

I felt a sudden chill.

"And April was the last one to see her," I murmured.

Zack exhaled. "Yeah."

The weight of it sat between us, heavy and unspoken.

Then, as if remembering something, Zack added, "You know, she was weird. April, I mean."

"Weird how?"

He hesitated. "That night in Amanda's room, she asked me a lot of questions. About my kidney donation, about my health. And . . . personal stuff."

"I remember. It *was* weird."

"At the time, I thought she was just making conversation. But now . . ."

Now, it felt like something else.

I swallowed, my pulse pounding. "Zack, I think she's done this before."

A pause. Then, quieter, "What are you saying?"

"I'm saying I don't think my mom's death was natural either."

Zack was silent.

Then, finally, he said, "V . . . don't mess with this. Just let it go."

I clenched my jaw. "I can't."

A long pause. "Yeah," he said quietly. "I figured."

Neither of us spoke for a few seconds.

Finally, I cleared my throat. "Thanks, Zack. For telling me."

"Yeah," he said. "Be careful, okay?"

"I will."

I hung up, remembering everything. Amanda wasn't terminal. She wasn't even supposed to die. It had been so unexpected and such a shock, I guess I blocked it, but April had been there.

I wasn't imagining things. I wasn't crazy. And come Monday, I was going to find out the truth.

13

RIDING A BIKE

"What we have once enjoyed deeply we can never lose. All that we love deeply becomes a part of us."
–Helen Keller

After talking to Zack, I needed to clear my head.

It was ten o'clock, and my stomach rumbled, but I wasn't ready to face Dad yet. I hadn't exactly been kind to him last night, and I definitely didn't want another conversation about college applications.

I stood in the hallway, listening. The distant hum of the TV drifted upstairs—Scotty, watching cartoons. But I didn't hear Dad's voice.

Hmm. I took a chance and tiptoed downstairs.

Scotty was sprawled out on the couch, a cereal box in his lap and Lucky curled up by his side. He glanced up as I entered, chewing noisily. "Good morning, V."

"Hey, squirt. Is that all you're having for breakfast? *Dry Cheerios?*"

"Yep."

"Why?" I asked, eyeing the untouched kitchen. "Where's Dad?"

"He said he left some tests at school and had to go grade them. He'll be back in a couple hours. He told me you were supposed to make me breakfast, but I heard you on the phone and didn't want to bother you."

I hesitated. Guilt pricked at my skin. "Oh. Thanks."

Scotty shrugged like it was no big deal, but it was. He'd been looking out for me, even though that was *my* job. I sighed and plopped onto the couch beside him, grabbing a handful of Cheerios from the box.

"Hey!" he said, his mouth half full. "Is *that* all you're having for breakfast?"

We both laughed.

It felt good to laugh with him. For a while, we just sat there, watching cartoons together like nothing had changed. Like we weren't two kids trying to figure out how to exist without her.

Then, quietly, he said, "Will you tell me a story about Mommy when you were little?"

I blinked, caught off guard.

"Please?" His voice was small, almost hesitant. "I miss her."

The words hit me like a tidal wave. For a second, I wanted to tell him no. That I couldn't do this, not right now, not when the grief still felt like it was suffocating me. But then I looked at him.

His eyes were wet, his fingers twisting the edge of his blanket like he was bracing for me to say no.

I exhaled, pushing past the lump in my throat. "Come here," I said, patting the cushion beside me.

Scotty scooted in closer, tucking himself against my side like he used to when he was younger.

I swallowed and forced a steady breath. "Okay. I'll tell you about the time Mom taught me how to ride a bike."

Scotty settled in, his head against my arm, as I began.

"I was seven. We lived in a different house then, and our front yard was tiny, so Mom took me to the park to practice. I'd been begging for weeks to get rid of the training wheels."

Scotty nodded, his fingers still fidgeting with the blanket.

"She was so patient with me," I continued, a small smile tugging at my lips. "She held on to the back of the bike the whole time, running behind me even though I kept wobbling and almost running her into the bushes. I must've crashed, like, ten times before I finally figured it out."

I laughed softly, the memory so sharp it almost felt like I was back there, hearing her laughter, feeling the warmth of her hands steadying me.

"And the first time I rode without her holding on, I didn't even realize she'd let go. I was so proud of myself, yelling, 'Mom, look! I'm doing it!'"

I paused. My throat tight.

Scotty lifted his head, watching me. "What did she say?"

I blinked fast, willing the tears to stay put. "She said, 'You've got this, Violet. You don't need me to hold on anymore.'"

Scotty didn't say anything for a moment. Then, in the smallest whisper, he said, "She was the best."

I pulled him closer, my voice barely holding steady. "Yeah. She really was."

There was a silence. It was full of everything we didn't know how to say.

Then Scotty shifted, looking up at me. "Do you think Mom's like Thunderbird?"

"What do you mean?"

"You know . . ." He hesitated. "Watching us. Protecting us. Like, even though she's not here anymore, she's still keeping the bad stuff away."

I swallowed hard, my heart twisting. How would I answer that?

I wanted to tell him *yes*. That Mom was out there some-where, keeping us safe, making sure we were okay. I wanted to tell him that she was always with us, that she hadn't really left.

But I didn't *know* that. And I didn't want to lie. So I squeezed his hand and said, "I think . . . I think Mom would do anything to protect us. Even now."

Scotty considered that. Then he nodded. "Yeah. I think so, too."

I pressed a kiss to his hair. "Come on," I said. "Let's make some real breakfast."

Scotty smiled. "Pancakes?"

I ruffled his hair. "Pancakes."

DAD WAS GONE for more than a couple of hours, but when he finally came back, he brought pizza as an olive branch.

We made up, sort of. No big conversation, no apologies—just a silent agreement to let it go.

Scotty decided we should have a movie night. He picked *The Lion King*.

Great. Another tearjerker with a dead parent.

Scotty was curled up on the couch in his dinosaur pajamas, with Lucky on his lap. Dad had one arm draped over Scotty's shoulders, absently rubbing his back. I was cozy in the easy chair beside them, wearing my favorite baggy T-shirt and sweats.

The scene on the TV was one I knew too well—Simba curling up beside his father's lifeless body, his tiny paws nudging at him, his voice breaking as he begged him to wake up.

Scotty sniffled, rubbing his nose against his pajama sleeve. "I don't like this part," he whispered. His voice barely audible over the movie.

Dad gave him a little squeeze. "It's okay, buddy. It gets better, remember? Just hang in there."

I glanced at Dad, and he met my gaze. For a second, it was like we were both thinking the same thing.

Does it get better?

The warmth of the moment—the closeness, the quiet comfort of it—made my heart hurt. We were all together, but it wasn't the same. Mom should have been here, curled up beside Dad, her head resting on his shoulder, her fingers absently braiding and unbraiding my hair like she used to.

The thought hit me with such force that I had to look away. I needed my mom, you know, to save me from the fact that she was *dead.*

My throat burned, the ache spreading through me like something toxic. I stood up. "I'm gonna head to bed," I mumbled.

Dad glanced at me, his expression unreadable, but he didn't say anything.

Scotty didn't look up from the screen. "Night, V."

I hesitated for a second. Maybe I should stay. Maybe I should sit back down, pull Scotty close, and remind him that I missed her, too. That he wasn't alone.

But I didn't. I left. I shut the door and leaned against it, closing my eyes as I let out a shaky breath.

The muffled sound of the movie drifted up from downstairs —the music swelling, the familiar voices—but it felt far away, like it belonged to someone else's life.

I'd seen that look on Dad's face before—tired, sad, holding it together for Scotty's sake. And Scotty, with his sniffles and over-sized dinosaur pajamas, just trying to find comfort in a story about grief and hope.

They were mourning, just like me. Maybe worse. So why couldn't I handle being around them?

Guilt gnawed at me, sharp and relentless. I *should* have stayed downstairs. I *should* have curled up next to Scotty, let him lean on me, told him it was okay to cry. I *should* have looked Dad in the eye and reminded him he didn't have to hold all of this alone. But I couldn't.

The grief was too big. The weight of it pressed against my ribs, suffocating, inescapable. So I did what I always did when the feelings got too messy to deal with—I reached for the case.

I crossed the room and pulled out Mom's hospice paper-work, unfolding the pages with careful fingers. The edges were creased, and the ink was smudged where my grip had lingered too long.

My stomach twisted as I scanned the notes. I'd read them all before, but I still searched—hunting for something I had missed, something that would make this *make sense.*

The words blurred slightly as tears pricked at my eyes. I blinked hard, inhaled sharply.

This is how I help, I told myself, clinging to the thought like a lifeline. *This is how I make it right.*

I forced a breath, pushing the guilt down, burying it beneath the weight of my obsession. There wasn't room for anything else right now—not grief, not guilt, not the hollow ache in my chest.

Just the investigation. Just the truth. And I *had* to find it. No matter what.

I HAD BEEN SEARCHING for hours. It must be early Sunday morning by now—I had no idea anymore. My room was dark except for the glow of my laptop screen, the only sound the click-click-click of my mouse as I scrolled through page after page of search results.

I'd tried everything.

• April Dawson complaints → Nothing.

• Hospice malpractice cases in California → A bunch of legal jargon I didn't understand.

• Hospice nurses under investigation → A few lawsuits, but none involving April.

I leaned back, rubbing my eyes. It couldn't just be me.

There had to be someone else out there who felt what I felt —who *knew* what I knew.

So I switched search tactics:

• Hospice care too much morphine

• Hospice death sudden decline suspicious

• Hospice nurse gave too much medicine

That's when I found it. A blog post. Tucked away in an old hospice support forum, buried five pages deep into my Google search.

"I Trusted the Wrong Person with My Father's Care."

The author: Rachel Collins.

I clicked on it.

"Rachel's Story."

The post was dated July 2016, written almost exactly two years before my mom died.

"I don't even know why I'm writing this. Maybe just to get it out. Maybe because I can't stop replaying the last days of my father's life and wondering if I should have asked more questions. Maybe because deep down, I already know the answer.

"My dad was placed in hospice care at St. Lucia's in San Diego after his cancer progressed. We were told he still had time. A few months, at least. He was awake, talking to us, even making jokes. We thought we'd get to say goodbye the right way.

"Then one night, a nurse—one we hadn't seen much before—gave

him more pain medication than usual. He was out of it immediately. And then, by morning . . . he was gone.

"I asked about it later. The hospice director said it was 'his time.' That it was 'a peaceful passing.' But it didn't feel peaceful. It felt like something was stolen from us.

"Maybe I'm just looking for someone to blame. Maybe this is all in my head. But if anyone else has ever felt like this . . . please tell me I'm not crazy."

I stared at the screen, my pulse pounding in my ears. Rachel Collins wasn't crazy. She wasn't imagining it.

She was me—just two years earlier.

April had been at St. Lucia's in 2016. April had been Rachel's dad's nurse. And he had died the exact same way as my mom.

My hands shook as I clicked on Rachel's profile.

She hadn't posted anything in over a year. I didn't know if she would ever see this. But I had to try.

I typed:

"Hi Rachel,

I know this is completely out of the blue, but I came across your post about your father's hospice care, and I think I might understand what you were feeling. My mom was in hospice, too, and I have reason to believe the same nurse might have been involved.

If you're willing to talk, please message me back.

Violet"

I hovered over the Send button. Once I sent this, there was no taking it back. This was real. I clicked "send."

Then I sat back and waited. For a long time. Nothing happened. I seriously had to get some sleep.

14

NOT QUITE THE TRUTH

"That it will never come again is what makes life so sweet."
–Emily Dickinson

Monday. At last, it was time for my appointment with Dr. Khatri.

As I pulled into the parking lot, I gripped the steering wheel hard, knuckles white. My heart raced like I was about to walk into a crime scene. I'd rehearsed what I was going to say at least ten times on the drive here, but now, standing in front of the glass doors, my mind felt blank.

I forced myself to go inside.

The receptionist looked up as I approached, offering a polite but practiced smile. "Hi, how can I help you?"

"I have an appointment with Dr. Khatri," I said, relieved that my voice sounded steadier than I felt. "Violet Jiménez."

She nodded, typing something into her computer before handing me a clipboard. "You can fill this out while you wait. We'll call you back in a few minutes."

The pen felt heavy in my hand as I absently filled out the form, my pulse drumming in my ears. Before I could even reread what I'd written, the door to the waiting room opened.

"Violet?"

I looked up. A nurse stood there, waiting. It was time.

Dr. Khatri stood as I entered, her sharp, assessing eyes softening when she saw me.

"Violet," she said warmly, gesturing for me to sit. "It's been a while. How are you holding up?"

I lowered myself into the chair across from her desk, sitting stiffly. "I'm okay."

The office was just as I remembered—clean, orderly, diplomas lining the walls, a small plant perched on the corner of her desk. But it felt colder now, the warmth I used to associate with this space stripped away.

Dr. Khatri folded her hands. "What can I do for you?"

I hesitated, my fingers twisting the hem of my sleeve. "I've been thinking a lot about my mom's last few weeks," I said carefully. "About hospice care."

Dr. Khatri nodded, her expression neutral. "That's completely natural," she said gently. "It's common to revisit those memories, especially when you're still processing everything."

I swallowed hard. "Do you remember the nurse, April Dawson? She was on my mom's care team."

Something flickered in her eyes—recognition, maybe? Or hesitation?

"Yes, I remember April," she said slowly. "She's been with the hospice organization for quite some time. Why do you ask?"

I chose my words carefully. "Mom wrote about her in her journal. She said she felt . . . uneasy sometimes. Like April was watching her too closely."

Dr. Khatri leaned back slightly, her brow furrowing. "Uneasy?"

I nodded. "She wrote that she didn't feel like anyone was really listening to her. Like . . . everyone was just waiting for the end."

A pause. Dr. Khatri's gaze held mine, unreadable.

"Hospice care is designed to provide comfort and dignity," she said finally. "It's not uncommon for patients to feel vulnerable or unsure, especially near the end. It's a difficult time for everyone."

She was choosing her words carefully. Too carefully.

I pressed forward. "What about the pain medication?"

Dr. Khatri's expression didn't waver. "Morphine and other medications play a crucial role in hospice care. Our goal is to keep patients comfortable while balancing their quality of life. Administering these medications requires great care and experience, which is why we rely so heavily on our dedicated nursing staff."

Smooth. Practiced. But it wasn't an answer.

"Did you recommend April specifically?" I asked, watching her closely.

Her lips pressed together, just slightly. "I trust the hospice organization to assign nurses who are experienced and compassionate. April has always been professional, as far as I'm aware."

Her tone was calm, measured. But something about the way she said it made my skin prickle.

"Is there something you're concerned about, Violet?" she asked, her voice steady but probing.

I hesitated. If I pushed too hard, she'd shut me down. If I played it too safe, I'd get nothing.

I forced a small shrug. "No," I said quickly. "I was just . . . curious."

Dr. Khatri nodded, but she studied me for a moment longer

than necessary. "If you ever need to talk more about your mom's care—or if you have questions about anything—please don't hesitate to reach out."

"Thanks," I murmured. My voice sounded hollow, distant.

She gave me a reassuring nod as I stood to leave.

The moment I stepped outside, I drew in a shaky breath, trying to steady myself. I'd hoped for answers. All I got were polite reassurances and carefully worded non-answers.

But her eyes—her hesitation—had given something away. Dr. Khatri knew something. She just wasn't saying it. And I wasn't done asking.

I SAT cross-legged on my bed, my desk lamp throwing a pool of yellow light over the chaos spread out in front of me: crumpled pages of hospice records, photocopies of treatment notes, and the handwritten list of questions I'd compiled.

Mom's handwriting was in there, too, from a card she'd signed for me before she got really sick. I'd shoved it in the stack, even though looking at it broke my heart. Her loopy, uneven cursive said, *"Love you to the stars and infinity—forever!"* like nothing had changed.

But everything had changed.

I stared at the papers, rubbing my temples. There had to be something I'd missed. Some detail I'd skimmed over. I couldn't shake the feeling that the answer was right in front of me, like a shadow just out of reach.

The hospice records were the worst. Each one was a catalog of her last days—what she ate, what she drank, what medications she was given, all reduced to cold, clinical notes. Every time I read them, it felt like losing her all over again. But I kept going.

I flipped through the pages slowly, scanning the same lines for what felt like the millionth time. Blood pressure readings. Pain scales. Dosages. My brain buzzed with frustration. How was I supposed to make sense of any of this?

A soft knock broke the silence. "V?" Dad's voice was low, hesitant, like he wasn't sure if I'd yell at him for interrupting.

I closed my eyes, taking a deep breath. "What?"

The door creaked open, and he stepped inside, holding a cup of tea in one hand. His dark eyes looked tired, lined with shadows that hadn't been there a year ago.

"I thought you could use this," he said, setting the cup on my desk.

"Thanks," I mumbled, not looking up.

He lingered, glancing at the mess of papers on my bed. I could feel his concern radiating off him, but I wasn't in the mood for another *we need to talk* speech.

"You've been up late a lot lately," he said carefully.

"I've got a lot of homework," I lied, still not meeting his eyes.

"V . . ."

"I'm fine, Dad. Just . . . go to bed, okay?"

He hesitated, like he wanted to say something else, but finally he just nodded and backed out of the room. The door clicked shut behind him, and I let out a long sigh.

I turned back to the paperwork, my stomach twisting. The guilt was immediate and heavy—I knew he was trying, in his own way. But I couldn't deal with him right now. I couldn't deal with anyone. Not until I figured this out.

I stopped on a page I'd skimmed over earlier—a treatment summary from Mom's last night. I picked it up and read it slowly this time, forcing myself to focus on every line.

Something caught my eye. I remembered what Dr. Khatri had said about morphine.

Morphine: 10 mg. I froze.

Ten milligrams. That was . . . a lot, wasn't it? Too much for someone Mom's size, for someone who'd already been on painkillers for months. My heart thudded in my chest as I scanned the page again, looking for context, some kind of explanation.

There wasn't one. Just a single note written in neat, professional handwriting:

Administered by Nurse A. Dawson.

April Dawson.

The name made me suck in my breath. For a moment, I couldn't move, couldn't breathe. The world tilted, my vision blurring as I stared at the words.

Morphine: 10 mg.

Administered by Nurse A. Dawson.

It wasn't a coincidence. It couldn't be. She'd been there, alone with Mom in those final hours, just like she'd been with Amanda. The pieces clicked into place, jagged and ugly, and for the first time, the thought I'd been avoiding finally solidified into something real:

Mom didn't just die. She was *killed.*

A choked sound escaped my throat, half sob, half gasp. I thought I'd cried all my tears already, but I was wrong. They came pouring out, hot and relentless, blurring the words on the page.

I clutched the paper in both hands, fingers trembling. My head spun, torn between grief and rage and a deep, hollow ache that felt like it would never go away.

The tea Dad brought sat untouched on my desk, the steam curling into the air like a ghost.

I sat there for what felt like hours, the treatment summary crumpled in my hands and my tears leaving blotchy stains on the paper. My chest felt hollow and full at the same time, like grief and fury were fighting for space inside me.

How could I not have seen it before? How could I have let her—*April Dawson*—walk out of that room, out of our house, like she hadn't just stolen the most important person in the world from me?

The guilt hit next, suffocating. If I'd been paying closer attention—if I hadn't been so tired, so numb, so caught up in my own useless hope that maybe, somehow, Mom would wake up and smile at me again—maybe I could've stopped it. Maybe I could've *saved* her.

I wiped at my face, trying to pull myself together, but the tears kept coming. I couldn't fall apart. Not now. Not when I finally had the proof I'd been looking for.

I grabbed my phone and snapped a picture of the treatment summary, saving it to a folder I'd labeled *Mom*. There were already pictures of her there—some smiling, some when she was sick, and some that I hadn't been able to delete from the funeral. But this? This wasn't a memory. It was evidence.

I stared at the photo on my screen, the name *Nurse A. Dawson* staring back at me like a challenge.

"Okay," I whispered, my voice trembling. "You want to play God? Fine. Let's see how that works out for you."

When I woke up the next morning, the anger was still there,

simmering under my skin, but it wasn't the wild, directionless rage I'd felt last night. This was sharper. Controlled.

I skipped breakfast, ignoring Scotty's confused look and Dad's half-hearted attempt to ask me if I'd slept okay. Instead, I grabbed my backpack and headed out the door early, earbuds in, already plotting my next move.

The first stop was school, because as much as I wanted to skip again, I couldn't afford another lecture from Dr. Sykes. Plus, I needed to use the library computers. My laptop at home was good for casual searches, but the school computers had access to better databases—hospital reviews, medical articles, maybe even staff directories if I could figure out how to dig deep enough.

By the time first period rolled around, I had three tabs open on Riverside Serenity Care alone. There wasn't much—just a handful of old reviews, most of them generic. "The staff was kind and caring." Blah, blah, blah.

But then I hit on something new. A blog post, written by a woman who'd lost her father at the hospice in 2016. She mentioned how quickly things had gone downhill during his last week, how the nurse—*April*—had assured her it was "natural."

Natural.

I clenched my fists, pulse racing like a freight train. That was her excuse every time, wasn't it? Natural. Expected. Peaceful. Like dying was a service she was offering, not a choice she was stealing. I printed out the article and headed to English.

15

QUESTIONS NO ONE WANTS TO ANSWER

"Do not be afraid of tears. Tears are what heal us when the heart has been broken."
–Unknown

The rest of the day passed in a blur. I sat through classes, but I wasn't *in* them. The lessons, the voices, the noise—it all faded into the background.

My brain was stuck in a loop.

Ten milligrams. Mom's name. April Dawson.

Over and over.

By the time I got home, my head was pounding. All I wanted was to collapse into bed and shut everything out.

But today was Tuesday. *Grief support group. Yay.*

I sighed, rubbing my temples. Before I could think too hard about that, I grabbed my notebook and flipped it open, pressing my pen hard against the page.

· Riverside Serenity Care

· *Patient reviews mentioning April*
· *Morphine dosages—patterns?*

I wasn't just reaching in the dark anymore. I had something real. A thread to pull. But I needed to confirm something. And I knew just who to ask.

I pulled out my phone and shot a text to Kal.

"Hey, can I come in early today? Need to talk to you about something."

She replied almost instantly.

"Yeah, of course. I'm free half an hour before group. See you then."

I exhaled slowly, gripping my phone.

Good. That gave me time. Now I just had to figure out what I was going to say.

KAL'S OFFICE smelled faintly of lavender and plumeria, a soft, almost delicate scent that made the room feel calmer—like it was trying to convince me everything would be okay. Sunlight slanted through the half-closed blinds, stretching golden lines across the muted green walls. In the corner, a plush beanbag sat beside a small table stacked with stress balls, fidget cubes, and motivational flyers.

Kal was at her desk, writing something onto a notepad, but when I knocked on the open door, she looked up. Her face broke into a warm, easy smile.

"V," she said, setting the pen down. "Come on in."

I hesitated for a second before stepping inside, shutting the door softly behind me.

I wasn't entirely sure why I'd come—what I thought I'd get out of this conversation. But Kal had been steady and approachable, and something about her made me feel like she might have answers. Or at least, that she wouldn't think I was completely crazy for asking the questions I couldn't get out of my head.

I sat down, fingers twisting in my lap. "I just . . . had some questions."

Kal leaned back slightly, folding her hands in her lap. "Questions about?"

I exhaled, glancing down at my hands. I hadn't planned this out. Not really. "About grief, I guess. Or . . . hospice care."

Her expression softened, her dark eyes kind but searching. "That's a big topic," she said gently. "Is there something specific on your mind?"

I swallowed. I wasn't ready to mention Mom's journal. Not yet. Not until I knew what I was looking for. But the words, "*If something happens to me,*" rattled inside my head, refusing to settle.

I forced myself to meet her gaze. "How do you know when someone's death was peaceful?"

Kal tilted her head slightly, studying me. "That's a hard question to answer," she said carefully. "But generally, a peaceful death is one where the person's pain is well managed, where they're surrounded by support, and where they feel safe and cared for."

I nodded, but it wasn't the answer I wanted.

Safe and cared for. Mom had been surrounded by nurses, but had she felt safe? Had she felt cared for?

"But, how do you know it wasn't rushed?" I asked, my voice barely above a whisper.

Kal's brows furrowed slightly, and she leaned forward. "Do you feel like someone's death was rushed, V?"

My pulse ticked up. "No," I said quickly. "I mean—not

really. I just . . . I've been thinking about it a lot lately. Like, how do we know people are ready? Especially in hospice care?"

Kal rested her elbows on the desk, her hands loosely clasped. "Hospice care isn't about deciding when someone's ready," she said. "That's up to the patient and their body. Hospice staff—doctors, nurses, social workers—they're there to ease suffering and support families, not to push anyone toward an ending."

Her words were calm. Steady. Logical. But they didn't quiet the gnawing doubt.

I hesitated, then forced myself to ask the question I wasn't sure I wanted the answer to.

"Do hospice nurses ever, um, make decisions for people?" I swallowed. "Like, about when it's time for them to go?"

Kal blinked, her expression unreadable for half a second before she straightened slightly.

"That's a complicated question," she said finally. "Nurses follow very strict ethical guidelines. They manage symptoms, provide comfort, and advocate for the patient's wishes. But ultimately, the timeline of someone's passing isn't something they control."

Her voice was gentle, but there was something else there. Something just beneath the surface.

I held my breath.

"V," she said after a pause, her voice quieter now. "Is this about your mom?"

My fingers curled into fists in my lap. "Kind of," I admitted. "I've been thinking about those last few weeks a lot. And reading some of the things she wrote. And I keep wondering if everything was really as it seemed."

Kal nodded slowly, considering me. "That's completely normal," she said. "When someone we love passes—especially in hospice—it's natural to wonder if there's something we missed. If we could have done something differently."

Her words felt like they were getting close to what I needed to hear—but not quite there.

I shook my head. "But it wasn't my decision," I said quickly. "And it wasn't hers, either." I hesitated, then forced the words out. "It was the nurse."

Kal's expression shifted, the crease between her brows deepening.

"Hospice nurses follow the patient's care plan," she said carefully. "That plan is usually made by the physician, the family, and the patient together. They don't act on their own."

Her voice was even, steady. But something flickered in her eyes—something uncertain.

I bit my lip. "What if they did?" I asked quietly.

Silence. I could feel her watching me, trying to piece together what I wasn't saying. After a long pause, she exhaled and leaned forward. "V, if you feel like something wasn't right, you should talk to someone about it. Your dad, maybe. Or the hospice organization."

I nodded, but I didn't say anything. Talk to Dad? Impossible. He was so sure of how everything had happened. Call the hospice company? The thought alone made my stomach turn.

Kal's voice softened. "You've been through a lot," she said. "And it's okay to have questions. It's okay to feel uncertain. But it's also important to take care of yourself while you process everything. Don't carry this alone, okay?"

I nodded again, but the knot in my chest only tightened. I left Kal's office with her words still echoing in my head.

They are there to ease suffering, not to push anyone toward an ending.

It was a nice thought. But Mom's journal said otherwise.

As I walked down the hallway, my hand brushed against the

strap of my backpack, where the journal was tucked away. I'd come here hoping Kal could give me clarity. Instead, I just felt more uncertain.

What if Mom had been right? What if something *had* happened to her, and no one had noticed? I glanced over my shoulder as I reached the stairs, half expecting to see Kal watching me from her office doorway.

But the hall was empty.

"You're not alone," Kal had said.

But I felt more alone than ever.

16

WAVES OF GRIEF

"Grief, like the ocean, is always moving. Some days it's calm, and some days it crashes over you. But no matter how rough it gets, you'll always find your way back to the shore."
—Kailani (Kal) Makai

I waited in my car until exactly 3:30. I wasn't in the mood for small talk, and the last thing I wanted was for someone to ask how I was doing. That question had no good answer. So I sat, watching the clock tick down until I had no excuse to stay put any longer. With a sigh, I grabbed my backpack and headed inside.

The group was already settling in—Zuri in her usual chair near the window, quietly watching the trees sway outside; Aiden, arms crossed, scowling at nothing in particular; Caitlyn chatting with Joon, who was making a ridiculous face behind her back. Melody sat with perfect posture, her notepad open on her lap, already poised to take notes like this was a class.

Kal greeted me with a warm smile as I slid into my seat.

"Aloha, V."

I gave her a small nod but didn't say anything.

Once we were all seated, Kal passed out a pamphlet. I scanned the list.

Coping with Depression:
Top Seven Self-Help Tips

1. Cultivate supportive relationships.
2. Take care of yourself.
3. Get regular exercise.
4. Eat a healthy, mood-boosting diet.
5. Challenge negative thinking.
6. Raise your emotional intelligence.
7. Know when to get additional help.

Common sense. Yet, I wasn't following *any* of it. I sighed and stuffed the pamphlet into my backpack.

"But the part of him that matters is gone," Caitlyn was saying, her voice thick with emotion. "I'll never see him again. I'll never get to hug him. Or pretend to like his burnt steaks."

Aiden exhaled sharply, his fingers tapping restlessly against his knee. "I think about my little sister and brothers," he said. "This is hard on them, too."

Kal nodded. "Have you heard the expression, 'Put on your own oxygen mask first'?"

"Of course," Joon piped up. "But it's not just an expression. It's literally part of the safety speech flight attendants give. You put your own mask on first so you don't pass out before helping anyone else, like kids."

"Exactly," Kal said.

Aiden frowned. "I don't get it."

Kal leaned forward slightly, her voice calm, steady. "In this case, it's a metaphor. When you're grieving, it's important to prioritize your own self-care—to allow yourself time to process everything. If you don't, it becomes harder to be there for the people who need you."

Aiden shook his head. "How is my seven-year-old little sister supposed to prioritize self-care? She needs help!"

"Yes," Kal agreed. "But you can't help her if you're barely getting through the day yourself."

"Besides," Joon added, "kids are weirdly resilient."

"Really?" I said. "I have a little brother. Tell me how resilient this is—he thinks our mom broke into a million pieces and is in the sky with the glass stars and Thunderbird, watching over us. You think that's healthy?"

Silence.

"It might be reassuring to him," Kal said after a moment. "A way for him to process her absence in a way that feels less final."

Aiden let out a short, bitter laugh. "Yeah? Well, it feels pretty final to me."

I nodded in agreement.

The room went quiet for a beat.

Kal let the silence settle for a moment, then said, "Grief, like the ocean, is always moving. Some days it's calm, and some days it crashes over you. But no matter how rough it gets, you'll always find your way back to the shore."

Aiden scoffed, running a hand through his hair. "Yeah? What if I don't?"

"You will," Kal said softly. "Maybe not today. Maybe not for a long time. But the waves don't stay this rough forever."

Aiden scowled but didn't reply. The rest of the group looked thoughtful, and I just tried to make sense of it all.

Then Kal spoke again, her voice gentle but firm. "All of you —the point is, taking care of your own physical, emotional, and mental health isn't selfish. It's a necessary step in being able to support the people around you."

I looked down at my hands, my nails digging into my palm.

I can't think about how hard this is on my dad right now. I have to put my own oxygen mask on first. Know what I mean?

I have to tell myself to get up. I have to tell myself to breathe. I have to make myself get through the day.

And then I have to do it again tomorrow. And the next day. And the next.

I DIDN'T FEEL like going home after group.

I should have. I should've gone back, had dinner with Dad and Scotty, maybe even started my English essay. But the thought of walking into the house—of sitting at the table, pretending I was fine—I just couldn't do it.

So, without thinking too much about it, I found myself driving toward Emma's.

By the time I pulled up in front of her house, I was already second-guessing myself. I hadn't texted her. I hadn't even planned to come here. What if she was busy? What if she didn't even want to see me?

But before I could talk myself out of it, the front door swung open.

Emma stood in the doorway, blinking at me in surprise. "V?" She tilted her head. "What are you doing here?"

I swallowed. "I—uh, I was just in the area."

Emma raised an eyebrow. "In the area?"

Okay. Weak excuse. I shifted on my feet. "I didn't feel like going home."

Her expression softened slightly, and after a brief pause, she stepped aside. "Come in."

The smell of fresh tortillas and simmering pinto beans filled the air, wrapping around me like a hug. My stomach twisted—not from hunger, but from the sudden familiarity of it. Warm, rich, comforting.

"Abuela's cooking?" I asked.

Emma nodded, leading me inside. "Yeah, she's making burritos. Want some?"

I shook my head. "Just water for me."

She went in the kitchen and came back out with a glass of water, handing it to me before taking a seat on the sofa. "So what's up?"

I took a sip and sat in the chair next to the sofa, stalling. "I went to grief group."

Emma's brows lifted slightly. "And?"

I shrugged. "And nothing. Same as always. Kal handed out some pamphlets, people talked about how sad they were, and Aiden got mad at the world."

Emma smirked faintly. "Sounds about right."

She studied me in silence, like she was waiting for me to *really* say something.

I sighed, setting my glass down. "I don't know why I came over."

Emma didn't answer right away. Instead, she reached for the bag of pretzels on the coffee table, popped one in her mouth, and said, "Well, do you wanna talk, or do you wanna eat snacks and watch bad TV until you feel better?"

A lump rose in my throat. It was such a simple offer. But after dodging her, avoiding everyone, and keeping my thoughts locked up tight, it felt . . . good.

"Bad TV," I whispered. "Definitely bad TV."

Emma grinned. "Good choice." She grabbed the pretzels, nodded toward the living room, and just like that, we were okay again.

17

ZURI'S CONNECTION

"The wound is the place where the light enters you."
–Rumi

At school the next morning, I was still thinking about the case. Obviously. When wasn't I?

I shut my locker and started zombie-walking toward English when I ran straight into Emma. *Literally.*

"Hey, sleepwalking again?" she teased, steadying me with a hand on my arm.

"Kinda." I rubbed my face. "I haven't been sleeping too well lately."

"Yeah, I know. Have you tried taking something to help?"

"You mean sleeping pills? No, I would never—"

"No, I mean, like, home remedies," she interrupted. "My abuela swears by manzanilla tea. She makes a whole thing out of it—lights a candle, mutters something under her breath. It's like a ritual." She laughed.

My stomach twisted.

"Oh. Maybe I'll try that," I said, forcing a small smile. Little did she know the real reason I wasn't sleeping.

Emma didn't push. Instead, she bumped my shoulder lightly. "Hey, last night was fun. We should do that again sometime."

"Yeah," I admitted. "I'd like that."

"I miss you, V."

I swallowed. "I know. I miss you, too."

As we settled into class, Emma's offhand comment lingered in my mind—her abuela's ritual. It sparked a memory, something Zuri mentioned in group last week. April praying in another language over her patients.

I never followed up on that. I didn't want to wait until the next group meeting. So, as soon as I slid into my desk, I pulled out my phone.

I scrolled through Waves of Hope's Instagram page until I found her.

Zuri M. | Book nerd | Trying to be okay.

Her profile was private, of course. But it was her. I hesitated for half a second, then tapped "message."

"Hey, Zuri. It's V, from Waves of Hope. I was thinking about what you said last week about your dad's nurse. I'm sorry if this is weird, but I'm trying to understand something about hospice care, and I was wondering if you'd be willing to talk more about it."

I hit "send" before I could second-guess myself.

For a long time, nothing. I stared at my screen, my heart pounding, half convinced she'd ignore me. I put my phone away and tried to pay attention to Miss Calloway's lecture. My grades were already slipping, so I should probably make an effort.

I WOULDN'T LET myself take my phone out again until the break after second period. This case was taking over my life—the last thing I needed was to flunk all my classes my senior year.

I slipped my phone out and took a deep breath, opening the Instagram app. There it was.

Zuri M.: *Hey, V. Sure, I guess. What do you want to know?*

I exhaled, my fingers shaking as I typed.

You said the nurse prayed in another language. Do you remember what she looked like?

Her response came immediately.

Zuri M.: *Um, yeah. Small, brown hair, kind of plain-looking? She prayed in Spanish over my dad. And she smiled a lot, but it was . . . idk, too much? Like she was trying too hard to act calm all the time. Why? Did you know her?*

That description fit April perfectly. I chose my next words carefully.

I might've had the same nurse for my mom. Do you remember her name?

Zuri M.: *I don't, sorry. But she worked nights most of the time. And I remember her saying something about being from South America? She talked about how death wasn't the end, just a transition or whatever. It kind of freaked me out, tbh.*

I felt goosebumps. April. It had to be her. The South America detail sealed it. Dad had mentioned once that she was from Colombia.

Thanks, Zuri. That helps a lot.

A pause. Then . . .

Zuri M.: *Are you okay? You seem . . . idk, intense?*

I stared at the message for a second before typing back:

I'm fine. Just trying to figure some stuff out.

Her response was a simple thumbs-up.

But I could feel her hesitation even through the screen. I didn't care. This was the confirmation I needed.

The bell rang, and I had to get to class.

Once home, it was time to go over all my clues, a big-picture view. I carefully took down the photos of happier times I'd tacked to my bulletin board and created space for an investigation board, like they do in the detective shows.

I tacked up Mom's and April's photos, with some important papers, then made sticky notes for each clue:

> Zuri's dad
> Hospice, prayed in Spanish
> "South America"
> Worked nights

I pinned them under April's name, then stepped back, staring at the board, chewing on the inside of my cheek.

More connections. More families. More people who had been alone with April in their final hours.

How many more were there? I grabbed my laptop and started digging.

I searched hospice directories, staff pages, old reviews. I dug through forums, local news articles, anything buried deep in Google's results.

Hours passed in a blur. The glow of the screen made my eyes burn, but I barely noticed.

And then—buried in an old staff list from a hospice in San

Diego—her name appeared.

April Dawson. Another hospice. Another pattern. Patients dying faster than expected.

I'D SKIPPED DINNER, ignored my family, and stayed awake from sheer stubbornness and caffeine. But it was worth it because I was getting closer. I could feel it. April had been working as a hospice nurse for years, transferring from hospital to hospital, always slipping away before any official complaints could stick.

And her patients? They all died *too fast*.

I had pages of notes, lists of names, flagged medical records. Mostly elderly patients, late-stage cancer, severe pain. It all lined up.

But then, I saw one name that didn't fit. Richard C. Hayes, age thirty-seven, stage two ALS.

I frowned, pulling up his file. He wasn't dying. Not yet. ALS was fatal, yeah, but it could take *years*. Most stage two patients could still function, still talk, still live. But according to the hospice records, Richard had died in his sleep—while April worked at the hospice in San Diego.

My stomach lurched. I double-checked the medication log. He'd been given morphine, but the dosage was normal. No overdose. No red flags.

Cause of death: *cardiac arrest due to respiratory failure.*

I bit my lip, flipping between files. It didn't add up. April's other patients were at the ends of their lives—in constant pain, no real chance left. Richard still had time. *So had Amanda.*

I wrote a note and stuck it to the board:

• Richard Hayes – stage two ALS – too early to die???

I stared at the name for a moment. Then I shook my head.

Maybe he'd had complications. Maybe his body gave out faster than expected. Maybe.

I sighed, rubbing my temples. It didn't matter. April was still the answer. Even if Richard wasn't a perfect match, he was under her care. That was enough for me.

I shut my laptop and pushed the papers aside, reaching for my phone to check the time. 12:37 a.m.

I needed sleep. Because tomorrow? Tomorrow, I was going to prove April Dawson was a murderer.

18

THE CRACKS BEGIN TO SHOW

"Grief is a tide, rising and falling on its own time.
It cannot be rushed, silenced, or wished away.
It will hold you, break you, and leave only when it's ready.
Those untouched by loss may never understand
how it rewrites your soul."
–Unknown

The smell of coffee and Pop-Tarts dragged me out of my room the next morning. I hadn't meant to stay up that late—again—but sleep felt like an afterthought lately. Who needed REM cycles when your brain was running on adrenaline and spite?

Scotty and Dad were at the table, munching on Pop-Tarts. Scotty had his tablet propped up next to him, something bright and cartoony playing on the screen.

I hovered in the doorway for a second, the tension in my chest squeezing tighter. It wasn't fair that they could just sit there, eating breakfast, watching cartoons, acting like everything was okay. Like Mom wasn't gone. Like she hadn't been stolen.

"You were up late," Dad said, glancing over his shoulder. His tone was neutral, but I could hear the question underneath it. *Why are you up late all the time? What are you doing in there?*

I shrugged, heading for the fridge. "Homework."

"That's what you said yesterday."

"And it was true yesterday," I shot back, grabbing a Pop-Tart. "Ah, the breakfast of champions."

Dad sighed. "V, look, I know things have been hard. For all of us. But you've got to—"

"I'm fine," I snapped, cutting him off. "You don't have to do the whole concerned-parent thing. I'm not Scotty."

Scotty looked up from his cartoons, his wide eyes flicking between us like a spectator at a tennis match. "I didn't do anything," he mumbled.

"No one said you did, buddy," Dad said gently, but I could see the tightness in his jaw. He turned back to me. "V, I'm just trying to help. You've been so closed off lately, and I . . ." He hesitated, his voice softening. "I don't want to lose you, too."

The words were like a dagger.

I stared at him, the guilt crawling under my skin like fire ants. He looked so tired. The dark circles under his eyes made him look older, his shoulders slumped like he was carrying the weight of the world—and I wasn't helping.

But instead of apologizing, I pulled back into myself, wrapping my arms around my chest like armor. "I'm fine," I said again, this time quieter. "I've just got a lot going on."

Dad opened his mouth, but before he could say anything else, I turned and left, muttering, "I've got to get ready for school."

I shut the door to my room and leaned against it, exhaling shakily. My head was pounding, my chest still tight from the conversation downstairs. I glanced at my desk. The papers were still there, scattered and chaotic, a physical reminder of everything I couldn't let go. My laptop was open to the hospice directory I'd found last night, the screen dark after hours of inactivity.

This wasn't supposed to feel like this. I'd thought that figuring it out—finding the connections, building the case— would make me feel closer to Mom. Like maybe, somehow, solving this would be a way to keep her with me. But it wasn't working. If anything, it was pulling me further away.

Emma walked on eggshells around me, barely talking about Miles, or soccer, or anything going on in her life. I'd walked out on family movie night, leaving Scotty and Dad with that sad scene. I'd been a terrible friend, sister, and daughter.

I didn't know who I was anymore, outside of this. Outside of the rage and the grief and the singular focus on *her*. April Dawson. The name burned in my mind like a brand. I hated her, hated everything about her—her fake smile, her calm demeanor, the way she whispered prayers over people she was stealing from their families.

But more than that, I hated myself. Because I'd been there. I'd sat in that room with Mom, holding her hand, thinking it was the end of her journey, her *natural* time to go. And I hadn't seen it. I hadn't seen *her*.

I grabbed the closest thing to me—a pen—and threw it across the room. It hit the wall with a dull thunk and fell to the floor. Not satisfying enough.

My legs gave out, and I sank to the carpet, my back against the door. The tears came back with a vengeance, spilling hot and fast down my cheeks. Silent sobs shook my shoulders as I pulled my knees to my chest, burying my face against them. I wanted to scream. I wanted to break something. But all I could do was sit there, trembling, while the weight of it all crashed down around me.

I didn't know how long I sat there. Long enough for the tears to dry on my face, leaving my skin tight and raw. When I finally stood, my legs felt like jelly. I rubbed my eyes and walked over to my desk. The bulletin board loomed over it, the names and sticky notes taunting me, daring me to give up.

I stared at April's headshot. "No," I whispered, my voice hoarse. "You don't get to win."

I grabbed a pen and scribbled a new note, pinning it to the board:

Next step: Find patients from San Diego hospice.
Track dates. Look for families willing to talk.

This wasn't just about Mom anymore. It was about everyone.

THE SCHOOL DAY passed by in an uneventful blur. I couldn't wait to get back home and work on the case. Finally, the bulletin board loomed over me, cluttered with sticky notes, printouts, and pins connecting dots in messy, overlapping lines. April Dawson's name was at the center, circled in red. Around her were smaller names, the ones I'd spent hours digging up: patients who had died in the last few weeks of her employment at the San Diego hospice.

Four names. Four people who were gone, just like Mom.

And maybe—just *maybe*—four families who could help me prove that this wasn't just a coincidence.

I stared at the list. Reaching out to Zuri had been one thing. We were in group together. Both grieving. It had been awkward, but at least I could pretend we were equals.

This? This felt different. These were strangers, older people who'd lived through so much already. What right did I have to ask them to dredge it all up again?

But then I thought about Mom, lying in that bed, her breaths shallow and uneven. I thought about the way April had smiled at me that night, calm and reassuring, like she wasn't stealing Mom from me.

I gritted my teeth, grabbed my phone, and looked at the first lead.

The name at the top of my list was Craig Ganz, a man in his sixties whose wife, Darlene, had died at the San Diego hospice three years ago. He'd posted a comment on a local news article about hospice care, something vague but critical: *"Not all hospices are as compassionate as they claim to be."*

I found his phone number buried in an old online directory, one of those sketchy people-search websites that probably broke ten privacy laws. It felt invasive. Creepy, even. But I needed answers.

I dialed the number before I could lose my nerve. The phone rang twice before a gruff, tired voice answered. "Hello?"

I swallowed hard. "Hi, Mr. Ganz. My name's Violet." My voice wavered slightly, but I pushed through. "I'm really sorry to bother you, but I'm trying to learn more about the San Diego hospice where your wife was a patient. I was wondering if you'd be willing to talk to me about your experience."

There was a long pause. My heart pounded in the silence.

"How'd you get my number?" he asked finally, suspicion creeping into his tone.

I hesitated. Lying felt wrong, but the truth—*I found it on a sketchy website while hunting down my mom's killer*—wasn't an option. "I found it online," I said, keeping my tone neutral. "I know this is out of the blue, and I understand if you don't want to talk to me, but . . . it's important."

He sighed, and I heard the faint creak of a chair. "Why are you asking?"

"My mom was in hospice care, too," I said quickly, leaning into the truth where I could. "She passed away recently, and . . . I have questions. About how it all happened. About the nurses. I came across your wife's name, and I thought maybe—"

"Maybe what?" His voice was sharp now, defensive.

"Maybe we had the same nurse," I said, my stomach churning. "Her name was April Dawson. Does that sound familiar?"

The silence that followed was thick and heavy. My pulse roared in my ears.

Finally, Craig said, "Darlene always liked her. She said she had a calming presence. But . . ." He hesitated, and I could almost hear the tension in his voice. "I thought it was strange, how fast everything happened at the end. She was stable one day, and then—"

He cut himself off, clearing his throat. "Look, I don't know what you're trying to figure out, but dragging all this up isn't going to change anything."

"But what if it does?" I blurted. "What if it wasn't natural? What if it wasn't supposed to happen like that?"

"Kid . . ." He sighed, and the weight in his voice hit me like a brick. "What are you hoping to get out of this? Justice? Closure? Because neither one's going to bring her back."

The words stung, but I refused to back down. "Maybe not," I said quietly. "But if April Dawson did something—if she's done this to other people—don't you think someone should stop her?"

There was another long pause. When he spoke again, his voice was softer, almost reluctant. "I remember her saying something strange once. Something about how suffering didn't have to last, and how some people needed a little help letting go."

My stomach dropped.

"Do you think you could write that down?" I asked, my voice trembling. "Or email me, maybe? Anything you remember about her?"

"I'll think about it," Craig said, his tone guarded. "But you should be careful, kid. If you dig too deep into this, you might not like what you find."

The line went dead before I could respond.

I set the phone down on my desk, my hands shaking. Craig's words echoed in my head. *You might not like what you find.*

Too late. I already didn't like it.

I stared at my bulletin board, at April's smiling photo pinned next to Mom's name. The connection was there, clear as day: April wasn't just a nurse. She was a *predator*, hiding behind her calm demeanor and her whispered prayers.

I scribbled a note under Craig's name:

Darlene Ganz: Stable one day, gone the next.
April's comments: Suffering doesn't have to last.

Another thread. Another victim.

But Craig's warning stayed with me, gnawing at the edges of my resolve. What if he was right? What if this was too big for me to handle?

I shook my head, pushing the thought aside.

"Doesn't matter," I whispered to myself, pinning the note to the board. "I'm not stopping."

I ACTUALLY TOOK a break and ate dinner with my family. Dad brought home tacos. But thankfully, he spared the small talk.

We ate on TV trays in the living room, while watching some kid show that had Scotty in giggle fits. It was good to see him happy, for a change.

Yet, all through dinner I couldn't turn my thoughts off. Craig's words played on a loop in my head: *"What are you hoping to get out of this? Justice? Closure? Because neither one's going to bring her back."*

I pressed my palms into my eyes, trying to block out the voice, the memories, the guilt. But it was useless. The doubts were already there, creeping in like shadows under the door.

What *was* I hoping to get out of this? What was I even doing?

I let out a shaky breath and stared at the TV, my eyes glazing over. Craig's voice had been so heavy, so certain, like he'd already made peace with what happened to his wife. He sounded tired—like he'd spent years trying to forget, only for me to drag it all back up again.

And for what? A few cryptic comments? Another fragile thread to pin to my wall?

I closed my eyes, and for a second, I was back at Mom's bedside. The beeping of machines, the smell of antiseptic, the faint rustle of April's scrubs as she moved around the bed. I remembered how calm she'd been, how she'd smiled at me like she *understood*.

I'd thought she was being kind. Now, all I could see was the lie in her eyes.

My stomach churned, and I shot up, grabbed my dishes, and hurried to the kitchen. "Get it together, V," I said under my breath. "You're not doing this for you. You're doing it for her."

But even as I said the words, they felt hollow. Was I really doing this for Mom? Or was it for me?

Craig had asked what I wanted—justice, closure, something else. I didn't know the answer. All I knew was that every time I looked at Mom's name on my bulletin board, I felt this gnawing ache in my chest, this desperate need to make sense of it all. To make it *matter*.

But what if he was right? What if digging into this just made everything worse? What if it made me worse?

I stood at the kitchen sink for what felt like forever, my thoughts spiraling in circles. The room felt quieter than it should have, like even the house was holding its breath.

Eventually, I turned on the water and rinsed off my plate. I threw away the fast-food wrappers and wiped down the counters. The truth was, I didn't know what I was hoping to find. I didn't know if justice or closure was even possible. But I *had* to keep going.

Because if I stopped—if I let the doubts win—then April Dawson would keep smiling, keep whispering her prayers, keep stealing lives from families who didn't even know they needed to fight for them.

I couldn't let that happen.

19
POP QUIZ

"Those we love never truly leave us.
There are things that death cannot touch."
–Jack Thorne, *Harry Potter and the Cursed Child*

The quiz landed on my desk with a satisfying thwap.

"Fifteen minutes," Mr. Grayson announced, shuffling back to his desk with a stack of ungraded assignments tucked under his arm. "No calculators for the first section. Show your work."

A collective groan rippled through the class. I barely noticed.

I stared at the page, blinking like the numbers might rearrange themselves into something I understood.

Sample mean . . . standard deviation . . . probability distributions.

My brain refused to cooperate.

I tapped my pencil against the desk, rereading the first question for the third time. Something about a survey and a confidence interval? Or maybe it was about expected values? I couldn't tell anymore.

Because all I could think about was April's name pinned in the center of my bulletin board. I'd spent half the night buried in hospice records, scouring forums, searching for other families she might have fooled. The idea that this woman—this smiling, soft-voiced fraud—could still be out there, slipping into other homes, sitting beside other dying patients, made my stomach twist.

How many more families did she manipulate?

The clock ticked. Loudly. Each second slipped through my fingers like sand. I scratched out a few half-hearted answers, but when Mr. Grayson called time, I had barely finished the first page.

He came around to collect the quizzes, pausing a beat too long when he reached my desk. "V, are you okay?" he asked quietly, his brow furrowed.

"I'm fine," I said, gripping the edge of my desk to keep from snapping.

He didn't look convinced, but he moved on. I slumped back in my seat, my face burning. Another failure. Another thing Mom would've been disappointed about.

I WAS HEADED for the exit, earbuds in, when Emma stepped in front of me.

I pulled out one earbud, arching an eyebrow. "What?"

She crossed her arms. "Have lunch with me?"

I hesitated. I usually went home for lunch—less noise, fewer people, no forced conversations—but Emma's expression told me this wasn't a request.

"Fine," I sighed.

The quad was its usual mess of chaos and stale cafeteria pizza. My stomach growled—I hadn't eaten since last night—so I grabbed an apple and a granola bar before following Emma to a table at the edge of the courtyard, under a tree where it was quieter.

She unwrapped her sandwich, watching me carefully. "Got any weekend plans?"

I shrugged. "Do you?"

Emma brightened. "Yeah, actually. Miles is coming home this weekend. His cousin's getting married, so his family's flying him in just for the wedding. He asked me to be his plus-one." She smiled, tucking a strand of hair behind her ear. "Isn't that great?"

"Super."

The word fell flat, dull, laced with something even I couldn't define.

Emma's smile faded. "What's with you?" she snapped. She wasn't just annoyed—she was hurt.

Guilt churned in my stomach, sharp and immediate. But then I thought about Mom. About April. About how close I was to figuring it all out.

I inhaled sharply. "I've just got a lot going on." I forced a lighter tone. "You wouldn't get it."

Emma blinked like I'd slapped her. "What's that supposed to mean?"

"Nothing. Just drop it, okay?"

Her jaw tightened. "No. I'm not dropping it."

I looked up. Her eyes burned with frustration, but there was something else there, too. Hurt. "You're my best friend, V," she said, voice rising slightly. "Or at least, you used to be. Now you're just ... I don't know. A stranger."

The words hit hard. I clenched my fists under the table,

forcing down the urge to lash out. "I'm sorry if I'm not the perfect friend you want me to be right now, but I've got better things to do than sit around eating pizza and talking about boys."

Emma's face crumpled.

For a moment, I wished I could grab the words and shove them back down my throat.

"Wow," she said quietly, pushing her tray away. "That's really what you think of me?"

I opened my mouth—to apologize, to explain, to fix it. But nothing came out.

Emma stood, grabbing her backpack. "You know what? Let me know when you're done being mad at the world. Maybe then we can talk."

I watched Emma walk away, my chest tightening, the weight of my own words crushing me from the inside out. *What's wrong with me?*

I had wanted to hurt her—no, that wasn't right. I had wanted her to understand that I wasn't the same person anymore, that I didn't have room for wedding dates and small talk. But instead of saying that, I'd made her feel like she didn't matter. And that wasn't true.

I shoved my uneaten granola bar into my backpack, suddenly feeling sick. Emma and I had been through everything together—best friends since first grade. She'd been there when Mom got sick. She'd sat next to me in the hospital waiting room, distracting me with stupid memes and vending machine snacks while I tried to hold on to hope that was already slipping through my fingers.

She had been there. And now? I was pushing her away like she was nothing. I squeezed my eyes shut, willing the lump in my throat to disappear.

I should go after her. Tell her I didn't mean it. Tell her I'm sorry.

My fingers twitched against the edge of the table, my whole body screaming at me to stand up.

But I didn't. I sat there, frozen, because part of me still believed what I said.

I *did* have bigger things to worry about. I *did* have better things to do than pretend everything was fine. But at what cost?

I glanced toward the quad entrance, hoping—*stupidly*—that Emma might turn around. That she'd give me a second chance to fix it before it festered into something worse.

But she didn't. She kept walking.

And I just sat there, my stomach twisting, regretting everything.

✶ ✦ ✷ ✦ ✶

BY THE TIME I got home, my stomach was still in knots. I tossed my backpack onto the couch and sank into it, rubbing a hand over my face. The house was quiet. Too quiet. *Where's Lucky?*

He always greeted me at the door, tail wagging, paws skittering on the tile as he ran up to me. Every day, without fail. But today? Nothing.

I straightened, scanning the living room. "Lucky?"

No sign of him.

I walked to the dog door. Unlatched.

My pulse ticked up a notch. I pushed through the back door and scanned the yard. "Lucky!"

No movement. No collar tags jingling. Nothing.

I ran to the gate. Still locked. That meant he hadn't gotten out, right? But then where—

Panic surged up my throat. Our family did *not* need one more bad thing to happen.

I yanked my phone out of my pocket and called Dad. Straight to voicemail.

My hands trembled as I fired off a text:

> LUCKY'S MISSING!!! Call me ASAP

Seconds later, my phone buzzed.

Dad.

I fumbled to answer. "Dad—"

"No, he's not." His voice was calm, amused even. "Check the note on the kitchen island. I'm still in class. Not all of us have half days." He hung up.

A second later, my phone vibrated again. A text.

DAD

I exhaled shakily, relief hitting so hard it left me lightheaded.

I sprinted back inside and found the note, scrawled in Dad's messy handwriting:

> V,
>
> Dropped Lucky off at the vet's this morning. Minor ear infection. They can board him till I get off work, or you can go get him early if you want. Your call.
>
> I'll bring Chinese food home for dinner.
>
> Love, Dad

I sagged against the counter, pressing a hand to my chest.

I was fine. Lucky was fine. But I needed to see him now.

Grabbing my keys, I headed for the door. Then—out of habit, I reached for my phone again, fingers already moving to text Emma.

You won't believe the heart attack I just had—

I stopped. Right. Emma wasn't speaking to me.

For a second, I just stared at the screen, the instinct to share clashing with the reality of our fight. I hated this. Hated the space between us, the way my own words had burned a bridge I didn't know how to fix.

I got in my car and typed out the message I should have sent much sooner:

I'm sorry. I didn't mean what I said.

I miss you.

I hit send. Then I waited. And waited.

Nothing. No three dots. No immediate *"It's okay."* No sarcastic *"Finally, you admit it."*

Just silence.

I threw my phone onto the passenger seat and backed out of the driveway.

The regret inside me turned from a dull ache to a stinging slap. Emma never ignored my texts. Not like this. Maybe she was just busy. Maybe she needed time.

Or maybe she was done with me.

I swallowed hard and shoved the thought down. *Fine.* I focused on the street ahead. At least Lucky still wanted to see me.

20
THE VET'S LEAD

"Sometimes, only one person is missing,
and the whole world feels empty."
–Alphonse de Lamartine

I pulled into the vet's parking lot, my nerves finally settling now that I knew Lucky was safe.

Inside, the air smelled like antiseptic. Muffled barks and meows filled the small waiting area. A couple sat near the door with a massive golden retriever sprawled across their feet. A woman in scrubs was trying to coax a stubborn cat out of its carrier.

Then—Lucky's bark.

I turned just in time to see his little brown and white body squirming behind the counter, ears perked, tail wagging so hard his whole back half wiggled.

"Lucky!" I breathed, relief washing over me again.

A vet tech—mid-twenties, red scrubs with black paw prints all over them, dark curls pulled into a messy bun—grinned as she scooped him up. "Someone's happy to see you." She set him on the counter, scratching behind his ears.

Lucky's tail thwacked against the countertop like a drumbeat.

"You have *no* idea." I reached out, running my fingers over his fur, grounding myself in the warmth of him. My good boy. My constant.

"He's been a good patient," the tech said with a grin. "Just a minor ear infection, nothing to stress about. We gave him his first round of meds—just keep up with the drops, and he should be fine in a few days."

"Thanks." I ruffled Lucky's fur, relief washing over me. At least one thing in my life wasn't falling apart.

She grabbed a clipboard and flipped through pages. "You're Violet, right? Your dad said you might come early."

"Yeah, that's me."

"Cool, just need you to sign here, and you guys are good to go."

I took the pen and signed my name. As I slid the clipboard back, the vet tech hesitated.

"Hey, random question," she said, tilting her head. "Didn't you go to Sierra High?"

I blinked. "Uh yeah?"

Her face lit up. "Knew you looked familiar! I think we had French together? Junior year?"

I studied her again. She did look familiar. "It was freshman year for me . . . Mia?"

"Close—Maria." She laughed, tucking a curl behind her ear.

"Right," I said, nodding. "Sorry, I'm—"

"Running on fumes?" she finished with a smirk. "Been there. Been *there*."

I huffed out a laugh, rubbing Lucky's head. "Yeah, something like that."

She leaned against the counter. "So, how've you been? You still at Sierra?"

"Yeah. Senior year. Just trying to make it through."

Maria nodded knowingly. "I feel that. Senior year was a mess for me. Family stuff, college apps, all of it. And my aunt—" She shook her head. "Sorry, you don't need my life story."

"No, it's fine," I said automatically. But then—*aunt?*

Something about the way she said it made my brain click into high alert.

Maria sighed. "It was just rough, you know? She passed a few years ago. Hospice care. In San Diego."

My heart stopped. San Diego.

My fingers tightened in Lucky's fur.

"San Diego?" I repeated, trying to sound casual. "Do you know where?"

Maria blinked, surprised by the question. "Hmm, some place called, like, St. Lucia's, I think?"

St. Lucia's hospice in San Diego? That meant April.

My mouth felt dry. "I—I'm sorry about your aunt."

"Thanks," Maria said softly. "She was young, too. It was sudden. I mean, we knew she was sick, but she wasn't supposed to go that fast, you know?"

I knew. Oh, God. I knew. "Yeah," I murmured. "I know."

Maria sighed. "Anyway, it sucked. But the nurses were nice. Well, most of them."

I forced my expression to stay neutral. "Most of them?"

She shrugged. "Yeah, there was this one—April, I think? Yeah, April Dawson. She gave me the creeps."

My pulse spiked so hard I thought Maria might hear it. I kept my face neutral, my fingers tightening in Lucky's fur. "What do you mean, she gave you the creeps?"

Maria made a face, like she was debating how much to say. "I don't know. She was just—off. She was super nice at first, all 'I'm here for your family' and 'We'll make sure she's comfortable,' but something about her felt fake."

My stomach twisted. "Fake how?"

Maria leaned against the counter, absently tapping her nails on the clipboard. "I guess it was the way she talked to us. She was too calm, you know? Like, unbothered. Even when things got bad, she had that same soft voice, that same creepy little smile."

I knew that smile.

"She talked a lot about death, too," Maria added. "Like, more than usual. I mean, I know hospice is all about end-of-life care, but she made it sound like some beautiful transition instead of —" She gestured vaguely, frustration in her voice. "Instead of what it actually is. Instead of my aunt dying."

I swallowed hard. This was it. This wasn't just a bad vibe or a misinterpretation. This was the pattern.

The same eerie calm. The same way of talking about death like it was inevitable, like it was just another step on a schedule she already had planned out. "Did she—" My voice caught. I forced myself to sound casual. "Did she handle your aunt's meds?"

Maria frowned, like she was trying to remember. "Yeah. Well, a few nurses did, but April was on shift when—" She broke off, shaking her head. "Never mind. Doesn't matter."

It mattered.

"Maria." I met her eyes, my pulse skyrocketing. "Did your aunt decline really fast?"

Maria hesitated, brows pulling together. Then she sighed. "Yeah. She did."

I barely breathed. "Like ... how fast?"

Maria's fingers drummed against the counter, her expression darkening. "She was stable for a while. Then April started her on some new med—morphine, I think?—and after that, it was like everything just . . ." She exhaled. "Like she just gave up. Like her body shut down overnight."

A chill ran through me.

Maria looked away. "I always wondered if they gave her too much, but the doctors said it was just the disease progressing. Said it happens sometimes, that it was 'her time.'" Her lips pressed into a thin line. "It didn't feel like her time."

I wanted to tell her *she wasn't crazy*. That she wasn't just imagining things. That it wasn't her aunt's time—it was April's decision. But I couldn't say that. Not yet. Instead, I forced my fingers to relax in Lucky's fur and took a slow breath.

"I'm really sorry," I said quietly. And I meant it.

Maria gave a small, tired smile. "Yeah. Thanks." She straightened, shaking off the heaviness of the moment. "Anyway, sorry for dumping that on you. It was forever ago."

"It's okay." I swallowed. "Really."

Maria glanced at the clock behind her. "Well, you're all set with Lucky. Just keep up with the ear drops and call if you need anything."

"Right. Yeah. Thanks."

She smiled and turned toward the back office, and I forced my legs to move, walking out of the clinic in a daze.

By the time I reached my car, my hands were shaking. I barely got Lucky into the passenger seat before gripping the steering wheel, staring out at nothing.

April Dawson. San Diego. Hospice. Morphine. Too much, too fast.

It was the same story. I exhaled sharply, my whole body vibrating with nausea, rage, and cold, hard certainty. She'd been doing this for years. And no one had stopped her.

I reached for my phone and pulled up my notes, my thumbs flying across the screen.

- San Diego – St. Lucia's Hospice
- Maria's aunt – April was her nurse
- Same pattern: "comfort," morphine, rapid decline
- Too fast. "Didn't feel like her time."

I chewed the inside of my cheek, heart pounding. This wasn't a coincidence. This wasn't just a hunch anymore. April Dawson wasn't just careless. She was a killer. But I needed actual proof.

21

THE BEST FRIEND CLAUSE

"To live in hearts we leave behind is not to die."
–Thomas Campbell

I barely remembered the drive home.

The second I stepped inside, I grabbed my laptop, Lucky trailing behind me as I shut my bedroom door and dove in.

San Diego. St. Lucia's Hospice. April Dawson. I searched everything.

Old job listings. Staff directories. Complaints. Anything that could tie April to another unexplained death.

Hours passed. The glow of my screen made my eyes burn, but I ignored it. I found breadcrumbs—bits of information buried three or four pages deep in Google searches.

- A brief mention of April Dawson on a staff page from 2015.

- A comment on a hospice review site: "My mother declined so fast after a new nurse took over her care."
- A news article about St. Lucia's receiving scrutiny for unusually high patient mortality rates that same year.

It was all adding up. But not enough. I needed proof.

I sat back in my chair, rubbing my eyes. My phone buzzed, and I grabbed it, half hoping it was another witness.

It wasn't.

EMMA.

Hey. I saw your text. I don't know what you
want me to say.

My stomach twisted. I stared at the message, my thumbs hovering over the letters.

I just want to talk.

A full minute passed. Then—

About what? How you don't have time for me
anymore?

I squeezed my eyes shut. I deserved that.

No. About everything.

Another pause.
Then:

Meet me at the park?

THE AIR WAS STILL thick with late-summer heat as I pulled in at the park, the setting sun painting everything in gold.

Emma was already there, sitting on the back of a bench with her feet propped up on the seat, her sneakers untied.

She didn't look up as I walked over, her fingers absentmindedly twisting a strand of hair.

I hesitated. Then sat down beside her, letting my flip-flops dangle from my toes.

Neither of us spoke at first.

Then Emma exhaled, still not looking at me. "So. What's *everything*?"

I stared at my hands. "It's not just about Mom."

Emma finally turned, her sharp brown eyes scanning my face. "Then what is it?"

I swallowed, my throat tight. "Do you remember when I told you I had a bad feeling about April?"

She nodded. "The hospice nurse, right?"

I nodded. "I've been looking into her. And, Em—" I sucked in a breath. "She's been doing this for years."

Emma frowned. "What do you mean?"

"I mean—" My voice cracked. "*She's killed people.* This isn't just about my mom. There are other families—multiple families —who've said the same thing. Their loved ones were fine, stable even, and then suddenly, they were gone. And guess who was with them when it happened?"

Emma's face paled.

"But . . . she overdosed my mom," I whispered.

The weight of those words hung between us, thick and suffocating.

Emma opened her mouth, then shut it. Finally—"Are you sure?"

"Yes."

She rubbed a hand over her face. "Oh my gosh."

"Yeah."

Emma looked down at her lap, her expression unreadable.

Then, after a long beat: "Okay."

I blinked. "Okay?"

"Yeah," she said, looking back up at me. "I mean, it's completely *insane*, and you sound like you belong in a Netflix true crime doc, but you're not an idiot. If you're sure, I believe you."

A lump rose in my throat. After everything—after me pushing her away, after being a total jerk—she still had my back.

I swallowed hard. "So, you're not mad at me?"

Emma scoffed. "Oh no, I'm *still* mad at you."

I let out a breathless laugh. "Fair."

"But," she continued, voice softer now, "I get it. This isn't just about grief for you, is it?"

I shook my head. "No. It's all I can think about."

Emma nodded, like she already knew that.

Then she clapped her hands against her thighs. "Okay. So what's the next move?"

I blinked. "What?"

She gave me a look. "You think I'm letting you do this alone?"

Warmth flooded through me.

I shook my head, smiling despite everything. "You *really* wanna get involved in this mess?"

Emma smirked. "Wouldn't be the first time."

And just like that, I had my best friend back.

EMMA BUZZED with energy as we walked to the parking lot, her phone clutched in one hand, texting Miles non-stop.

"Okay, tell me the truth," she said, tucking her phone into her pocket. "Do I look okay?"

I gave her a once-over. Fitted baby blue tank top, white jean shorts, sneakers instead of sandals—because, of course, soccer came first. Her dark hair was braided over one shoulder, a few strands already escaping.

"You look fine," I said, rolling my eyes.

She huffed. "Fine? Not exactly the confidence boost I was looking for, V."

I smirked. "You look hot. Miles is gonna forget what state he's in the second he sees you."

"Better." She grinned, unlocking her car. "I mean, it's just a wedding. Not *our* wedding."

I choked. "Oh wow, calm down. You've been dating for three months."

"Four. And they've been four *amazing* months," she corrected, dramatically flipping her braid over her shoulder. "And hey, don't look at me like that. I'm just saying it's nice. I *like* him, V."

I leaned against her car door, arms crossed. "I know you do."

And I meant it. I could see it all over her face. She actually lit up when she talked about Miles, her first real boyfriend.

"Doesn't hurt that he's gorgeous and has a ridiculously perfect jawline," she added, grinning.

I rolled my eyes. "Yeah, yeah. We get it. Miles is a god among men."

Emma laughed, leaning against the car next to me. For a second, things felt normal.

But then she gave me a look. "You sure you're gonna be okay this weekend?"

I shrugged. "Why wouldn't I be?"

"Because you literally look like you're plotting someone's murder half the time."

"Not someone's *murder*—exposing a *murderer*."

Emma sighed. "V . . ."

I held up a hand. "It's fine. Seriously. Go have your romantic weekend."

She hesitated, then bumped my shoulder. "You know, you could text me every once in a while. Just to remind me you haven't gone full true crime podcast yet."

"I'll think about it."

She rolled her eyes, pushing off the car. "Okay, creep, I gotta go. Miles is waiting."

I smirked. "Go be disgustingly adorable. Give my regards to the happy couple."

"Will do." She paused, one hand on the door handle. "And, V?"

"Yeah?"

"Try to do something fun this weekend. For once."

I gave her a flat look. "We clearly have different definitions of fun."

She snorted. "Figures. See you Monday, weirdo."

And just like that, she was gone.

22

DOWN THE RABBIT HOLE

"Grief does not change you, Hazel. It reveals you."
–John Green, *The Fault in Our Stars*

I watched Emma's car disappear down the road, feeling sort of sad. Like I was standing still while the whole world kept spinning around me. She had a weekend of fun, laughter, and romance ahead of her.

And I had nothing.

I could've gone home. I should've gone home. Instead, I found myself driving aimlessly, looping through side streets, past neighborhoods I didn't recognize, past places that didn't mean anything to me. I didn't want to go back to my quiet house. I didn't want to sit in my room, staring at my bulletin board, thinking about how many families April had fooled.

But eventually, I ran out of road. So I went home.

Lucky greeted me at the door, wiggling happily, and I gave him a quick scratch before heading to my room.

I opened my laptop. Time to work.

* * * * *

I SPENT the entire weekend digging.

I barely left my room except for food and bathroom breaks. I stayed up until 3:00 a.m. both nights, my screen the only light in the darkness, my search history a mess of hospice records, medical blogs, and archived complaints.

By Sunday night, my head throbbed, my eyes burned, and I felt like I was *this close* to finding something real.

And then, at 11:34 p.m., my phone buzzed.

RACHEL COLLINS

Hi Violet. I got your message.

My heart stopped.

I inhaled sharply and grabbed my phone, my hands shaking as I read the rest of her message.

I don't usually talk about this anymore, but I know exactly what you mean. My dad wasn't supposed to go that fast either. We were told it was "the natural progression," but I've never believed that. If you're serious about this, I can tell you what I know.

I sat up so fast my laptop nearly slid off my bed.

Yes. Please. Anything you can tell me would help.

A few agonizing minutes passed before she responded.

Let's talk tomorrow. I'll call you when I'm free.

I barely breathed.

This was it. A person who actually wanted to talk to me.

Another victim. Another family who suspected April had taken something from them.

I wasn't just chasing ghosts anymore. I had a name. A voice. A witness.

And come tomorrow, I was going to find out everything she knew.

By the time Monday afternoon rolled around, I had almost convinced myself that Rachel Collins wasn't going to call.

I had checked my messages at least fifty times since yesterday. Nothing. Maybe she'd had second thoughts. Maybe she didn't want to dig up old wounds.

I got it. I really did. But I also needed answers.

So when my phone finally buzzed as I drove home from school, and her name flashed on the screen, my stomach dropped.

I pulled into the nearest parking lot—an old strip mall with a donut shop, a nail salon, and a laundromat—my hands shaking as I put the car in park and answered.

"Hello?"

For a second, silence. Then—"Is this Violet?"

Her voice was lower than I expected. Careful. Like she was testing the waters before saying too much.

"Yeah," I said, gripping the steering wheel. "Rachel?"

"Yeah."

I swallowed. "Thanks for calling."

Another pause. Then, straight to the point, "You said your mom and my dad had the same nurse?"

I exhaled. "April Dawson. She worked at St. Lucia's in 2016, right?"

Rachel let out a hollow laugh. "Oh, she worked there, all right."

My stomach twisted.

"What do you mean?"

Rachel sighed, and I heard shuffling, like she was pacing or sitting down. "I mean, she was everywhere. She was on the floor more than the other nurses. Always checking in, always hovering. People thought she was just thorough, but my mom and I thought it was weird. Like she was waiting for something."

A chill. I gripped the steering wheel. "You said in your post that your dad was supposed to have months left, but he declined overnight. Was April on duty that night?"

Rachel hesitated. Then—"Yes. She was."

I closed my eyes, my heartbeat thudding in my ears.

Rachel sighed. "I always thought it was too fast, you know? He was still talking, still laughing with us that day. Then suddenly, he's gone? And April was the one who gave him his meds that night? I told myself I was imagining things. That it was just bad timing."

I gritted my teeth. "You weren't imagining things."

Another pause.

Then Rachel asked, "Have you ever heard of Meredith Greyson?"

I blinked. "Who?"

"She was April's supervisor at St. Lucia's. One of the only people who didn't think she was some perfect angel of mercy."

"What happened to her?"

Rachel's voice tightened. "She tried to report April."

Every hair on my arms stood up. "Tried?" I echoed.

Rachel let out a sharp breath. "Yeah, she noticed a pattern. Patients declining too fast. April always being the last one with them. So she went to management. And three months later, she was dead."

A cold wave of dread washed over me. "What kind of dead?" I asked, already afraid of the answer.

"Fell down her stairs. At home." Rachel's voice was flat. "Broke her neck. They ruled it an accident."

She *fell down the stairs.* Or at least, that's what everyone *believed.* I forced myself to sound calm. "And no one thought that was suspicious?"

Rachel gave a bitter laugh. "Of course *I* did. And a few of the other nurses. But there was no proof. No forced entry. No signs of a struggle. They said it was a 'tragic accident.'"

I swallowed hard. April was a hospice nurse. She knew how to make deaths look natural. But what if hospice wasn't the only place she was killing people?

Rachel sighed. "After Meredith died, April left. Just—transferred to another facility. Riverside, I think?"

Another chill ran through me. Riverside Serenity Care. Another unexplained death.

I inhaled sharply. "Rachel, do you know if Meredith left any notes? Like, anything she wrote down before she died?"

Rachel hesitated. "No. But I know someone who might."

I snapped to attention. "Who?"

"Jillian Sosa," Rachel said. "She was close with Meredith. And after she died, Jillian quit. Just walked out. She wouldn't talk about why, but I always thought it had something to do with April."

I grabbed my notebook from my backpack on the passenger seat and scribbled the name down. Jillian Sosa. A nurse who might have seen exactly what Meredith uncovered.

I pressed my phone tighter to my ear. "Do you know where she is now?"

"Not exactly," Rachel admitted. "But I think she moved back to Orange County."

My breath caught. Orange County. Where April was now.

Where my mom had died. This wasn't a coincidence. This was something real.

Rachel's voice softened. "Violet . . . you're really doing this, aren't you?"

I swallowed hard. "Yeah. I am."

A pause. Then, quietly, "Be careful, okay?"

A shiver crawled down my spine. Rachel wasn't telling me to drop it. She wasn't telling me to let it go. She knew.

Just like I did. I nodded, even though she couldn't see me. "I will."

We said our goodbyes. I hung up. And then I sat there, staring at the name in my notebook.

Jillian Sosa. She knew something. And I was going to find her.

23

A WARNING

"Once the storm is over, you won't remember how you made it through, how you managed to survive. You won't even be sure whether the storm is really over. But one thing is certain: When you come out of the storm, you won't be the same person who walked in."
–Haruki Murakami

When I pulled up in Emma's driveway, the sun had started dipping behind the palm trees, washing everything in shades of orange. My brain was still buzzing from my call with Rachel, but I needed to talk to someone who wasn't just a voice on the other end of the phone. I needed Emma.

I didn't even bother texting first. I just got out of my car, marched up the driveway, and knocked. A few seconds later, the door swung open.

"V?" Emma blinked at me, eyebrows raised. She was in her

usual post-practice uniform—soccer shorts, a UNC T-shirt, and sneakers. "What are you doing here?"

"Why weren't you in English this morning? Did you even go to school today?" I pushed past her into the house.

"Nice to see you, too," she muttered, closing the door behind me. "I told you, Miles was in town."

I arched an eyebrow. "Interesting. Oh yeah, how was the wedding? Never mind, you can tell me later. I found something."

I turned in time to see her abuela peeking out from the kitchen. She gave me a small nod before going back to whatever smelled amazing on the stove.

Emma crossed her arms. "You want food?"

"Don't distract me with carbs."

She smirked. "Okay, but you *do* want food."

"Fine. But later." I began pacing the length of her living room. "I just got off the phone with Rachel Collins."

Emma's smirk faded. "The blog girl?" she asked.

I nodded. "She told me something insane. About April. About her old boss."

Emma sighed and flopped onto the couch, pulling her legs up. "Okay. Lay it on me."

I sat beside her and took a deep breath. "So, April worked at St. Lucia's, right? Rachel's dad was one of her patients. And guess what? There was a nurse there—her boss—who suspected something was off. She tried to report April."

Emma's expression tightened. "And?"

"And she died before she could."

Emma's eyes snapped to mine. "What do you mean, *died*?"

"Fell down the stairs at her house," I said grimly. "Broke her neck."

Emma's mouth parted slightly.

"Rachel thought it was suspicious," I continued, sitting on

the sofa. "I agree. And so did another nurse—her friend, Jillian Sosa. She worked at St. Lucia's, too, and after her boss died, she quit. Just disappeared. No one knows why."

Emma exhaled slowly, processing. "So let me get this straight," she said, counting on her fingers. "You have Rachel, who already suspected April. You have this Jillian lady, who also thought something was shady. And you have this boss, who thought April was up to something and then mysteriously fell down the stairs?"

"Yes."

Emma let out a low whistle.

I turned to face her fully. "I need to find Jillian."

She looked at me for a long second. Then she sighed, rubbing her temples. "V . . ."

"Don't 'V' me right now," I said.

"I have to 'V' you right now," she shot back. "Because you are *obsessed*. Do you even hear yourself? You're talking about tracking down some random woman who quit hospice *years ago*. How do you even plan on finding her?"

I paused. I hadn't gotten that far yet.

Emma sighed again, softer this time. "Look, I get it. This is important to you. And I know you're probably right. But you are going so deep into this, and I don't want to see you lose yourself over it."

I swallowed. "I'm fine."

She made a face.

"I *am*," I insisted. "I just—I need to do this, Emma."

Her expression softened. "I know," she said quietly. "But can you at least promise me something?"

"What?"

She nudged my leg with her foot. "Promise me that you'll eat something before you start this next round of detective work."

Despite everything, I smiled. "You're such a mom."

"And *you* are running on caffeine and spite," she shot back, standing up. "Come on. You're not leaving here without at least a tortilla."

I let her pull me to my feet, my mind still racing with possibilities.

* * * * *

I LEFT Emma's house feeling lighter. Not because I wasn't still neck-deep in this case, but because she'd grounded me, just a little. Reminded me that I still had a life outside of hunting down serial killers. That feeling lasted about five minutes.

Until I got the text.

UNKNOWN NUMBER

You need to stop asking questions.

I froze, my stomach twisting as I stared at my phone screen.

The streetlight above me flickered, buzzing faintly in the warm September air. I got in my car, rolled up the windows, and locked the doors. For the first time since I started all this, I felt exposed.

I glanced around. Nothing. A few cars parked along the curb. A porch light on across the street. A distant bark from someone's backyard.

Nothing out of the ordinary. But suddenly, the quiet didn't feel safe. It felt wrong.

Who is this?

The message delivered. But no reply.

I exhaled slowly, my fingers tightening around my phone. This could've been anyone. Maybe even April.

But then again, April had no reason to be subtle.

April had stared me down in my own house, poured my dad a cup of coffee, looked me in the eye after killing my mother. She wouldn't send some vague "back off" text. This had to be someone else.

I glanced over my shoulder again, my pulse skipping. The street still looked empty. But was it?

I shoved my phone in the center console, turned on the ignition, and backed out of Emma's driveway.

My heart was beating triple-time. I forced myself to take a breath. Think logically.

Option 1: This was just some sick prank. Unlikely.

Option 2: April sent it. Maybe she finally caught on that I wasn't just *grieving*—I was investigating.

Option 3: It wasn't April at all.

That thought sent a new wave of unease through me. *What to do next?*

Should I call Emma? Tell her I got some creepy text right after leaving her house?

Was it time to bring Detective Lomeli into this yet? Did I have enough proof for him to believe me?

Instead, I did neither. I pulled over, grabbed my phone and went into my settings, disabled read receipts, and blocked the number.

If whoever this was wanted me to stop, they clearly didn't know me. Because all they'd done was make me more determined than ever.

I checked my mirrors and pulled out onto the street again. As I turned the corner, my headlights caught something in my rearview mirror.

A car. Black. Parked down the block.

Had that been there before? I didn't know. And that terrified me.

BY THE TIME I got to school the next morning I had almost convinced myself the text was nothing. Some sick prank. Some hospice worker who caught wind of my questions. Maybe even April.

Whoever it was, they were just trying to scare me. That's all it was. But then I felt it. That prickling sensation at the back of my neck.

I was walking across the quad, earbuds in, heading toward the library before first period. I wasn't even thinking about the case—just zoning out to some old *Veronica Mars* soundtrack playlist when I caught the feeling. Like I was being watched.

I slowed. Took a sip from the coffee I barely remembered pouring. Scanned the crowd, careful not to look like I was looking.

And that's when I saw him. Dark blue scrubs. Salt-and-pepper hair. Tan skin. Maybe early fifties.

I didn't recognize him. But he recognized me. Because the moment our eyes met, he turned too quickly—pivoting toward the parking lot, walking away like he hadn't just been staring at me. I yanked out my earbuds. *That was random!*

Was that a teacher? A school nurse? A hospital employee?

I sped up, stepping between a group of juniors who were laughing too loudly about some TikTok video. I didn't take my eyes off him. He was heading for the faculty lot.

I picked up my pace. Whoever he was, he had no reason to be here. And yet, he was here. Watching me.

And then—he was gone. Slipped into the driver's seat of a

black sedan—the same make and model I'd seen parked down Emma's block last night. My heart pounded.

Before I could even think, I yanked my phone out of my back pocket and snapped a photo of the license plate. Then the car pulled away. I stood there, coffee forgotten, my hands shaking.

This wasn't just a text message. This wasn't just a prank. Someone was following me. And I had proof.

24

GETTING THROUGH THE DAY

"Tears are words the heart can't express."
–Gerard Way

I spent the rest of the morning in a daze. I kept replaying the moment over and over—the man in scrubs watching me, the car pulling away, the text from last night. I had proof that someone was following me. I had a photo of the car, the license plate. And yet, I was stuck in class, analyzing poetry.

Ms. Calloway was in a mood. Her turquoise reading glasses were perched at the end of her nose, and she paced the front of the classroom, waving a copy of *Hamlet* like a battle flag.

"Tragedy," she said, "is driven by indecision. The inability to act. The delay that allows fate to do its worst."

I stared at my notebook. I hadn't written a single word.

"V," Ms. Calloway's voice cut through my thoughts.

I snapped to attention. "What?"

A few people snickered.

Ms. Calloway arched an eyebrow. "Since you seem deep in thought, why don't you tell us—what is Hamlet's fatal flaw?"

I exhaled slowly. "His inability to act."

"Good," she said. "And do we sympathize with him for that?"

I hesitated. Because honestly? No. Hamlet knew something was wrong. He knew who had killed his father. But instead of doing anything about it, he monologued. Over and over, waiting for the right moment. And what happened? Everyone died.

I met Ms. Calloway's gaze. "I think it's frustrating. He could've stopped it. But he waited too long."

Ms. Calloway smirked, pushing her glasses up. "And that, my dear students, is why tragedy is so tragic. When we watch someone march toward disaster and think—if only they'd moved sooner."

I stared at the blank page in my notebook. If only.

WHEN THE BELL RANG, I caught up to Emma as she walked toward the door.

"Hey," I said.

"Hey, what's up?"

"I think someone's following me."

That got her attention. She spun to face me. "Wait, what?"

I hesitated, glancing around. The hall was crowded, students shoving past us to get to class. This wasn't the place for details.

"I'll tell you everything later," I said. "Just—be careful, okay?"

Emma frowned. "V, what are you getting yourself into?"

I didn't have an answer. Because this was supposed to be about April. But if someone was following me, watching me—it meant the case was bigger than I thought.

I ALMOST SKIPPED SUPPORT GROUP. I didn't want to sit in a circle and talk about my feelings. I wanted to be out there, finding Jillian Sosa, getting answers.

But skipping would mean more questions from Dad. So I went.

Kal had jazz music playing softly when I walked in. The smell of herbal tea filled the room, and the usual group was already gathering—Zuri, Aiden, Caitlyn, Joon, Melody.

I took a seat.

"Aloha, how's everyone doing today?" Kal asked, settling into her chair.

Zuri gave a small shrug. Aiden stared at the carpet. Caitlyn launched into a story about how her aunt had been 'smothering' her with attention.

I barely listened. I was still thinking about the text, the man, the car.

And then—Zuri's voice pulled me back.

"I've been thinking a lot about my dad lately," she said quietly, twisting the hem of her sleeve between her fingers. "I miss him so much. I can't eat. I can't sleep, or I sleep too much and don't want to get out of bed. I know I'm depressed, but I don't know what to do about it. No offense, but that pamphlet you handed out last week didn't help at all."

A few quiet chuckles broke the tension, but Zuri's face was serious.

"I've felt my depression creeping back in, like a worn, soft robe. And I let it. I let it wrap around me because, honestly? It's easier. It hurts to think. It hurts to feel. I've tried ignoring it, stuffing it back down, distracting myself with stupid games on my phone, TV, Instagram. But nothing really helps. I'm not getting anything done—my homework, my chores—because I can't focus. And then I get mad at myself for being useless. This sucks!"

No one spoke. But no one needed to. We all got it.

Kal let the silence settle before saying, "Depression is often tied to our grief about the past, while anxiety is linked to our fear of the future. But right here, in the present—this exact moment—you are safe. Here, neither depression nor anxiety can control you. The key is learning how to exist in this moment, not in the past or future."

Zuri gave a small nod, but her hands still clenched the fabric of her shirt.

"I just want my mom to hold me," Melody said suddenly, her voice barely above a whisper. "Like she did when I was little. When I'd fall off my bike or have a nightmare about monsters under my bed. She would stroke my hair and whisper, 'It's okay, my love. I've got you. Everything's going to be okay.'"

Her voice cracked.

"But nothing is okay. She's gone. And now I'm supposed to figure out how to survive without her, without her warmth, her laugh, her stupid jokes that weren't funny but somehow always made me smile."

Caitlyn reached over and squeezed Melody's hand. She didn't say anything. She didn't have to.

Kal nodded. "Grief isn't something you can run from. If you try, it will follow you, finding cracks to slip through. The only way out of it is through it."

"Great," Joon said, crossing his arms. "Love that for us."

A few of us chuckled weakly, but then his face grew serious.

"You know what I don't get?" Joon asked. "Why do people say, 'passed away' or 'passed on'? What does that even mean? Did he pass me on the sidewalk? Did he pass out? Pass a test? Pass a freaking kidney stone?"

Aiden snorted.

"That all makes it sound like they're still alive, like maybe they could just 'pass back' someday. Man, even passing wind is a temporary thing."

Despite myself, I let out a quiet laugh.

"But no. Death is final," Joon said, his voice hardening. "Nobody 'passed' anywhere. They're dead. They died. I can't visit him. I can't call him. Stop trying to soften it."

Aiden exhaled sharply. "Don't even get me started on 'She's in a better place.'"

A couple of heads nodded.

"Don't you dare tell me my mom is in a better place now, like she's happier without her family. That's not cool." He clenched his fists. "She didn't leave us. She had four kids, for crying out loud. I'm the oldest, and I can't take care of us all. She was ripped away from us, from her children."

The room felt heavy, like we were all suffocating under the weight of our losses.

Kal let Aiden's words settle before she spoke. "People say 'passed away' or 'passed on' as a way to soften the pain, not erase it. To some, the word 'died' feels too harsh. And 'a better place'—" She sighed. "It's meant to be comforting. But that doesn't mean you have to find comfort in it. Grief is personal. No one else gets to decide what helps you."

Aiden looked down, his jaw tight.

I swallowed hard. I hadn't spoken this whole time, hadn't contributed to the conversation, but it was pressing against me now. A lump in my throat, a tightening in my chest.

Maybe this was why I hadn't wanted to come. Because grief demanded to be felt. And I wasn't sure I was ready to feel it.

25

JILLIAN SOSA

"You don't go around grief, you go through it."
–Helen Keller

By the time I left support group, I was buzzing with too many thoughts. I missed Mom. But the case. I had to press on. I had to put my grief on hold for just a little longer.

The thoughts were swirling: The text. The man. The car.

And now? Jillian Sosa. I spent an hour digging through online records, searching for her name. Nothing.

I tried again. "Jillian Sosa, RN, California." "Jillian Sosa, hospice nurse."

And then—there it was. A LinkedIn page. Her profile picture was a smiling woman in her late forties, dark curls pulled back, wearing a stethoscope.

But the most important part? Current Location: Orange County, CA. Still here.

My hands shook as I clicked on her work history.

- St. Lucia's Hospice (2014–2016)
- Riverside Serenity Care (2016–2017)
- Lakeview Hospice (2017)

I stared. She had worked at the same hospice centers April had.

And then—she had left hospice care completely. Her most recent job? She was a home health care nurse for private clients only.

I exhaled slowly, gripping the edge of my desk. She had run from something. I clicked the contact button.

But before I could type a message—

My phone buzzed.

UNKNOWN NUMBER

I told you to stop.

Not this again. I turned to my window. The blinds were half open. The street outside was dark.

But the longer I stared, the more certain I was. Someone was out there. Watching.

I BARELY SLEPT. Even after I slammed my window shut and triple-checked the locks, I kept jerking awake at every sound. Every creak of the house. Every car passing outside.

I'd spent the whole night staring at my phone, debating what to do. Should I tell Dad? Call Emma? Bring Lomeli in on this? Would he believe me?

Turns out, I did none of those things. Because I wasn't stopping. Whoever was watching me—whoever was sending those texts—they were scared. And that meant I was close.

* * * * *

I sent the message before school Wednesday morning.

ME

> Hello Ms. Sosa, My name is Violet Jiménez. I'm looking into something that happened at St. Lucia's, and I think you might be able to help me. Could we talk?

It was the vaguest, least threatening version of what I actually wanted to say. I didn't expect a response.

But three hours later, toward the end of AP Stats, my phone buzzed.

JILLIAN SOSA

Who gave you my name?

My pulse jumped.

> Rachel Collins. She said you worked with Meredith Greyson.

I held my breath, staring at the screen. Nothing.

I barely heard Mr. Grayson lecturing about probability. My fingers tightened around my phone, heartbeat in my ears.

Then—three dots appeared.

JILLIAN SOSA

I don't talk about that.

> Please. I think April Dawson was involved in my mother's death. If you know anything I need to hear it.

I watched, practically vibrating in my seat.

Three dots. Then nothing. Then—

JILLIAN SOSA

I get off work at 7. Meet me at Café Rico on
Tustin. Don't be late.

* * * * *

BY THE TIME I pulled into Café Rico, the sun was just starting to set. The sky was streaked with pinks, and the lot was nearly empty—just a couple cars, a handful of people inside.

Jillian was already there. I recognized her immediately from her LinkedIn photo—forties, dark curls pulled back, tired eyes that flicked toward the door the second I walked in. She was watching me. Assessing.

I took a slow breath and walked over.

"You're Violet?" she asked, voice low, guarded.

I nodded. "Thanks for meeting me."

She studied me for another second, then motioned for me to sit.

I slid into the booth across from her. Up close, I could see the worry lines around her mouth, the way her fingers tapped restlessly on the table. She looked nervous. Good. Because that meant she knew something.

"Rachel shouldn't have given you my name," she said.

"She didn't want to," I admitted. "But she thought you might have answers."

Jillian exhaled, rubbing a hand over her face. "I left all that behind," she said.

"Meredith tried to report April, didn't she?" I said, leaning forward. "And then she *fell* down the stairs."

Jillian's fingers froze mid-tap. She didn't confirm it. But she didn't deny it.

I swallowed hard. "Jillian, please. My mom was under April's care at Lakeview Hospice. And before that, Amanda—my ex's sister—died at UCI. I know April has done this before. I just need to prove it."

Jillian stared at me for a long moment. Then she reached into her bag and pulled out a small, worn notebook. She slid it across the table.

My breath caught.

"Meredith kept notes," Jillian said quietly. "She started noticing patterns. She knew April was overdosing patients. She tried to get the hospice director to listen, but no one wanted to believe it."

My hands shook as I flipped through the notebook. Pages of dates, patient names, medication logs. And then, at the very bottom of one page—

"April Dawson: Too many coincidences."

"She was right," I whispered.

Jillian nodded, her jaw tight. "She always was."

A chill ran through me. This was it. The proof. The case against April was solid.

But as I stared at the notebook, something inside me itched. Because this almost felt too easy.

I looked back at Jillian. "Did Meredith ever mention another nurse? Someone else at St. Lucia's?"

Jillian frowned. "Like whom?"

"Never mind." I didn't know. It was just a hunch.

26

THE WARNING GETS REAL

"Sadness gives depth. Happiness gives height.
Sadness gives roots. Happiness gives branches."
–Osho

Emma agreed to meet me Friday night so we could go over the notebook together. The house was quiet except for the hum of the AC and the occasional bark from a neighbor's dog. Dad and Scotty were at his soccer game—Dad coaching, Scotty probably scoring a goal and then dabbing like his sports heroes. That meant I had the house to myself for the first time all week.

Well, almost. Emma was sprawled out on my bed, flipping through the notebook Jillian had given me.

"So this is it?" she asked, holding it up. "The thing that's gonna take April down?"

I sat cross-legged on the floor, my own stack of notes spread out in front of me. "It's enough to get Detective Lomeli's attention."

Emma skimmed a few pages, brow furrowing. "Wow. Meredith was thorough."

"She was," I agreed, flipping through my notes. "And she died for it."

Emma didn't respond to that.

I glanced up at her. "You okay?"

She exhaled. "Yeah, it's just that this is all getting really real."

"It's been real."

She gave me a look. "You know what I mean. You have actual evidence now. This isn't just chasing theories and pissing off hospice workers. This is going to lead to an *actual arrest.*"

I nodded, pressing my fingers into my temples. "I know." But something still didn't seen right.

I stared at the notebook in front of me. The dates. The names. The patterns. April was guilty. I knew that. She had killed patients.

But I kept circling back to one thing. "This doesn't explain Amanda," I said abruptly.

Emma looked up. "What do you mean?"

"Amanda wasn't terminal," I said. "She wasn't even in hospice. She was supposed to recover. But she died anyway." I pointed at the notebook. "These other patients were all end-stage. April saw herself as some kind of angel of mercy, but Amanda? That doesn't fit her pattern."

Emma frowned. "So what are you saying?"

I hesitated. "I don't know."

Emma sighed. "V . . ."

"I just—I feel like I'm missing something."

Emma flipped to the last page of the notebook, her fingers tracing over Meredith's final notes. "Maybe Jillian will remember something else," she suggested. "Or the police will find something once you show them this."

"Maybe," I said, but doubt was already creeping in. Something about this was still wrong. Still incomplete.

And then—a noise. A sharp, muffled sound from outside.

We both froze. I sat up straighter, listening.

Emma glanced at me. "Did you hear that?"

Another sound. A dull thunk.

I scrambled to my feet, my pulse spiking. Emma moved fast, too, tossing the notebook onto my desk.

"What was that?" she whispered.

I didn't answer. Instead, I grabbed Dad's old baseball bat from under my bed and motioned for Emma to follow.

We crept down the hall, every step slow, silent.

I reached the front window and peeked through the blinds. Nothing. The street was still, the neighbor's porch light flickering across their empty driveway.

But then—I turned toward the driveway. My stomach dropped. The driver's side door of my car hung open. Someone had been inside. I spun toward Emma, my heart lodged in my throat. "Stay here," I whispered.

"No way," she whispered back.

We went outside together.

The night air was warm and heavy, the streetlamp buzzing faintly. My car sat there, driver's door slightly ajar.

I crept forward, bat tight in my grip, Emma right behind me. I reached the door. Peeked inside.

The glove compartment was open. Papers were scattered across the seat. But nothing was taken.

I scanned the interior—back seat, floorboards. And then I saw it. A single sheet of paper on my dashboard. I reached for it, my hands shaking, and turned it over. Four words.

YOU WERE WARNED. STOP.

Emma swore under her breath.

I felt my stomach drop. This wasn't April. This wasn't just a warning text. Someone else had been here and rummaged through my car. Someone else wanted me to stop.

Emma swallowed. "V?"

I crumpled the paper in my fist. "Yeah?"

Her voice was quiet. "I think we need to tell your ol' pal, Lomeli."

"Yeah. Maybe." My breath came in unsteady bursts as I tried to process the words. *You were warned. STOP.*

Beside me, Emma let out a slow, shaky breath. "V," she said carefully, like she was trying not to freak out, "this is bad."

No kidding. I swallowed hard, my eyes sweeping over the quiet street. The houses all looked the same, dark windows, empty driveways, the occasional flickering porch light. Nothing looked out of place. But I knew better.

I glanced at Emma. "Do you think it was April?"

Emma hesitated, shifting her weight. "I mean, maybe? But why break into your car? If she wanted to scare you, wouldn't she just—" She cut herself off, frowning. "I don't know. It just doesn't seem like her style."

That was the problem. April wasn't the type to send cryptic messages or lurk in the shadows. She was the type to look someone in the eye while she lied to their face.

I turned back to my car, scanning the mess inside. "Whoever it was, they were looking for something."

Emma got closer. "Did they take anything?"

I checked again. Nothing obvious was missing. The registration and insurance were still in the glove box, my emergency twenty-dollar bill still tucked into the center console. Whoever had done this hadn't been after money or paperwork. Just . . . *information.*

"We should go inside," Emma murmured. "Just standing out

here feels—" She shook her head, wrapping her arms around herself.

I didn't argue. I locked the car and followed her up the porch steps. The second I pushed open the front door, Lucky barreled into my legs, sniffing me frantically, his little body trembling.

"Hey, bud," I murmured, running a hand down his back. His ears were pinned flat, tail wagging in short, anxious bursts.

Emma bent down and scratched behind his ears. "He's freaked out," she said, frowning.

"He's not the only one!"

Emma shut the door behind us and immediately grabbed one of the dining room chairs, shoving it under the doorknob.

I gave her a look. "That's not going to stop anyone from getting in."

She crossed her arms. "Yeah, well, it makes me feel better, so shut up."

I let it slide. Lucky was still glued to my legs as I walked back toward my room. I scratched his head absently, but my mind was still spinning.

We didn't talk much after that. I tried to lose myself in the notebook, flipping through Meredith Greyson's careful notes, but I kept catching Emma glancing at the window like she expected someone to be staring back. Lucky curled up at my feet but kept shifting in his sleep, his ears twitching at every little sound.

I heard the front door open and glanced at my phone's clock. 10:04 p.m. I jerked up so fast I nearly knocked the notebook onto the floor. Emma tensed beside me, clutching a pillow like she might throw it at an intruder.

Then Scotty's voice rang out. "Dad, did you see that goal? It was *sick!*"

I exhaled, pressing a hand to my chest. "Ohmygosh."

Emma let out a nervous laugh. "I think my soul just left my body."

I rolled my eyes, getting to my feet. "Come on, let's go act normal."

"Define normal," she said, but she followed me downstairs.

Dad and Scotty were in the living room. Dad had his duffel bag slung over one shoulder, still in his coaching gear, and Scotty was grinning ear to ear, holding up a small golden trophy.

"I scored the game-winning goal!" Scotty announced before I could even open my mouth. "Coach said it was *sick!*"

Dad ruffled his hair. "It was pretty sick," he admitted. "Best goal of the night."

Scotty beamed. Then his eyes flicked past me and landed on the chair wedged under the doorknob. His smile faded into confusion. "Uh, why is the chair like that?"

Dad frowned. His gaze moved from the chair to me, eyebrows raised. "Planning on keeping out the Big Bad Wolf?"

Emma coughed. "It's, um, a home security measure?"

Dad did not look impressed. "I'll give you points for creativity." His expression sharpened slightly. "Everything okay?"

I hesitated a fraction too long. "Yeah," I said finally. "Emma just freaked herself out watching *Paranormal Activity*."

Emma shot me a glare but rolled with it. "Yeah, it was *so* stupid, but I got all paranoid, and you know, better safe than sorry, right?"

Dad sighed, shaking his head. "You two and your horror movies."

Scotty was still squinting at us suspiciously, but then Lucky launched himself at him, tail wagging frantically.

Scotty immediately forgot about the chair. "Lucky! You missed *the sickest* goal ever!"

Lucky barked like he understood, then jumped on Scotty, knocking him onto the couch in a fit of giggles.

Dad watched them for a second before turning back to me. "Don't stay up too late, okay?"

I nodded. "We won't."

He gave me a look.

I flashed him my best *see, I'm totally responsible* smile.

He sighed and headed upstairs, Scotty and Lucky tumbling after him.

The second they were gone, Emma turned to me. "*Paranormal Activity*? That's what you went with?"

"It was better than *a possible serial killer* just broke into my car," I shot back.

Emma groaned, rubbing her face. "You have to tell Lomeli."

"I will," I promised. "On Monday."

She narrowed her eyes. "You swear?"

I sighed. "I swear."

Emma still looked skeptical, but she didn't argue. Instead, she said, "Fine," and made her way toward the kitchen. "Now, let's eat something. This much stress calls for kettle corn."

I followed her, feeling the tension finally start to ease.

For tonight, at least, we were safe.

But Monday?

Monday, I was telling Lomeli *everything*.

27

ALMOST NORMAL

"Grief is the proof of love."
–Unknown

I woke up to the smell of bacon and coffee, the kind of Saturday morning scent that usually meant Dad was feeling sentimental or guilty about something.

Emma was already at the kitchen table, flipping through my heavily annotated copy of *The Stranger* for AP English. She had her bare feet propped up on another chair, a half-empty glass of orange juice beside her.

"Morning," she said, not looking up as she turned a page.

I grunted in response, rubbing my eyes as I collapsed into the chair across from her. My brain still felt foggy from lack of sleep, but the smell of food made my stomach rumble.

Dad set a plate in front of me—eggs, toast, bacon. Classic *guilty dad breakfast.* He only went full short-order cook mode when he either felt bad about something or wanted information.

I stabbed a piece of bacon with my fork. "What's the occasion?"

Dad gave me a knowing look as he poured himself another cup of coffee. "Everything okay? You and Emma were up late."

"We were watching *10 Things I Hate About You* and eating kettle corn," I said through a mouthful of bacon. "Very high-risk behavior."

Dad didn't laugh. Instead, he gave me his 'funny but also deeply concerned' look, the one that usually came right before a "V, I'm worried about you" speech.

Emma kicked me under the table. A warning.

I quickly washed down my bacon with orange juice and put on my best innocent expression. "We were just having a girls' night, Dad. You know, *rebelling* by quoting Shakespeare and gushing over Heath Ledger."

That finally earned me a half smile. "Sounds terrifying."

"Right?"

Before he could press any further, Lucky dashed into the kitchen at full speed, zooming in circles before launching himself against my legs.

I scooped him up, pressing my face into his warm fur. My good boy. A perfect, wiggly distraction.

"Geez, Lucky, dramatic much?" Emma laughed as she reached over to scratch his ears.

"He knows when I need an emotional support animal," I said, rubbing his belly.

Dad watched us for a beat, then sighed. "All right, well, I've got to get Scotty moving. His game's at eleven, and I'm not dealing with another last-minute 'I can't find my cleats' meltdown."

Emma groaned. "Ugh, same. My game's at noon. I should probably head out soon."

I nodded, not quite ready for them to leave. Because once

they were gone, I'd be alone with my thoughts again. And I wasn't sure that was a good thing.

BY MIDNIGHT, I was deep into a Reddit black hole, the kind where time blurred and my mind started playing tricks on me.

I told myself I was just researching.

But really? I was spiraling.

I kept telling myself, *One more article, one more thread*, but each one led to another, and another, and another—until suddenly, it was past midnight and my eyes burned from the glow of my laptop screen.

I scrolled through case studies, forum posts, and crime articles, my stomach tightening with each new tab I opened.

- "Hospice nurse arrested for overdosing patients." (Not April.)
- "How serial killers avoid detection."
- "How do you know if someone is following you?"

That last one hit too close to home. I clicked the thread anyway.

Most people don't notice they're being followed at first. The brain rationalizes small details—seeing the same car in multiple locations, a person in your peripheral vision, footsteps that match your pace.

My fingers tightened around my laptop.

By the time you realize it's real, they've already been watching you for a while.

I snapped my laptop shut.

The screen went black, plunging my room into darkness

except for the sliver of moonlight spilling through my blinds. I exhaled slowly, pressing my palms into my eyes.

I needed to sleep. I needed to turn my brain off, just for a few hours. But my thoughts weren't cooperating.

I flopped onto my back, staring at the ceiling. The shadows up there felt sharper than usual, like they had edges that could cut.

The notebook sat on my desk, untouched since Emma left.

And on my nightstand?

The crumpled "You were warned. STOP." note.

I reached for it, smoothing out the creases, visually tracing the words for the hundredth time. The handwriting was slanted, rushed. Impersonal.

Who wrote it? April? Someone else?

I turned it over, half hoping for some kind of hidden clue, but it was just a plain piece of paper. A simple message with a single goal—to scare me off.

It should have worked. It almost did. But instead, it just made me more determined. I wasn't stopping. But I also wasn't sleeping.

I TRIED to be normal on Sunday. That's what you're supposed to do after a week of paranoia and late-night crime research, right? Act normal. Be normal.

So, I took Lucky on a long walk through the neighborhood, letting him sniff every bush and lamppost like it was his job. I threw a load of laundry in the machine, folded my T-shirts, and actually hung up the clean clothes instead of letting them sit in the basket till they wrinkled.

I ignored six unread texts from Emma and didn't check my email to see if Rachel had followed up with anything.

For a little while, I even tried to pretend that life was just *life*. But pretending didn't last long. By mid-afternoon, I was pacing my room, flipping through Meredith's notebook for the hundredth time.

Every page was filled with painstakingly detailed notes. Names, dates, dosages. Some were circled, others underlined twice in thick black ink. Meredith had seen what April was doing—*before* anyone else had.

But she hadn't lived long enough to stop it. I flipped back to one page. Not a chart. Not a medical note. Just one sentence.

Someone else knows.

I stared at it, my fingers tightening around the edges of the paper. It didn't list a name. No initials. No explanation. Just a quiet warning buried in the middle of her pages, like she had meant to come back to it. Like she had been waiting for something to confirm her suspicion.

A strange feeling settled in my stomach. I knew what Meredith had thought—she had been watching April. She had seen patterns. But this note . . .

It didn't say, "April knows."

It didn't say, "April did it."

It said, "Someone else."

I tapped my pen against my knee, thinking. Maybe she had meant a coworker. Someone who had also noticed the pattern but stayed quiet. That made sense, right?

Or maybe she had meant a patient's family. Someone who had realized, too late, that their loved one shouldn't have died when they did. I closed the notebook, rubbing a hand over my face. I was probably overthinking it.

I believed April had killed at least seven people. I had proof for some of them.

This wasn't a question of *if* she was guilty. It was a question of when the police were going to take her down.

But still, something about that one page bothered me.

"Someone else knows."

Who? And why hadn't Meredith written anything else?

28

NOT YOUR AVERAGE MONDAY

"If you think grief has a time limit,
you have likely never lost a piece of your heart."
—Donna Ashworth

Monday dragged like it was moving through quicksand. English was a blur. Ms. Calloway spent the first thirty minutes going off about tragic flaws and the inevitability of fate, pacing in front of the whiteboard like she was delivering a monologue of her own.

"Tragedy," she said, "is driven by *hesitation*. By characters who see the truth but fail to act."

I kept my head down, scrawling nonsense in the margins of *Hamlet* while she grilled other students. I was too wired on caffeine and sleep deprivation to contribute anything meaningful.

Next to me, Emma was actually paying attention, nodding like she followed along.

I wished I could focus. But all I could think about was the notebook in my backpack.

- April worked at St. Lucia's → Patients died unexpectedly.
- April worked at Riverside Serenity Care → More patients died.
- April worked at Lakeview & UCI → Mom died. Amanda died.
- Meredith saw it.
- Meredith died.

And at the bottom of the page in Meredith's notebook— "Someone else knows."

Who? I tapped my pen against my desk. Click. Click. Click.

Emma nudged me. "You good?" she whispered.

No. "I'm fine," I said.

She shot me a look but didn't push. Before she could say anything else, Ms. Calloway called on her to break down Hamlet's motivations, and I let her handle Shakespeare while I counted down the hours until I could bolt out of here.

By LUNCHTIME, I had officially given up on pretending to be a normal person. Instead of going home, I sat in my car, flipping through Meredith's notebook again, double-checking my notes. April's pattern was clear.

So why did I feel like I was still missing something? My eyes lingered on that one page for what felt like the thousandth time. *"Someone else knows."*

It didn't say April. It didn't say *I* know. It said someone else.

A sharp knock on my window nearly made me jump out of my skin.

Emma.

I rolled my eyes and cracked the window. "You scared me! I thought I was about to get murdered in broad daylight."

Emma smirked. "Relax, I'm not that sick of you yet." She glanced at the open notebook on my lap. She sighed. "V, you're going to the police after school. You have *actual* evidence. Can you please, just for, like, thirty minutes, stop obsessing?"

I exhaled. "I *am* going to the police, but that doesn't mean I should stop thinking about this."

Emma groaned. "Fine, whatever. But eat something before you pass out in front of Lomeli." She reached through the window and shoved a yogurt and an apple into my lap.

I stared at them.

"That's your compromise," she said. "You can keep being a weirdo detective, but you have to eat."

I sighed but bit into the apple anyway. "Happy now?"

"Ecstatic," she deadpanned. She lingered for a second, kicking at a rock near my tire. "Hey, are you nervous?"

I hesitated. Then nodded. Because yeah. I was. Lomeli was going to be pissed. I just hoped he would listen.

WHEN I PULLED into the police station parking lot, my hands were ice-cold against the steering wheel. I was running on three hours of sleep and two cups of coffee. I had Meredith's notebook in my backpack.

And a sinking feeling that Detective Lomeli wasn't going to take this well.

I sat there for a moment, staring at the double glass doors of the station, trying to steady my breathing. This was it.

Everything I'd put together—the pattern, the patients, the warnings—*it all led here.*

I took a deep breath, unbuckled my seat belt, and got out of the car. It was time to tell him everything.

29

LOMELI'S LAMENT

"Grief is not as heavy as guilt, but it takes more away from you."
–Veronica Roth, *Insurgent*

Walking into the station felt different this time. I'd been here before. Plenty of times. This wasn't new territory. But today, it felt heavier.

Maybe because this time, it was about Mom.

I tightened my grip on my backpack strap as I stepped through the doors. The front desk officer, Martinez, recognized me immediately. His eyes flicked to my bag, then back to my face.

"You again," he said, leaning back in his chair. "What is it this time? More bodies? A conspiracy? The FBI on speed dial?"

I forced a smile. "I like to keep things exciting."

Martinez sighed, like he was already exhausted by my presence. "Let me guess—you want Lomeli?"

"Preferably before I die of old age, yeah."

He muttered something under his breath and picked up the phone. A few seconds later, he waved me toward the hallway. "You know the way."

I did. I walked past the bullpen, past desks stacked with case files, past two detectives arguing over whether or not it was their turn to bring donuts tomorrow. I pushed open the office door just as Detective Andrew Lomeli stood from his chair, arms crossed, eyes sharp.

"Violet Jiménez," he said in that exasperated, amused, and somehow still vaguely concerned way he always said my name.

I let the door shut behind me. "Detective Lomeli."

He shook his head. "Every time I see you walk in here, my blood pressure spikes. You know that, right?"

"Maybe you should look into meditation," I offered. "Or green tea. I hear it's good for stress."

His mouth twitched, almost like he wanted to smile, but he didn't take the bait. Instead, he sat back down and gestured to the chair across from his desk.

"All right, let's hear it," he said. "What kind of trouble have you gotten yourself into this time?"

I sat, unzipping my backpack. "No trouble. Just *evidence.*"

That got his attention. His gaze flickered to the notebook in my hands. "What am I looking at?"

I set it down on the table. "A hospice nurse. April Dawson. She's been killing patients for years."

Lomeli didn't say anything at first. Instead, he reached for the notebook, flipping through the pages slowly, his expression unreadable.

I watched his fingers skim over Meredith Greyson's careful notes—lists of patients, dates, dosages. He turned a few more pages before stopping near the back.

I didn't need to look to know what he'd found.

"Someone else knows."

He let out a slow breath, rubbing his thumb against his jaw. Then he closed the notebook, set it down, and looked me straight in the eye.

"How long have you been working on this?"

"Three weeks," I admitted. "Give or take a few all-nighters."

Lomeli sighed. "Of course you have."

I leaned forward. "Look, I know you don't like when I get involved in cases, but I'm telling you—this is real. This woman has been bouncing from hospice to hospice for years, and every time, her patients die faster than expected. The patterns are in there. Meredith Greyson saw it, and she tried to report it. And then—"

"She fell down the stairs," Lomeli finished, voice flat.

I stiffened. He already knew. I narrowed my eyes. "You've looked into this before."

Lomeli exhaled slowly, rubbing a hand down his face. "Meredith Greyson's death was ruled an accident."

I scoffed. "And you believed that?"

He glanced back to the notebook. "I had my doubts. But doubt isn't enough to build a case."

I gestured to the notebook. "Well, now you have more than doubts."

Lomeli was quiet for a long time. Then he tapped a finger against the cover. "You're sure about April?"

"Yes."

"You're sure about these patterns?"

"Yes."

He studied me for a second, then nodded—just once, sharp and certain. "All right."

I blinked. "Wait, *that's it*?"

He arched an eyebrow. "What, were you expecting me to call you crazy and throw you out?"

"A little, yeah."

Lomeli let out a dry chuckle. "You ever think that maybe, just *maybe*, I actually trust your instincts by now?"

I didn't have an answer for that. Because honestly? No. I hadn't thought that.

He shook his head and stood, tucking the notebook under his arm. "I'll look into it. But you"—he pointed at me—"are staying out of it."

I opened my mouth to argue, but he cut me off.

"I'm serious, Jiménez. This is not some high school mystery club project. You're talking about a *serial killer.*"

I hesitated. "I thought you said you trusted my instincts."

"I do," he said. "Which is exactly why I'm telling you to *back off.* If you're right about this, then Dawson is dangerous. And if you're wrong?" He tilted his head. "Then you're still a teenager investigating medical homicide cases in your free time, which is not normal."

I crossed my arms. "Normal is overrated."

Lomeli pinched the bridge of his nose. "I swear, kid, one of these days—" He stopped himself, shaking his head. "Just go home. Let me do my job."

I hesitated. "You'll call me if you find something?"

He gave me a long look. "You're seventeen," he said flatly. "I don't think I'm *legally* allowed to call you about an active investigation."

"Off the record?"

"Violet."

I sighed. "Fine."

He walked me to the door, but just as I stepped into the hallway, he said, "For what it's worth, I do think you're onto something."

I turned back.

He wasn't looking at me—he was looking at the notebook in his hand, flipping it open to Meredith's last entry.

"Someone else knows."

Something in his expression shifted. Like maybe, just maybe, he *already* knew who that *someone else* was.

I wanted to ask. I wanted to push. But before I could, Lomeli snapped the notebook shut. "Go home, Jiménez."

So I did. But I had a feeling this wasn't over. Not even close.

FOR THE FIRST time in weeks, I slept. Real, actual, *deep* sleep.

Not the restless kind where my brain replayed hospital hallways and whispered warnings. Not the kind where I jolted awake every hour, convinced someone was outside my window.

I had told Lomeli *everything*. I had done my part. And now, for the first time since Mom died, I felt like I was actually getting somewhere.

So after dinner—where Dad asked me about school and Scotty showed me a YouTube video of some soccer player I didn't recognize—I showered, crawled into bed, and let myself *shut down* for the night.

I barely even moved until morning.

30
MOVE ON?

"We don't see things as they are; we see them as we are."
–Anaïs Nin

Tuesday morning, I woke up feeling like a real person again. Amazing what some much-needed sleep would do. The weight in my chest was still there, of course. Grief didn't just *go away* overnight. But I didn't feel like I was walking through quicksand anymore.

I actually ate breakfast instead of just shoving a banana or a granola bar into my backpack.

Dad looked a little surprised. "You sleep okay?" he asked as I grabbed my keys.

"Yeah, I actually did," I admitted.

He gave me a slow, skeptical nod. "Good."

Even Scotty seemed less annoying than usual. He sat at the kitchen table, half watching a cartoon on his tablet while Lucky curled up at his feet.

I scratched Lucky's head on my way out. "Be good, okay?"

His tail thumped against the floor, and for once, I let myself believe that things might actually be turning around.

I HAD PLANNED on skipping support group. It wasn't exactly high on my list of priorities right now. But I knew if I bailed, Kal would call me, and I wasn't in the mood to explain myself. So I went.

The room was already filling up when I walked in. The usual group—Zuri, Aiden, Caitlyn, Joon, and Melody. I dropped into a chair near the back and pulled my sleeves over my hands.

Kal gave me a small nod, like she was glad to see me but wasn't going to call me out for ignoring her check-in text last week. She started the meeting the way she always did—with her 'Aloha' greeting and some quote about grief. This time, she added, "Grief is not linear. It's messy, and it doesn't follow a straight path. Some days are easier. Some days are harder. Some days, you think you're okay, and then—out of nowhere—it hits you again."

I picked at the frayed hem of my sleeve. I knew that already. I was *living* it.

Zuri spoke first, sharing a memory about her dad taking her to Disneyland as a kid. Then Caitlyn talked about how her aunt was making weirdly specific life plans for her, like she was supposed to "take over the family business" even though Caitlyn had *zero* interest in selling real estate.

Then Aiden spoke. "I feel like people expect me to be better by now," he said, arms crossed. "Like it's been *long enough*."

Kal nodded. "How long is 'long enough' supposed to be?"

Aiden let out a dry laugh. "I don't know. Ask everyone who keeps telling me to 'move on.'"

I got that. People didn't say it *outright*, but I could feel it sometimes. The expectation that I should be past the worst of it. That I should be functional again. That I should be focusing on college applications and senior year and moving forward.

Like I was supposed to just accept that Mom was gone. I took a slow breath, shifting in my seat.

Kal glanced at me. "V?"

I hesitated. Then, before I could stop myself, I said, "I actually slept last night."

A few people looked over.

Kal's expression stayed even. "That's good."

"Yeah," I said. "It just—hasn't happened in a while."

No one asked why. No one pushed. They just *let it be.*

"Hey, I had another thought," I said. "Remember a few weeks ago when we talked about Disney characters? And how they always had to grow up too fast because they were orphaned?"

A few people nodded.

"Well," I continued, "at least *they* had help. A wise-cracking sidekick, a magical animal to guide them along—something. No one tells you how to grow up in real life. No one hands you a map and says, 'Here's how to live without them.' It's just . . . this. Sitting in a too-bright room, talking about our feelings, hoping that somehow, eventually, it starts to make sense." I let out a frustrated sigh.

No one spoke for a second.

Then Joon, the group's class clown, chuckled. "Yikes. That's bleak—even for us."

A few people laughed, but it wasn't mean. It was the kind of laugh that said, "*I get it*".

Kal gave me a soft, understanding look. "You're right, V. There's no magical guide. No easy answers. But you *do* have something—*someone.* You have people who care. Even if they don't have all the answers, even if they don't always know what to say. You don't have to figure it out alone."

I swallowed. I wanted to believe that. But sometimes, grief felt *exactly* like being alone.

Still, I nodded. "Yeah. I know." And for once, no one asked me to say more.

BY THE TIME I pulled into my driveway that night I wasn't expecting anything out of the ordinary. I'd done what I needed to do. I'd gone to support group. I was planning to study for a quiz in Government tomorrow that I was *probably* going to fail, but whatever.

Yet, my stomach felt tight, like I was bracing for something I couldn't name yet. The street was quiet. Too quiet.

Dad's car wasn't in the driveway yet—he and Scotty were probably still at dinner after soccer practice. The porch light was on, but that was normal. Nothing seemed out of place.

Still, something about the night felt wrong.

Lucky must have sensed it, too, because the second I stepped inside, he bolted toward me, paws scrabbling against the floor, whining as he pressed his nose into my leg.

"Hey, bud," I murmured, bending down to scratch his ears. "What's up?"

His tail wagged, but his body stayed tense, like he was on high alert.

I shut the door behind me, my pulse picking up. Was someone here? I stood still, listening. The house settled around me—the faint hum of the fridge, the tick of the clock above the stove, the usual creaks in the walls. Nothing.

I was being paranoid. Still, I checked the locks, double-checked the windows. Everything was exactly how I left it.

I exhaled, trying to shake the feeling crawling up my spine. "Okay, Lucky. False alarm. We're good."

He didn't look convinced.

I dropped my backpack onto the counter and grabbed a glass from the cabinet. Water. That was what I needed. Hydration. Rational thinking. Not paranoia.

But when I opened the fridge—I froze.

Something was wrong. My throat went dry. Because sitting on the middle shelf, right next to the milk, was a single unlabeled prescription bottle.

I hadn't put it there. And I knew for a fact it hadn't been there this morning. My stomach twisted. My fingers trembled as I reached for it, half expecting it to disappear like some kind of hallucination. But no—it was real. Cold from the fridge, the amber plastic smooth against my palm.

I turned it over. There was no name. No pharmacy label.

Just one word written in black marker across the front.

STOP

The bottle slipped from my hand, clattering onto the floor.

Lucky barked, startled by the sound, but I barely heard him.

Because I knew what this was. Even without a label, even without opening it—I knew.

Hospice patients. End-of-life care. A controlled substance used to ease suffering in final days. Morphine.

A bottle of morphine had been placed inside my fridge. Inside my house. Someone had been here.

And this time, they weren't just warning me. They were sending a message.

31
IT'S TOO REAL

*"The pain of grief is just as much part of life as the joy of love:
it is perhaps the price we pay for love, the cost of commitment."*
–Dr. Colin Murray Parkes

I squeezed my eyes shut, inhaling through my nose, forcing my brain to catch up. *Okay. Think.* I grabbed the closest dishtowel and carefully picked up the bottle, my hands shaking as I set it on the counter.

I stepped back, my heart pounding so hard it drowned out everything else. The house was silent, but not in the way it usually was. This silence felt wrong.

Lucky was still watching me, ears twitching at every tiny sound. He had been alone in the house when it happened. Someone had walked right in.

I grabbed my phone with numb fingers. Opened my messages. My brain was screaming at me to call Lomeli. *Now.*

But instead, I typed one word.

ME

Awake?

It took three seconds for my phone to vibrate.

I answered immediately. "Emma—"

"What's wrong?" she interrupted. "I can hear it in your voice. What happened?"

I opened my mouth, but the words stuck. My throat felt tight. I turned back to the counter, staring at the bottle.

"Someone was in my house," I finally said.

A sharp inhale on the other end of the line. "What?"

I swallowed hard. "I just got home. And—" My voice shook, so I stopped, exhaling slowly. "They left something."

"What do you mean?"

I pressed my fingers to my temple, trying to stop my head from spinning. "A bottle of morphine."

Dead silence. Then Emma's voice came through, shaky but firm. "Call Lomeli."

"I—"

"Now, V. Right now."

I squeezed my eyes shut, fighting the overwhelming urge to break down right there in the kitchen.

"I'll stay on the phone," Emma added, like she could tell I was on the verge of losing it. "Just—just put me on mute and call him. Please."

My fingers fumbled as I pulled up Lomeli's number. My breath hitched when I realized my hands were still shaking.

I hit the button to make the call.

Lomeli picked up on the second ring.

"Lomeli."

"It's me." My voice wasn't steady.

A pause. Then, sharper, "Violet?"

I gripped the edge of the counter. "Someone was in my house."

Another pause. Shorter this time. "Explain," he said, his voice clipped, all business now.

I forced a breath through my teeth. "I came home twenty minutes ago. The door was locked. Everything looked normal. But—" I swallowed. "There was a bottle of morphine in my fridge. Unlabeled. Someone left it there with a note. One word. 'STOP.'"

Lomeli didn't say anything at first. But I could hear his breathing change.

Then, "You're home now?"

"Yes."

"Alone?"

I glanced down at Lucky, who was still hovering near my feet, tail low, ears twitching.

"Just me and Lucky."

Another pause. Then, more serious this time, "I'm on my way."

I exhaled slowly.

"Don't touch the bottle again," Lomeli added. "In fact, don't touch anything. Just stay put."

"Okay."

He hung up without another word.

I pulled the phone back to my ear. Emma was still there.

"V?"

"He's coming."

Emma exhaled. "Good."

For a moment, neither of us said anything.

Then Emma's voice softened. "I can come over if you want."

I swallowed. "No, it's okay. I don't want you near this."

"You really think that's gonna stop me?"

"Emma—"

"Fine," she huffed. "But I'm waiting up. You're calling me the second he leaves."

"Okay," I whispered.

Then I hung up and sat on the kitchen floor next to Lucky, pressing my forehead against my knees. Waiting.

LOMELI ARRIVED TWENTY MINUTES LATER.

By then, I had forced myself to breathe normally, but my hands still felt cold. I opened the door before he could knock.

He wasn't alone. Another officer stood behind him—someone I didn't recognize.

Lomeli stepped inside first, his sharp eyes immediately scanning the room.

"Show me," he said.

I led him to the kitchen, where the bottle still sat on the counter.

Lomeli pulled a pair of gloves from his pocket and put them on, then picked up the bottle carefully, turning it over in his hands. His expression didn't change, but I could tell he wasn't happy. He passed it to the other officer. "Bag it."

The officer pulled out an evidence bag, slipping the bottle inside.

Lomeli turned back to me. "Nothing else was touched?"

I shook my head. "No. The doors were locked. No signs of forced entry."

Lomeli's jaw tightened. "Which means they either picked the lock—"

"—or they had a key," I finished.

Neither of us said the third option out loud. That *whoever it was had been inside before.*

Lomeli ran a hand down his face. "No more staying here alone."

"Dad and Scotty were supposed to be back by now," I said, glancing at the time. "They must've grabbed a bite after practice."

"You're telling him about this," Lomeli said, not giving me an option.

I nodded. "I know."

He hesitated, scanning my face like he wanted to say something else. Then he sighed, lowering his voice.

"Violet," he said, "you're in real danger now."

Something about the way he said it made my stomach turn.

"This isn't just some scare tactic anymore. This is a direct threat."

I nodded slowly. "I know."

Lomeli exhaled through his nose. "Then do yourself a favor and listen to me for once. Let *me* handle it."

I swallowed hard. "And if you can't?"

Lomeli didn't answer. But the look on his face said he wasn't sure anymore. And that scared me more than anything else.

THE FRONT DOOR opened just as the other officer finished sealing the morphine bottle inside an evidence bag. I flinched at the sound, my pulse still too fast, too wired, but it was just Dad and Scotty. Their voices drifted into the house—Dad saying something about hydration and Scotty excitedly talking about his "amazing" header goal.

Then—silence.

I turned to see them standing in the entryway, both frozen.

Dad took in the scene—Detective Lomeli in the kitchen,

another officer with an evidence bag, me standing too stiffly in the middle of it all. His brows pulled together. "What's going on?"

Scotty blinked between us, still clutching a Taco Bell bag, like his brain hadn't caught up yet. "Why are the police here?"

I swallowed, glancing at Lomeli, who gave me a look that said, *Your turn, kid.*

I turned back to Dad. "Someone was in the house," I said. Flat. Quiet.

Dad's face went completely still.

Scotty, though—his eyes went huge. "Wait—*what*?"

Dad set his keys on the entryway table with deliberate control. "Explain."

I did. I told him about coming home, finding the bottle, the note, knowing someone had been here. I left out the part where I debated not calling Lomeli, but otherwise, I told him exactly what happened.

Dad didn't say a word. He just stood there, shoulders rigid, mouth pressed into a hard line, absorbing it all.

Scotty wasn't so quiet. "But—how? How'd they even get in?"

"We don't know yet," Lomeli said, stepping in. "There was no sign of forced entry, which means whoever it was either picked the lock or had access to a key."

Scotty's face paled. "That means they could come *back*."

Dad finally moved, putting a steady hand on Scotty's shoulder. "They're not coming back," he said firmly. Then he turned to Lomeli. "What happens now?"

Lomeli sighed. "We'll process the evidence, check for prints. We'll also have patrols in the area tonight in case whoever did this tries anything else."

Dad's jaw tightened. "That's not enough."

Lomeli's expression stayed unreadable. "It's what we can do for now."

Dad exhaled sharply, then turned to me. "You're not staying here alone again. Not until we figure this out."

"I know," I said, my voice small.

Scotty still looked uneasy. "Can we get a security system? Like, with cameras? And the loud alarm kind?"

"Yes," Dad said immediately, ruffling Scotty's hair. "Absolutely."

Lomeli glanced at me. "Violet, do you have any idea *who* might've done this?"

I hesitated. "April?"

"Who?" Dad said. "Wait, Hannah's hospice nurse?"

I forced a breath through my nose. "Yeah, I think so. I'll tell you about it later." I gave him an 'I'm so sorry I've been keeping you in the dark' look and hoped he'd let it go—for now.

Lomeli didn't look convinced. "I'll be honest with you, kid— this feels too messy for Dawson."

I stiffened. "Messy?"

Lomeli nodded. "April's good at blending in. Keeping things quiet. Everything you've told me about her? She's controlled. Careful. This?" He gestured toward the bagged evidence. "This is a statement. And it's a risky one."

"You think it's someone else?"

Lomeli didn't answer right away. He just looked at me, long and careful. Then—finally—he sighed. "Right now, I'm considering *all* possibilities."

That wasn't a no.

I glanced at the bagged morphine bottle.

"Someone else knows." The words from Meredith's notebook rang in my head like an alarm.

Lomeli clapped Dad on the shoulder. "I'll have officers checking the area tonight. And I'll update you as soon as I know more."

Dad gave a stiff nod. "Thanks."

Lomeli's eyes flickered back to me. "Stay out of this, V. For real, this time."

I swallowed and nodded. "Yeah."

I think we both knew I was lying.

Lomeli sighed, shaking his head before motioning to the other officer. "Come on. Let's get this processed."

I watched them go.

Dad locked the door behind them.

Scotty still looked unsettled. "Are we gonna be okay?"

Dad put a hand on his back. "Yeah, bud. We are." But he didn't look at me when he said it.

And I wasn't sure I believed it.

32

TIME TO SPILL

"Grief has no timeline. It's not linear. It's not one-size-fits-all."
–Liz Newman

The morning air felt too still, too careful. When I walked to my car, I spotted a police cruiser parked across the street. Dad must have called in a favor.

I didn't know whether to feel relieved or paranoid. I'd avoided Dad and stayed upstairs till it was time to leave for school, but I knew I couldn't dodge him forever.

Speaking of dodging, I wasn't even inside the building before Emma caught up to me.

"Okay, what's going on?" she said, falling into step beside me. "What?"

"You didn't call me last night!" she hissed, glaring. "You promised you'd call after Lomeli left, and then—radio silence."

I winced. I had promised. But after the cops left, I'd been too drained, too numb—and honestly? I hadn't known how to explain any of it over the phone.

"Em," I sighed. "It was late—"

"That's not an excuse," she cut in, her voice rising slightly. "Someone broke into your house, V! That's kind of a big deal!"

I glanced around the hallway, hoping no one was listening. "Keep your voice down."

She scowled. "Not until you tell me everything."

I sighed. "Fine. Tonight. I'll come over after dinner—if I can."

Her eyes narrowed, suspicion flickering across her face. "What's that supposed to mean?"

"Dad and Scotty came home while Lomeli was there. I have to come clean. It's time to tell him about April."

Emma's eyes widened. "Oh—"

The tardy bell rang. We had to get to class. It was only 8:00 a.m., and I already felt wrung out.

BY THE TIME third period rolled around, I was barely paying attention. Mr. Grayson was going over probability formulas, but I couldn't focus. Because my phone had just buzzed.

I glanced down and felt my stomach drop.

UNKNOWN NUMBER

You're not listening.

Before I could even process that, another message came through.

A photo.

I clicked on it, blood turning to ice.

The image was dark, grainy—but clear enough. A shot of my backyard, taken last night.

I snapped my head up, heart pounding. My breath felt shallow, trapped.

Whoever this was—they'd been watching.

Mr. Grayson's voice faded into the background. The classroom blurred. I clenched my phone in my hand, forcing myself to think. I needed to get out of here. I needed to do something. And I knew exactly where I had to go.

The second the bell rang, I shot out of my seat and ran to my car. I'd miss fourth period again, but so what? I was just a TA. Miss Torres would understand. She always did.

BUT DAD HAD OTHER PLANS. Before I even made it past the office, my father blocked my path, arms crossed. "Where do you think you're going, Violet Hemingway Jiménez?"

I gulped. Dad *never* addressed me by my middle name. That had only been Mom's thing. "Um—"

"Save it," Dad interrupted. "No more excuses, okay? Honey, when will you realize I'm on your side? Stop avoiding me, stop shutting me out, and *please* stop lying to me." He sighed, his shoulders sagged with exhaustion. His eyes held something deeper than frustration. Hurt? No. *Disappointment.*

"Come on, let's go to my classroom and talk. As you know, I'm free now—fourth period is my prep."

I followed him, knowing I had to tell him everything. That didn't make it any easier.

The familiar scent of old books and dry-erase markers filled the empty classroom. Posters of historical figures lined the walls, watching in silent judgment.

Dad shut the door and leaned against his desk, arms crossed, his sharp, disappointed teacher look pinning me in place.

I swallowed hard, hovering near the front row of desks. My fingers tightened around the strap of my backpack, like holding on could keep me from unraveling.

"You're in a lot deeper than I thought," Dad said, his voice quieter now. Not angry. Just worn out.

I shifted. "Dad, I—"

"Start from the beginning." His eyes met mine. "The *real* beginning, V."

There was no getting out of this. No sidestepping. No excuses.

So I told him. All of it. I started with Mom's journal and the uneasy feelings she'd had around April. I told him about Amanda, Trina's grandmother, and Zuri's dad. About the pattern I'd uncovered.

I finished with Lomeli's involvement, the break-ins to my car and our house, and even the text threats.

He didn't interrupt. He didn't react right away. He sat there, listening, his face growing tighter with every new piece of information.

And when I finally finished, he let out a long, shaky breath.

"Violet," he said, rubbing his hands over his face. "Do you have *any* idea how dangerous this was?"

I looked away. "I had to know," I said quietly.

Dad exhaled. "And now that you do?"

I hesitated. "They're planning to arrest April soon, maybe even today. I was going to—"

"No." His voice was firm.

I snapped my eyes up to meet his.

Dad shook his head. "You are *not* going anywhere near this again, Violet. Do you hear me? *This is over.*"

"Dad—"

"I mean it." His voice cracked slightly. "You think I haven't noticed how all this has affected you? You think I don't see you unraveling? You don't sleep. You barely eat. You've been keeping all of this to yourself."

My throat tightened. "I didn't want you to worry," I whispered.

He let out a bitter laugh. "I'm your father. Worrying about you is my full-time job."

I hated this. I hated how raw it felt. Exposed.

I'd spent weeks chasing the truth, following every lead, running on pure determination and grief. But now that the chase was ending? It felt like all that was left was the loss.

Dad's eyes softened. "I know you, honey. I know why you had to do this. And I know—I know how much you miss her."

A lump lodged in my throat.

He reached out, his voice gentler now. "You don't have to do this alone anymore."

I swallowed hard. "I don't know how to stop."

He nodded, like he understood exactly what I meant. Then he said something that almost knocked the wind out of me.

"You're not your mom, Violet."

I blinked. "What?"

Dad sighed, his shoulders sagging. "She always tried to control what she couldn't. Always carried too much on her own. I loved that about her—it's what made her *her*. But I don't want that for you."

Something cracked in my chest.

Dad shook his head. "You don't have to spend your whole life trying to fix things, V. You don't have to carry the weight of the world. You just have to *live*."

My eyes stung with unshed tears. This was supposed to be the part where I fought back. Where I argued. Where I told him I wasn't like Mom.

But for the first time, I didn't want to argue. I just felt tired. And maybe, just maybe, he was right.

Dad opened his arms, and I fell into them. He wrapped them around me and held me. "Go home directly after school, okay?"

I nodded into his chest, unable to speak.

33

APRIL'S LAST SHIFT

"Although the world is full of suffering,
it is also full of the overcoming of it."
–Helen Keller

I should have gone home. Dad's words still echoed in my head, lingering like an aftershock: *"You don't have to fix everything, V."*

I should have listened. But I didn't.

Lomeli had told me to stay out of it, to let him handle it. So, naturally, I did the opposite. Because there was still one last thing I needed to do. One last person I needed to face.

The drive to UCI Medical Center passed in a blur, my hands gripping the wheel too tightly, my pulse a steady drumbeat of anger. I wasn't stupid—I knew this was reckless. But I had to do it anyway.

Inside, the hospital was quiet, sterile, the fluorescent lights buzzing faintly overhead. Each step felt heavier than the last as I made my way through the halls.

And then I saw her.

April Dawson stood near a patient's room, flipping through a chart like it was just another shift. Like she wasn't about to lose everything.

I walked up slowly, stopping a couple feet away.

She looked up. Her smile flickered, just for a second. "V," she greeted me, her voice polite, cautious. "I wasn't expecting you."

I didn't return the smile. "Did you expect to get away with it?"

Her fingers froze on her pen. A heartbeat of silence. Then— deliberately—she put the pen in her pocket. "Why don't we talk somewhere private?"

Calm. Collected. In control. Like she was still managing me.

I gritted my teeth. "No, we're doing this here."

April exhaled, as if she was already tired of the conversation. "You seem upset—"

"*Upset?*" My voice shook with anger. "You broke into my house! You left a bottle of morphine in my refrigerator and told me to stop."

April's face didn't move. She just tilted her head slightly, as if studying me. "That wasn't me."

"I don't believe you."

"I don't threaten people, V."

"You're right—you just *kill them.*"

That got a reaction. A tiny flicker of something passed through her eyes—guilt? Sadness? Then it was gone. "You don't understand," she said softly.

"Then make me understand." My hands curled into fists.

April swallowed, her gaze dropping for half a second. Then she met my eyes and said, calmly, "I never wanted to hurt anyone."

"But you killed all those people! Amanda. My mom. How many others were there?"

Something flickered in her eyes. Something that almost looked like pity.

It made me want to scream.

"I never hurt your mother, V," she said softly.

I laughed, sharp and hollow. "Right. Because you think you *helped* them, right? That's what you told Lomeli, isn't it?"

Her lips pressed together.

"You think you were some kind of savior," I spat. "But you're just a murderer with a God complex."

For the first time, her composure cracked. "You don't understand," she whispered, voice nearly trembling. "I watched people suffer. I watched them die in pain while their families sat there, powerless. Do you think I *wanted* this? That I did it for fun?"

I shook my head, rage burning through me. "No. You did it because you couldn't stand to feel helpless. You did it because you convinced yourself it was mercy—because it made *you* feel better. Not them."

She flinched. Because she knew I was right. Her gaze dropped to the floor. "I only ever ended suffering," she murmured. "I only ever—"

"You didn't kill my mom?" I interrupted.

She hesitated. Then—"No," she whispered.

For some reason, that made me even angrier. "Then why did you just stand there and watch?" My voice cracked. "She was scared, April. She didn't want to go yet. And you—you were waiting for it."

April closed her eyes, like hearing it hurt too much. Like she couldn't face what she'd actually done.

"I didn't touch her dose," she whispered. "I swear to you, I didn't."

For a long second, I stared at her. And somehow, a part of me believed her. Still, I knew exactly what she was—a killer.

I was about to say something more when footsteps echoed behind me—hurried, deliberate. More than one person.

April's posture stiffened as she looked past me.

I turned.

It was Lomeli. And behind him, two officers.

April exhaled, slow and resigned. Like she *knew*. Like she had been expecting this moment all along.

I stepped back as Lomeli moved in, his voice steady, professional. "April Dawson, you're under arrest for the murders of multiple patients under your care."

April closed her eyes and stood there as the officers swarmed in, pinning her arms behind her back. She didn't resist. Didn't speak. Didn't even look at me.

Lomeli glared at me.

I braced for a lecture, but instead, he sighed. "You just couldn't stay out of it, huh?"

"Not really my style."

He huffed, shaking his head.

I watched as they cuffed her hands behind her back, as they led her through the hospital doors and into the waiting squad car.

I should have felt satisfied. Instead, I just felt empty.

Because something about this felt odd. Like I was missing something huge.

And I had a sinking feeling the real story wasn't over yet.

I ARRIVED at the police station about twenty minutes later and sat in one of the stiff plastic chairs near the front, my arms crossed, foot bouncing rapidly.

April Dawson had just been arrested.

I should have felt relieved, but I didn't. Because something wasn't right.

Lomeli emerged from one of the back offices, his expression unreadable. He walked over and leaned against the desk near me, arms crossed. "You good?" he asked.

I let out a slow breath. "I don't know."

Lomeli watched me for a beat. Then he nodded toward the hallway behind him. "We're in the process of booking her now. Should be in holding within the hour."

I nodded, still trying to shake the unease in my chest.

"You did good work, Jiménez," Lomeli added.

I blinked at him. That was unexpected. "You're not gonna yell at me for showing up at UCI?"

Lomeli sighed. "Oh, I absolutely am. Just, not right now."

I let out a weak laugh, but my stomach still twisted itself into knots.

"You don't think she did it," I said suddenly.

Lomeli's gaze didn't waver. "I think she's guilty of something. But I also think there's a chance she's not the only one."

My chest tightened.

"Someone else knows." That single sentence from Meredith's notebook had been bothering me for days.

I swallowed. "So what now?"

"Now," Lomeli said, "we see what April tells us."

A cold chill ran through me. Because when they had arrested her—when they had read her rights, cuffed her, taken her away—April hadn't resisted.

She hadn't even looked surprised. She had just stood there, silent, waiting. Like she had already made peace with it. Like she had known all along.

I wasn't sure what that meant yet. But I knew one thing for sure. This wasn't over.

Not even close.

34

IT'S NOT OVER

"Out of suffering have emerged the strongest souls; the most massive characters are seared with scars."
–Khalil Gibran

By the time I pulled into Emma's driveway, my hands were still shaking. I had barely turned off the engine when the front door flew open.

Emma marched toward me, arms crossed, jaw set.

I barely had time to get out of the car before she was in my face.

"You have to be kidding me."

"Emma—"

"You went to UCI?! Alone?! To confront a *literal* killer?!"

"Technically, she didn't try to kill me—"

Emma threw up her hands. "That's your defense?!"

I opened my mouth—then immediately shut it.

Because, okay. *Fair point.*

Emma let out a sharp breath and put her hands on her hips,

pacing. "I swear to God, V, one day you are going to give me an aneurysm."

"I didn't plan on getting arrested with her, if that helps?"

Emma whipped around so fast, I actually took a step back.

"That helps zero percent."

I sighed, rubbing a hand down my face. She wasn't wrong.

"I needed to see her," I admitted. "I needed to look her in the eye and know for sure."

Emma narrowed her eyes. "And? Do you?"

I hesitated. That was the problem. Because April had looked guilty. She had confessed to me, in her own twisted way.

But something about just didn't feel right.

"I don't know," I said finally.

Emma's shoulders dropped slightly, some of the fight bleeding out of her posture. "I thought this was supposed to be over," she said.

I thought so, too. I wanted it to be. But in my gut, I knew the truth. It wasn't.

Emma must have read something in my face because her expression shifted. She didn't yell again. She sighed, rubbing her temples. "Please," she said, quieter this time. "Just stop doing reckless, borderline illegal things for one week. Just one. I'm begging you."

I let out a breath. "I'll try."

Emma gave me a look.

"Fine," I said. "I'll strongly consider it."

She sighed again. "That's the best I'm getting, isn't it?"

"Yup."

She shook her head, but there was no real heat behind it anymore. "C'mon. We're eating ice cream and watching something aggressively stupid before my head explodes."

I let her pull me toward the house. Because for one night—

just one—I could pretend like things were normal. Even if I knew they weren't. Even if I knew this wasn't over.

FOR THE FIRST time in weeks, I woke up without that immediate, suffocating sense of dread pressing against my head. I hadn't dreamed of hospital beds or whispered warnings. I hadn't spent the night scrolling through crime forums or waking up in cold sweats.

I'd crashed at Emma's after watching an insultingly bad reality dating show, eating way too much cookie dough ice cream, and pretending—for a few hours—that my life was normal. And now?

The sun was shining. April Dawson was in custody. Maybe, finally, *this nightmare was over.*

I sat up, stretching, feeling almost human again.

Emma shuffled into her room from the bathroom, flopped onto the bed, and yawned. "Look at that. You survived the night without committing a felony. Progress."

I rolled my eyes. "Please, I was too full of cookie dough to commit crimes."

She smirked, tossing a pillow at me. "You staying for breakfast?"

I hesitated. "Better check in with Dad real quick. On a tight leash after what I pulled last night, and, well, the last few weeks."

By Friday afternoon, my sense of peace had completely shattered.

Because that was when I saw the headline on my phone.

"BREAKING: Patient Death at Lakeview Hospice Under Investigation."

My stomach dropped. I pulled the article up so fast I nearly dropped the phone.

"Authorities confirm that an elderly patient at Lakeview Hospice was found deceased early Friday morning. While details remain undisclosed, sources suggest an internal review is underway regarding the patient's care in their final hours. Officials have not commented on whether this incident is connected to Wednesday's arrest of nurse April Dawson, who remains in police custody."

I felt cold all over. April was already in custody. So how was another patient dead?

My fingers felt numb as I sent the link to Emma.

ME

It's not over.

The reply came seconds later.

EMMA

I'm calling you.

A second later, my phone buzzed.

I picked up.

"V," Emma said, her voice tight. "What's going on?"

"I don't know, but I need to find out."

I heard her exhale sharply on the other end.

"You're not gonna do anything stupid, right?"

I didn't answer. Because honestly? I wasn't sure anymore.

35
THERE'S A 'HIM'

"Hope smiles from the threshold of the year to come,
whispering, 'It will be happier.'"
–Alfred Lord Tennyson

When I parked outside the police station—again—I was fuming. I marched through the front doors like I had a personal vendetta against the floor tiles. Martinez barely had time to react before I breezed past him.

"Jiménez," he called after me, exasperated. "You can't just—"

I ignored him. I knew exactly where Lomeli's office was. And when I threw open the door without knocking, he didn't even flinch. He just let out a long, exhausted sigh.

"You again."

I dropped my phone onto his desk, screen glowing with the article headline.

"April's in custody," I said. "So explain this."

Lomeli barely glanced at the screen. "I saw it this morning."

I stared at him. "And?"

"And we're looking into it," he said evenly, leaning back in his chair.

I narrowed my eyes. "You don't think it's connected?"

"I didn't say that."

I exhaled sharply. "Then say something, Lomeli, because I know you're thinking it."

He gave me a long look. Then he tapped his fingers against his desk, considering. "I thought you'd be celebrating," he said finally. "You got what you wanted. Dawson's in custody."

I hated that he said it like that. Like this was some personal victory instead of *a murder investigation.*

"You think I care about a win?" I shot back. "Someone else just died. This isn't over."

Lomeli's jaw tightened. Then he stood, walking over to his filing cabinet, pulling out a manila folder.

"Do you know what's in here?" he asked, turning back to me.

I crossed my arms. "Enlighten me."

He flipped it open. "Official patient records. Death certificates. Hospice reports. All tied to Dawson."

I stared at him. "And?"

"And," he said, tossing it onto the desk in front of me, "none of them match what happened last night."

I frowned. "What do you mean?"

Lomeli sat down again, rubbing his temple. "Dawson's patients died *fast*—yes. But they were all end-stage. All expected to die soon. Even if she sped up the process, none of them should've lived much longer."

I swallowed. "But this patient—"

"Wasn't end-stage," he finished.

My stomach turned. April's whole twisted, messed-up justification for what she did was that she was *helping.* She only took patients who were already dying. But this patient?

They weren't supposed to go yet.

I sat down slowly. "Then we have the wrong person."

Lomeli rubbed his jaw. "Or we only have *half* the person."

My pulse spiked. Because for the first time, he was actually saying it.

April wasn't working alone. This was even bigger.

I leaned forward. "Then let me help."

Lomeli gave me a look. "No."

I scowled. "Lomeli—"

"You've done enough," he said firmly. "You gave us Dawson. Now let *me* do my job."

I clenched my jaw. "So what? You want me to just sit back and do nothing?"

"Yes."

I scoffed.

He sighed. "Listen to me. Whoever did this last night isn't just reckless. They're confident. Confident enough to kill again *while we have a suspect in custody.* That means they're not scared of us. And that?" He leveled me with a serious look. "That's what makes them dangerous."

I swallowed. Because he was right. This was different. But that didn't mean I was giving up. It just meant I had to play this smarter.

I grabbed my phone off the desk, standing.

Lomeli sighed again. "You're not gonna listen to me, are you?"

I met his eyes. "Nope."

"Good grief," he muttered. But this time, he didn't try to stop me. Because I think, deep down, he knew.

I DIDN'T GO HOME after leaving the police station. I went to Emma's. This was quickly becoming a habit.

She must've heard my car pull up because by the time I made it to the front door, it swung open.

Emma took one look at my face and sighed. "That bad?"

"Worse," I said, walking in past her.

I barely got my shoes off before she dragged me into the kitchen, pulling out two sodas from the fridge and shoving one into my hand.

"Okay," she said, leaning against the counter, arms crossed. "Tell me everything."

So I did. I told her about Lomeli, about the new death at Lakeview, about how it didn't fit April's pattern. And when I was done, she let out a long breath.

"Okay," she said slowly, eyes narrowing like she was solving a puzzle. "So either April somehow orchestrated a murder from behind bars, or—"

"Or there's someone else," I finished.

Emma nodded. "So what do we do?"

I blinked at her. "We?"

She caught the look and rolled her eyes. "Oh, don't even start. If you think I'm letting you run around solo with some copycat murderer on the loose, you're dumber than your AP scores suggest."

I actually laughed. First real laugh all day.

Emma smirked. "Okay, genius. Where do we start?"

I hesitated. Because I didn't actually know. For the first time in weeks, I didn't know what the next step was. And then—

Something clicked. I sat up straighter. "Meredith's notebook."

Emma frowned. "Didn't you give it to Lomeli?"

"Yeah, but—" I hesitated, searching my memory. "I read it so many times, Em. I know it cover to cover. But I was *so focused on April* that I ignored everything else."

Emma's brow furrowed. "Okay, so what else was in there?"

I closed my eyes, focusing. Trying to picture it. Trying to see it differently.

Meredith had been meticulous. Every patient. Every nurse. Every shift change.

And then, at the very end—

My eyes flew open. "Jillian Sosa."

Emma blinked. "Who?"

I grabbed my phone, pulling up Google. "I didn't pay attention to her name before because she wasn't a patient. She was a witness."

I typed as fast as I could, scanning results.

And then—there. An old article. A comment at the bottom.

"I tried to report him. No one believed me."

Emma leaned over my shoulder, squinting. "*Him?*" she echoed. "Him?!"

I stared at the screen, pulse racing. "April's not the only one," I whispered. "She never was."

Emma exhaled sharply. "So let's find Jillian."

I nodded. Because this time, we were going straight to the source.

I sat cross-legged on Emma's bed, staring at Jillian Sosa's contact in my phone. I had already met her once—a quick, hesitant conversation in a coffee shop. She'd been nervous, guarded, like she was looking over her shoulder the whole time. Now, I needed her to talk again. And this time?

Emma was coming with me. She sat beside me, chewing on the end of a pen, watching as I hovered over Jillian's number.

"Okay, so what's the plan?" Emma asked. "You just gonna call her and be like, 'Hey, remember how you were already terrified last time we spoke? Well, bad news—it's worse than we thought.'"

I shot her a look. "That was *almost* helpful."

Emma shrugged. "Just trying to mentally prepare."

I sighed and finally hit the call button.

The line rang twice. Then Jillian picked up.

"Violet?" Her voice sounded tired. Stressed.

I swallowed the guilt creeping up my throat. "Yeah," I said. "I'm sorry to call so late. I need to talk to you. Again."

A pause. Then—"I figured you might."

That caught me off guard. "You saw the news," I guessed.

Jillian let out a humorless laugh. "Of course I did. And I bet I know exactly why you're calling."

I glanced at Emma, who was listening intently.

I tightened my grip on the phone. "Can we meet?" I asked. "Tomorrow? Please. It's important."

Another pause.

Then, a resigned sigh. "Same place?" she asked.

"Yeah," I said quickly. "And—" I hesitated. "I'm bringing my friend. Her name's Emma. I trust her."

Jillian was silent for a long time. Then—"All right. Tomorrow morning. But that's it, Violet. I can't keep doing this."

My chest tightened. "Okay," I said softly. "Thank you."

She hung up.

I set my phone down and let out a slow breath.

Emma raised an eyebrow. "So, we're meeting the possibly traumatized key witness to a serial murder case early on a Saturday morning. Love that for us."

I shot her a look. "You don't have to come."

Emma scoffed. "Oh, please. Like I'm letting you do this alone."

I exhaled, feeling something strange—relief. For the first time in this whole mess, I wasn't doing this alone.

36
WEEKENDS OFF?

"You will survive and you will find purpose in the chaos.
Moving on doesn't mean letting go."
–Mary VanHaute

Emma and I pulled into the coffee shop parking lot just after 7:15 a.m. The morning sun was already too bright, too sharp, making everything feel more real than I wanted it to. I spotted Jillian immediately—same table, same nervous energy. She was hunched over a coffee cup, fingers tapping anxiously against the paper sleeve, her dark hair pulled into a messy bun.

She looked tired. Worse than last time.

Emma parked, cut the engine, and gave me a sideways glance. "Last chance to tell me to stay in the car."

I snorted. "Like you'd listen."

She smirked. "Correct."

We got out and headed inside. The moment Jillian saw us, she tensed.

I hesitated for half a second, then slid into the seat across from her. Emma sat beside me, setting her bag on the table.

"Hey," I said carefully.

Jillian's fingers tightened around her cup. "I don't know why I'm here."

"You do," I said.

She exhaled sharply, shaking her head. "This is a mistake."

"Jillian," I said, leaning forward slightly. "You said you tried to report *him* once. Who?"

Her jaw clenched. "I shouldn't have left that comment."

"But you did." My voice was steady. "Because you wanted someone to see it. Someone to *listen*."

Jillian swallowed hard. "I can't—"

Emma, who had been silent until now, suddenly spoke.

"We're not the cops," she said simply. "We're not gonna throw you in front of a judge or make you testify. We just want to know the truth."

Jillian studied Emma carefully. Then, finally, she let out a long breath. "It was years ago," she murmured.

Emma and I both stilled.

Jillian's gaze drifted somewhere past us, like she was already back there. "My dad was at St. Lucia's. He had congestive heart failure, but he was stable. We thought we had months left. Maybe even a year."

I didn't breathe.

Jillian's voice was low, careful. "And then, one night, everything changed. They said it was sudden. That his heart gave out. But I—" She hesitated. "I knew something wasn't right. He was fine that morning."

A sick feeling curled in my stomach.

"They didn't want an autopsy," she whispered. "The doctors called it a natural progression of the disease. Said it happens all the time. But something felt . . . wrong." She took a slow breath, fingers tightening around her cup. "I tried to tell someone," she continued. "The hospice director. The hospital liaison. They wouldn't listen. They said I was grieving. That I was in denial. The only person who believed me was my friend Doug."

I swallowed hard. "Who did you suspect?" I asked.

Jillian blinked, looking back at me. "I didn't have a name back then. Just a feeling."

"But now?"

She hesitated. Then—"April Dawson worked the night shift."

Emma and I exchanged a quick glance.

"Did you ever meet her?" I asked.

Jillian nodded slowly. "Once. She was nice. Too nice." Her fingers tensed. "But it wasn't just her."

"What do you mean?"

Jillian exhaled sharply, shaking her head. "It wasn't just one nurse," she whispered. "There was always another one. Someone else in the background. I didn't know his name, but he was there. Every shift. Every patient that died unexpectedly."

My pulse spiked.

Emma sat up straighter. "Wait—*him*?"

Jillian nodded. "I only saw him once or twice. He wasn't my dad's primary nurse, but he was there." She let out a bitter laugh. "But no one ever talked about *him*. It was always about April. She was the one patients and families remembered because she was so friendly."

I tensed. April wasn't the only one. She had always been the face. The one everyone saw.

But Jillian had seen someone else. And that meant April wasn't working alone.

Emma let out a slow breath, like she was processing all of this in real time. "Do you think she knew?"

Jillian hesitated. "I'm not sure."

I felt sick. If April had known about him, this other nurse—then how many more people had they hurt?

The pieces clicked into place. April killed some patients, but someone else had been right there with her. Someone who was still out there.

I met Jillian's gaze. "Do you remember anything else about him?"

She hesitated, brows furrowing. "He was older, I think. Late forties? Maybe fifties. He had this"—she gestured vaguely—"calm energy. Like nothing ever got to him. It was almost unsettling."

Emma frowned. "And no one ever questioned him?"

Jillian shook her head. "Not once. He just blended in."

I swallowed, staring down at the table. It made sense. Too much sense.

April was reckless. She had let herself get sloppy. That was why she got caught.

But this other guy? He was smarter. And now? He was still free.

Jillian rubbed a hand down her face. "I don't know what you two are planning to do with this information, but—" She swallowed. "Be careful. If he's still out there, and he knows you're digging—"

She didn't have to finish the sentence. We already knew. Emma and I exchanged a glance.

Jillian had just confirmed what I had been too afraid to say out loud. This really wasn't over.

Emma and I drove straight to the station. We didn't stop for food. We didn't take a detour.

Jillian had just confirmed what I already suspected. April Dawson wasn't the only one. And now? The real killer knew I was closing in.

"This guy—whoever he is—he's still working," Emma said. "Still doing this. And no one's looking for him because everyone thinks April is the whole story."

I swallowed hard, staring out the window. "We're telling Lomeli."

Emma shot me a look. "Yeah, no kidding. It's literally the only semi-responsible choice you've made this week."

I almost smiled. Almost. My mind was spinning too fast.

Jillian had seen another nurse. A man. Someone who had been working alongside April, blending in, going unnoticed.

I pulled out my phone and scrolled through the old articles again. So many of them focused on April. Her shifts. Her patients. Her demeanor. But who else had been there?

I skimmed the staff lists from St. Lucia's, Lakeview, and UCI, but none of the names stood out—yet.

Because I'd been looking for April. Now, I had to look for someone else.

WE STORMED through the front doors of the station so fast they didn't even bother trying to stop us this time.

Lomeli was standing near his desk, flipping through a case file.

He looked up just in time to see me drop into the chair across from him. Emma took the seat beside me, arms crossed.

"Good, I was hoping you'd be here," I said. "Don't you ever take weekends off?"

"Do serial killers?" Lomeli replied.

"Good point. Detective Lomeli, you remember Emma?"

"Of course. Good to see you again, Emma."

"You, too," Emma said, sheepishly.

Lomeli sighed. "Now that the pleasantries are out of the way, what brings you here—again?"

"We met with Jillian Sosa this morning."

Lomeli's expression didn't change. "I see."

"She confirmed something," I said, voice tight. "She saw another nurse. A man. He was working the same shifts as April. He was there when her dad died. And if he was there for that—"

"He was probably there for other deaths, too," Lomeli finished.

My pulse spiked. Because he wasn't brushing me off this time.

Emma leaned forward. "You already suspected this, didn't you?"

Lomeli was quiet for a long moment. Then, finally, he exhaled sharply and rubbed his temple. "April's arrest made waves," he admitted. "Which means more reports are coming in. And some of them?" He met my eyes. "They don't fit her pattern."

A shiver ran down my spine. "So you know," I said.

Lomeli sighed. "I *suspect.* Knowing and proving are two different things."

Emma narrowed her eyes. "So prove it."

Lomeli let out a dry laugh. "You think it's that easy?"

I clenched my fists. "Lomeli, if this guy is still out there, he's going to kill again."

Lomeli's jaw tightened. "I know."

The weight of those two words settled over us like a storm cloud. Yet, for the first time, he wasn't telling me to back off. Because he knew. And that meant this was bigger than any of us realized.

37

CONNECTING THE DOTS

*"Courage doesn't always roar. Sometimes courage is the quiet voice
at the end of the day saying, 'I will try again tomorrow.'"*
–Mary Anne Radmacher

Emma and I left the station in tense silence, Lomeli's confirmation hanging over us like a storm cloud ready to break. Someone else was involved. April wasn't the only one. And this wasn't over.

Emma drove too fast, her fingers locked around the steering wheel like she might snap it in half. "So," she said finally, "we were right."

I let out a slow breath. "Yeah."

Emma shook her head. "This is insane. How is someone getting away with this? How has nobody caught him before now?"

Because April made it easy. She was reckless. Sloppy. The face of the operation—the one everyone remembered, the one they noticed. But the other guy?

He disappeared into the background.

"We need a name," I said.

Emma shot me a sideways glance. "And how exactly are we supposed to get that?"

I stared at my phone, my mind spinning. Lomeli was buried in paperwork and red tape. I wasn't.

I pulled up my search history—all the old staff lists I'd combed through before.

Except this time, I wasn't looking for April.

I was looking for him.

A nurse who worked at St. Lucia's in 2014. And Riverside Serenity Care in 2016. And Lakeview and UCI in 2017.

Emma leaned over, reading my screen. "You really think we'll find him like this?"

"It's a start."

She exhaled slowly. "Okay. So where do we start?"

"The patients."

April's known victims. The ones Lomeli had records on.

"Every patient who died suspiciously," I said, "we cross-check their nurses."

Emma blinked. "That's actually a really good idea."

I smirked. "Try not to sound so surprised."

She rolled her eyes, but I could tell she was already on board.

We drove back to my house, grabbed our laptops, and started digging.

A FEW HOURS LATER, we were really close to a breakthrough. The list of nurses was shrinking. Every name I crossed off felt like I was getting closer, getting warmer.

Then—my phone buzzed.

A text from Lomeli.

And I knew. Even before I read it, I knew.

LOMELI

We need to talk. Another patient just died.

My stomach plummeted.

Emma saw the look on my face. "What?"

I turned my phone around so she could see.

Her face drained of color. "V," she said slowly, "who was it?"

I swallowed hard. I didn't know yet. But I was about to find out. My hands felt too cold as I gripped my phone. I stared at Lomeli's message, my pulse pounding in my ears. Another patient just died.

Emma was still looking at me, waiting. "V," she said, more urgent this time. "Call him."

I swallowed hard and hit dial.

Lomeli picked up immediately. "Violet."

"Who?" I asked.

A pause. Then—"Doug Holloway."

I squeezed my eyes shut, trying to process. "Doug—"

Jillian's friend. Her one ally after her dad's death. The only other person who had tried to report something was wrong back then. And now, he was dead.

Emma stiffened. "Oh my Gosh."

I barely heard her. My breath was coming too fast, my chest too tight. "When?" I asked, forcing my voice to stay even.

"Tonight," Lomeli said. "He was at Lakeview. Nurses found him unresponsive. No clear cause of death yet, but—"

"But it wasn't natural," I finished flatly.

Lomeli didn't answer right away. Then, quietly—"I don't think so, no."

Emma was still staring at me, trying to read my face. "V," she whispered. "This isn't a coincidence."

She was right. Doug Holloway wasn't just another victim. He was a message.

Jillian had barely mentioned him. She'd said he was a friend. And now? He was gone.

A chill crawled down my spine.

The real killer knew we were looking. And *he* wasn't just watching anymore—he was cleaning up loose ends.

I DIDN'T THINK. I called her. I owed her this.

Jillian picked up on the second ring. "Violet?" She sounded uneasy, like she already knew something was wrong.

I swallowed the lump in my throat. "Jillian," I said, "it's Doug."

A pause. "What about him?"

I closed my eyes, gripping the phone tighter. "He's ... dead."

"No," she said, her voice fragile. "No, that's—no, he was *fine*—"

"I know," I whispered. "But it happened tonight. At Lakeview."

A sharp intake of breath. "Lakeview," she repeated. Almost a whisper.

Emma was watching me, arms crossed, jaw set. She didn't say anything, but she didn't have to.

Jillian's breathing had changed. It was erratic, shallow.

I waited.

"No, no, no," she said, more to herself than to me. "Not Doug, not him, too."

Doug had been the only one who had believed her. The only one who had fought with her, not against her. And now, he was gone.

Jillian let out a shaky breath. Then, too quiet—"They know."

"What?" I shook off a sudden chill.

"They *know*, Violet," she said, stronger this time. "Whoever did this—whoever you're looking for—they know you're getting too close. This is bad. This is really, really bad."

I closed my eyes, gripping the phone. "Jillian, listen to me. If Doug was targeted, that means—"

"It means I'm next," she cut in. The fear in her voice made my stomach twist.

"Jillian, we won't let that happen," I said, trying to keep my voice steady. "But we need to know *everything*. If you're holding something back—"

"I'm done talking about this." The words came out flat. Final.

I blinked. "Wait, what?"

"I should have kept my mouth shut," she said, mostly to herself. "I knew this was dangerous. I knew it, and now Doug is —" Her voice broke on the last word.

"Jillian, we can still—"

"No," she snapped. "No, we can't. You don't get it, Violet! You have no idea who you're dealing with!"

Something cold curled in my chest. "Then tell me," I pressed.

She let out a harsh, bitter laugh. "What, so you can keep playing detective? So you can end up like Doug?"

The words hit like a slap.

Emma, who had been silent this whole time, suddenly leaned in, voice calm but firm.

"Jillian, we can't ignore this," she said. "You can't just pretend this isn't happening."

Jillian exhaled sharply. "I'm not pretending. I'm stopping. I'm done, Violet. Don't call me again."

The line went dead.

38

THEY'RE LISTENING

"A note for anyone who needs to hear this: We don't 'get over' or 'move on' from grief. We make space for it. We carry it. We learn to live with it. And, sometimes we thrive in spite of it."
–Anonymous

I stared at my phone, too stunned to move.

Emma's eyes darkened. "She's scared."

I nodded slowly. "Yeah, me, too."

"Which means we're getting close."

Before I could respond, my phone buzzed again.

But it wasn't Jillian.

My stomach dropped as I read the message.

UNKNOWN NUMBER

Last chance. Stop now.

My breath hitched.

Emma was already reading over my shoulder. "V," she whispered, "look at the time stamp."

I did. And my blood went cold. The message had been sent five minutes ago.

The exact moment we had mentioned Doug's name. They weren't just warning me. They were listening.

"Last chance. Stop now."

It wasn't just a threat. It was a reminder. They knew exactly what we were doing. Exactly what we were talking about. *And they were listening.*

"Okay," Emma said, slow but certain. "That's bad."

I nodded.

The silence stretched, until finally, Emma let out a sharp breath and snatched the phone from my hands. She scrolled back to the text, eyes flicking over it. "Is there an IP address? A weird country code?"

"No," I said. "Just 'Unknown Number.'"

She gritted her teeth. "Coward."

I barely heard her. My mind was spinning, unraveling. Because if they'd heard us—if they had been listening in real time—then that meant . . . I sucked in a sharp breath. "Emma."

She looked up. "Yeah?"

My eyes darted around the room. My heart was pounding now, too fast, too loud.

"What if they're not just watching us?" I said. "What if they're *hearing* us?"

Her face drained of color. "You mean—"

I nodded, my throat tightening. "They're listening. *Right now.*"

Emma moved fast. Within seconds, she grabbed my laptop, my phone, and her phone and yanked the battery out of her device. "Okay," she said, all business. "Let's assume worst-case scenario. Where would someone plant a listening device?"

My mouth was too dry. "I don't know."

Emma paced, restless. "Okay, okay, think. We've been talking about this mostly in your room."

I nodded, trying to force my brain to work. But my thoughts were a tangled mess.

"Could they have bugged it?" I whispered.

Emma was already scanning the walls, eyes darting to outlets, the vent, smoke detector. She opened her laptop, quickly googling, then held it up. "We can check for frequencies."

"For what?"

She turned the screen toward me. "If they planted something wireless, we can scan for unusual signals."

I grabbed my phone, opened my settings, and checked for unfamiliar Bluetooth connections. Nothing.

Emma scanned the room again. "What about your bulletin board?"

We searched it. Nothing. We searched everything we could think of. Nada.

We decided to get out of there, especially if the room was bugged. I opened the door to go downstairs when Lucky, who'd been curled up, sleeping on the floor, got up to follow us.

Emma and I stopped, staring at each other. We both got the idea at the same time.

I knelt down and unclipped Lucky's collar, then turned it over in my hand. A tiny black dot was embedded in the buckle.

Emma locked eyes with me. "V," she whispered. "They bugged your dog."

I STARED at the tiny black dot on Lucky's collar, my pulse a steady roar in my ears. I knew it was a listening device. They hadn't just been watching. They'd been listening to everything.

Emma and I exchanged a glance, both of us frozen.

Then she hissed, "Get me something sharp."

I scrambled to my desk, grabbing a pair of scissors. My hands were shaking.

Emma snatched them from me and started prying at the tiny device, her jaw clenched so tight I thought she might crack a tooth.

Lucky, blissfully unaware that he'd just been a freaking wiretap, wagged his tail and licked Emma's arm.

I pressed a hand over my mouth, trying to keep my breathing steady.

Emma finally popped the device loose and dropped it onto my desk like it was a dead bug. It was so small. Just a little black circle, no bigger than a button. But it was everything. It meant that this wasn't just someone sending anonymous threats. They were in my life. In my space.

"How long has this been here?" I whispered.

Emma didn't answer right away. She pulled out her phone and took a photo of the device, zooming in on any markings. "Looks like a standard GSM bug. Cheap. Easy to hide. Runs off a SIM card."

I swallowed hard. "How long?"

Emma let out a slow breath. "Could be days. Maybe weeks?"

I felt sick. *Weeks.* Weeks of them listening. To my house. My conversations. My life.

They listened to me talking about the case, to Jillian.

My breath hitched. "Emma."

She glanced up, face still tight.

I held up my phone. "That text. They sent it right when we mentioned Doug's name."

Emma's eyes widened.

I grabbed the bug off the desk, heart pounding. "They knew what we were saying in real time. Which means—"

Emma's expression darkened. "They heard us figure it out."

A sharp, terrified chill ran down my spine. The moment we had realized April wasn't the only one. The moment we had realized someone else was still out there. That was when they sent the text.

They had been listening. And they had responded.

Emma swallowed. "We have to go to Lomeli. Now."

For once, I didn't argue. I grabbed my keys.

EMMA DROVE. I was too busy staring at the tiny bug in my palm, my stomach twisting. Someone had been listening. For days, maybe longer. They'd heard everything.

Every theory. Every lead. Every name.

They had known when we were getting too close. And now?

Doug was dead. And we might be next.

Emma's knuckles were white against the steering wheel as we sped toward the police station.

"We're telling him everything, right?" she said.

"Everything," I confirmed.

For once, I wasn't about to hold anything back.

MARTINEZ BARELY HAD time to react before we stormed past him —again.

"Jiménez—"

"Not now," I snapped.

Lomeli was at his desk, flipping through a file. He barely looked up before sighing. "What now?"

I slammed the bug down onto his desk.

Lomeli looked down at it. Then back to me. "Explain," he said evenly.

I took a breath. "Someone bugged my dog."

Silence.

Emma crossed her arms. "Yeah, you heard her."

Lomeli just stared at us, then slowly picked up the device. Turned it over in his palm. His jaw tightened. "When did you find this?" he asked.

"As long as it took to bring it here, ten minutes or so," I said. "They've been listening, Lomeli. Everything we've said, they've heard."

Lomeli's expression darkened. He stood, grabbing his coat. "Martinez!"

The younger officer appeared instantly. "Sir?"

"Get a tech team to Jiménez's house. Now. I want a full sweep. If there's one of these, there could be more."

Martinez nodded sharply and disappeared.

Lomeli looked back at us. "You're sure this was planted before tonight?" he asked.

Emma and I exchanged a glance.

Then I nodded. "They texted me right after we talked about Doug. It was in real time."

Lomeli muttered something under his breath. Then he ran a hand down his face. "This isn't just about covering tracks anymore," he said finally.

My chest tightened. "What do you mean?"

Lomeli's eyes met mine. "Whoever this is, Jiménez—they're watching *you*."

39

THE SEARCH

"The depth of love reflects the depth of grief felt."
–Tara Coyote

By the time we pulled into my driveway, two police cruisers were already parked outside. Their red and blue lights flashed against the darkened windows of my house, bathing everything in an eerie, pulsing glow.

I felt cold all over.

Emma put the car in park and exhaled. "You ready?"

I wasn't. But I nodded anyway.

Lomeli led the way as two tech specialists followed behind him, carrying equipment I didn't recognize. The house felt too quiet. Like it knew what was happening.

"Lucky's collar was just the start," Lomeli said. "If they planted one bug, they could've planted more."

I felt Emma tense beside me.

I tried to breathe normally, but my chest felt tight. Whoever did this had been inside my house. Moving through my space. Touching my things.

The officers started sweeping the living room first, running a signal scanner over the walls, the furniture—anything that could hide a transmitter.

I watched every pass of the device, bracing for the worst.

At first, nothing. Then—BEEP.

One of the specialists froze.

Lomeli's head snapped up. "Got something?"

The officer nodded, holding up the scanner, watching the signal spike. Then he turned toward the bookshelf. The officer knelt, pulling a small black device from between two books. It looked identical to the one we'd pulled off Lucky's collar.

My breath hitched. How long had that been here?

I barely felt my feet moving as they swept through the rest of the house. Kitchen? Clear. Bathroom? Clear. Scotty's room? Clear.

They stepped into my room. And I knew. Before the scanner even beeped, I knew. This was where I had pieced it all together. Where I had been making connections, saying names out loud.

Of course they'd want to listen here.

Another officer ran the scanner over my nightstand. Then my desk. BEEP.

The tech froze.

And I stopped breathing.

The officer reached up, fingers pressing against the underside of my desk. And then—he pulled off a second bug that had been taped there.

Lomeli's face was stone cold. "Son of a bitch," he muttered.

* * * * *

EMMA'S FACE had gone pale. "V," she whispered. "Whoever did this wasn't just listening."

I swallowed hard. "What do you mean?"

Emma met my eyes. "They weren't just watching from a distance," she said.

My blood turned to ice as I realized exactly what she meant. This person hadn't just been following me. They had been inside my house. And that meant they could come back—at any time.

I sat on the edge of my bed, thinking about the tiny black devices the police techs just found. Bugs.

The one from the bookshelf, from under my desk, and the one Emma and I found on Lucky's collar. Three.

Someone had been in my house, moved through my space, placing the bugs so precisely, knowing exactly what they were doing. I felt cold all over.

Emma paced in front of me, her arms tightly crossed, her sneakers scuffing against my rug. She kept shaking her head, muttering under her breath.

Lomeli stood near the door, his arms crossed, his expression unreadable.

The house was still full of cops. Some were sweeping for more devices. Others were outside, talking into radios.

It didn't matter. I didn't feel safer. I felt watched. Scared.

I was never alone. Not here. Not in my car. Not anywhere.

Lomeli let out a long, slow breath. "You're getting police protection," he said. No argument, no room for negotiation.

Emma stopped pacing. "How does that help?" she demanded. "Whoever did this already got in. What's stopping them from doing it again?"

Lomeli's jaw tightened. "It won't happen again."

Emma scoffed, throwing her arms out. "And we're just supposed to believe that?"

He met her glare with a steady look. "Yes."

"How long?" I asked.

"As long as necessary," Lomeli said.

"And then what?"

"Then," he said, "we catch whoever did this."

BY THE TIME Detective Lomeli and his officers finally cleared out, exhaustion weighed on me like a lead blanket. My limbs ached, my head throbbed, but my mind refused to quiet. Sleep felt impossible.

Emma had insisted on staying over. She'd tried to play it off, making some offhand comment about how it was too late to drive home, but I could see the tension in her face, the way she lingered near me, the way her eyes flickered to my bedroom door every so often, as if expecting someone to walk through it. She was scared.

And honestly? So was I.

I lay on my back, staring at the ceiling, my thoughts racing too fast to catch. Doug was dead. Jillian was terrified. And the killer?

They were still watching me. That meant they knew. They knew I was close.

Outside, a car rumbled into the driveway. A few seconds later, the front door creaked open, and I heard Dad and Scotty step inside. I glanced at the clock—11:06 p.m. They were just getting home from the tournament in San Bernardino, exhausted from a long day of games, oblivious to everything that had happened while they were gone.

I stayed frozen in bed as I listened to them move around downstairs. The shuffle of cleats being kicked off. The low murmur of Dad asking Scotty if he wanted something to eat. The faint hum of the fridge opening, then closing. Normal sounds. Ordinary sounds.

But nothing about tonight was ordinary.

I turned onto my side, my gaze landing on my desk—only to remember the bugs weren't there anymore. The police had taken them when they left, tiny pieces of evidence bagged and tagged, but their absence didn't make me feel any safer.

Those bugs had been inside my house. *Inside.* I swallowed hard. That wasn't the part that scared me the most.

Whoever planted them hadn't just gained access. They'd had time.

Time to slip inside unnoticed. Time to set everything up. Time to listen. Time to do more.

A shudder ran through me. I sat up so fast that Emma stirred in her sleeping bag, blinking groggily in the dim light.

"Wha—?" she mumbled, rubbing her eyes.

But I wasn't listening. My hands were already moving, grabbing my phone, swiping to my notes, scrolling past a mess of frantic thoughts and scattered clues. I was looking for something specific.

The day I found the first warning note.

"You were warned. Stop now."

My stomach plummeted as I found the date. It was before I had even gone to Lomeli the first time. Before I had spoken to Jillian. Before I had put even half the pieces together.

Which meant—they had been inside my house *before that.* I swallowed hard. They had known from the start. They had been one step ahead of me this entire time. And if they were still watching me? It meant they were waiting. For what?

40
THE NOTE

"To weep is to make less the depth of grief."
–William Shakespeare, *Henry VI*

By the time the first pale light of dawn crept through my blinds, I had given up on sleep entirely. I rolled onto my back, staring at the ceiling, my mind still circling the same horrifying realization I'd come to in the middle of the night. The anonymous texts, the surveillance, the warnings—they had started before I ever went to Lomeli. Before I had spoken to Jillian. Before I had put anything together. Which meant they had been watching me from the beginning. What did they want?

Beside me, Emma shifted in her sleeping bag with a groan, throwing an arm over her face. "Ugh. Morning already?"

I sat up, rubbing my eyes. "Not like we slept."

Emma peeked at me from beneath her arm, her dark curls a tangled mess. "You were out for, like, twenty minutes. I counted."

I snorted. "Okay, stalker."

She managed a smirk but didn't deny it.

A knock at my door made us both flinch.

"Girls, you want breakfast?" Dad's voice carried through the wood, rough with exhaustion.

For half a second, I'd forgotten he and Scotty got home late. It was after eleven by the time they'd stumbled in, lugging muddy cleats and half-empty Gatorade bottles from the all-day soccer tournament in San Bernardino. Dad had barely asked any questions before crashing into bed, completely unaware of the chaos he'd missed.

Emma sat up, rubbing her face. "Tell me you have coffee," she called.

"I'll make some," Dad replied, already walking away.

I let out a breath and stood, stretching out my stiff back. "You coming?"

"In a minute," Emma muttered, still half buried in her sleeping bag.

I didn't push. I just stepped into the hallway, Lucky trotting at my heels, his tail wagging as he scurried down the stairs ahead of me. At the bottom, I scooped up one of his chew toys and tossed it toward his bed. But as I straightened up, something near the front door caught my eye.

A single folded piece of paper. No envelope. No name. Just sitting there, waiting.

A cold, electric jolt shot through me.

Emma must have heard my sharp intake of breath because when I turned around, she was there. Like she just appeared at the bottom of the stairs. She followed my gaze. "V," she whispered. "Don't."

But I was already reaching down, my hands trembling as I picked it up and unfolded it.

The message was short.

LET'S TALK. MIDNIGHT. UCI PARKING GARAGE, CENTER ROW.

No threat. No warning. Just an invitation.

My stomach twisted violently. This was it. This was what they wanted.

And I had no idea if I was walking into a trap. But I knew one thing for sure. I was going.

I stared at the note.

Emma was beside me in an instant. "Absolutely not," she said.

I barely blinked. "Emma—"

"No." She ripped the paper from my hand, crumpling it into a tight fist. "This is insane, V. You are not going to some empty parking garage at midnight to meet a literal murderer."

She wasn't wrong. This was stupid. Reckless. Exactly the kind of move Lomeli had warned me against.

But it was also the only move I had. I swallowed hard. "I have to go."

Emma's eyes blazed. "No, you don't. You can take this to Lomeli. Let him deal with it!"

I shook my head. "If I tell Lomeli, the meeting won't happen. They'll know. They'll back out. And we might not get another chance."

Emma let out a sharp breath, pacing the living room. "Man, I hate it when you make sense."

"I need to do this, Emma. They want something. And right now, that's my only advantage."

She stopped pacing. Her face was tight, frustrated—but then she exhaled sharply and snapped her fingers. "If we're doing this, we're doing it smart."

I blinked. "We?"

She shot me a look. "Obviously we. There is no version of reality where I let you do this alone."

A small, relieved breath left my chest. I hadn't even realized how much I needed her until that second.

Emma folded her arms. "Okay. Plan time. How do we do this without you, ya know, dying?"

Before I could answer, Dad's voice rang out from the kitchen. "Girls! Come eat before it gets cold."

Emma and I locked eyes. The tension from our argument hadn't lifted, and neither of us had a solution yet. But we had to act normal. At least for the next twenty minutes.

I shoved the crumpled note into the pocket of my sweats, pressing my lips into a thin line. "Let's go before Scotty eats everything."

Dad had made scrambled eggs and toast. Basic, easy. But I could tell from the stiffness in his posture, the way he kept rubbing a hand over his face, that he was exhausted from the tournament.

Scotty, on the other hand, had energy that could run laps around all of us for days. He was already halfway through his second plate when we sat down.

"Yo, V, you should've seen the game," he said, waving his fork for emphasis. "Last ten seconds of the match, I took a shot from midfield. It was sick."

Dad huffed out a tired laugh. "It was reckless."

"But it *worked*," Scotty shot back, grinning.

I nodded absently, my mind elsewhere. Across the table, Emma nudged my foot under the table, giving me a warning look.

I knew what she was thinking. *Don't say anything about the note. Don't be stupid.*

I shot her a look back. *I'm still going.*

Her eyes narrowed. *Not alone.*

She stabbed a piece of toast a little too aggressively, and Dad raised an eyebrow at her. "You okay, Emma?"

She forced a bright smile. "Yup! Great. Love breakfast. Love being awake."

Dad frowned but let it go, turning back to Scotty, who was still talking about his game.

Emma's knee bumped mine under the table. This time, when I met her gaze, there was no arguing, no stubbornness. Just a silent promise.

Whatever happened next, we were in this together.

WAITING WAS THE WORST PART. Sunday stretched on forever, slow and unbearable.

There was no school to distract me, no errands to run, nothing to do but sit with the knowledge that in just a few hours I'd be face-to-face with someone who had been watching me for weeks. Someone dangerous. Someone who might not let me walk away.

Dad and Scotty had left for the afternoon—Scotty had some "mandatory team bonding" pizza party, and Dad, exhausted but still in Dad mode, had to tag along since he was one of the coaches. That left Emma and me alone in the house, stuck in an endless cycle of pretending to watch TV, scrolling mindlessly through our phones, and rehashing the plan so many times it started to feel unreal.

At one point, Emma insisted we watch something funny. "You need a distraction," she said, plopping onto the couch and cuing up some old sitcom we used to binge in middle school.

I stared at the screen, not processing a single word.

By five, Emma was flipping through a book she wasn't really reading.

By seven, I realized I hadn't eaten since breakfast, but the thought of food made my stomach turn.

By eight, I gave up pretending to be normal and paced the hallway instead.

And by ten, we had it figured out.

Emma sat on my bed, firing off a text. Her face was set with determination.

Me? I was so nervous my palms wouldn't stop sweating.

"So let's go over it again," she said, all business. "You drive there. I follow in my car. I keep my distance, park somewhere hidden, but close enough to see you."

I nodded.

She continued. "You keep your phone on, speaker open, so I can hear everything."

Another nod.

"And if anything feels even remotely off, you walk away."

I hesitated.

Emma narrowed her eyes. "V."

"Fine," I said. "I walk away."

She studied me like she didn't quite believe me. "And Lomeli?"

I exhaled. "I text him after the meeting. If I make it out alive."

Emma rolled her eyes. "Not funny."

I smirked. "A little funny."

Emma shook her head, but her face was tight. I could tell she hated every second of this. She tucked her phone into her hoodie pocket. "We leave at eleven-thirty."

I nodded.

And just like that, the plan was set.

Now, all I had to do was go through with it.

41
MIDNIGHT MEETING

"When he finally died, my heart felt like it just broke into a million pieces... even though we knew it would happen, it was still so hard to accept and watch him go."
–YY Chan

The drive to UCI was suffocating in its silence. Emma followed me, just like we planned, her headlights visible in my rearview mirror, never too far, never too close. Just enough distance to avoid suspicion. The streets were empty at this hour, the world stripped down to a hushed, eerie quiet, like the universe itself was holding its breath.

I wasn't calm. My hands gripped the steering wheel so tightly my knuckles ached, but still, my palms were cold, clammy. My pulse thrummed in my ears, in my throat, in my fingertips. A constant, relentless beat.

Because in five minutes, I was going to meet them. Whoever had been watching me. Following me.

Whoever had killed Doug.

And maybe—

Whoever had killed my mom.

A sharp swallow barely forced down the rising nausea in my gut. I had spent the entire day waiting for this moment, hours stretching endlessly as I paced my room, as I ran through every possibility, every outcome. It had been agonizing, the weight of the unknown pressing down on me.

But now, here it was. No more time to second-guess. No more time to back out.

I could do this. I had to.

The garage was mostly empty when I pulled in, a vast, open space swallowed by concrete and shadows. The fluorescent lights overhead buzzed faintly, flickering every so often, making the dark corners stretch and breathe.

I parked near the center, right where the note had told me to.

Emma pulled in farther back, barely visible behind a row of abandoned cars. Close enough to see me, far enough to stay hidden.

My phone was tucked into my hoodie pocket, on speaker, the call with Emma still open.

"You okay?" her voice whispered.

"Fine," I murmured, though I couldn't stop trembling.

I stepped out of the car, leaving the door slightly ajar. An escape route. Just in case.

I waited.

I wasn't sure how long. Maybe thirty seconds. Maybe an hour.

Every distant sound made my skin prickle—the hum of a streetlamp, the faint echo of a car passing in the distance, the rhythmic tap of water dripping from a rusted pipe. My pulse thrummed harder with each passing second.

Then, just as the clock on my dashboard switched to 12:00 a.m.—a figure stepped out of the shadows.

A breath caught in my throat.

He moved slowly, deliberately, his steps unhurried, like he had all the time in the world. Like he wasn't afraid. Like he had done this before.

I couldn't see his face at first, just the broad outline of him, the way the dim light barely caught on the edges of his frame.

But then—he stepped fully under the light.

And I saw.

Ian Langley.

A nurse. Mid-fifties. Calm. Professional.

Someone I had seen in the hospice records but never thought twice about.

Because April had been the face. April had been the distraction. But Langley?

Langley had been there all along.

A slow, measured smile curved his lips, like he could see the realization flicker across my face.

"Violet," he said smoothly. "Or should I call you V?"

My pulse spiked. He knew my name.

I forced my expression to stay neutral. "You invited me."

Langley tilted his head slightly. "I did."

Silence stretched. A heavy, unbearable thing.

I forced a breath. "You've been watching me." My voice was even, controlled.

He smiled like I had told a joke. "You say that like it's a bad thing."

A slow, creeping dread settled deep in my stomach. This was wrong. All of this was wrong.

April had been careless. She had left trails. She had wanted recognition. Langley?

Langley had never been caught. Because Langley had never been reckless. Until now.

Until this.

I clenched my hands into fists. "You killed Doug Holloway."

Langley didn't react. Didn't flinch. Didn't deny it.

His gaze stayed steady on mine, calm, unreadable. "Doug was an inconvenience," he said simply.

A slow, sinking horror gripped my chest.

I swallowed hard. "You're the reason Jillian's dad died."

A faint shrug. "One of many."

My stomach turned.

April hadn't been the only one. She hadn't even been the worst one.

Langley had been doing this for decades.

My breath was shallow now, heart pounding so fast I thought he might hear it. "Why now?"

His eyes flickered, amusement curling at the edges. "Why reveal myself?"

I didn't answer. Because, yes, that was exactly what I was asking.

He had spent years blending in. Years avoiding detection. Why would he break his pattern now?

Langley studied me for a long moment, considering his words. "I was curious," he admitted. "To see how far you'd go. To see if you'd actually find me."

A slow, creeping chill ran down my spine.

I hadn't found him. *He had let me.*

I had been playing his game this whole time.

Langley took a step forward.

I didn't move.

"But now that you have," he murmured, almost pleasant, "I'm afraid you've reached the end of your little investigation."

Every nerve in my body went on high alert.

My fingers itched toward my phone. Emma was listening. She had to be.

I kept my voice steady. "If you were going to kill me, you wouldn't have invited me here."

Langley actually smiled. "No. I wouldn't have."

Somehow, that was worse.

He took another step, and this time, I stepped back.

Langley noted it. He liked it.

"Here's what's going to happen," he said, his voice too smooth, too sure. "You're going to let this go. Walk away."

I dug my nails into my palms. "Or what?"

His eyes darkened. "You have a little brother, don't you?"

The world tilted. A sick, suffocating dread slammed into my chest. He was threatening Scotty.

Langley took one last step forward, lowering his voice.

"I leave no loose ends, V," he murmured. "And that includes you."

Something inside me snapped. I turned and ran.

My feet pounded against the pavement, each frantic step jarring through my legs as I ran, lungs burning, my heartbeat a wild, erratic hammer against my ribs. The cold night air sliced through me, sharp and unforgiving, but I didn't stop.

I didn't dare look back.

I didn't have to.

I felt him watching me.

Not chasing.

Just watching.

The parking garage was a maze of concrete and fluorescent lights, the sound of my own ragged breathing echoing off the empty walls. My sneakers squeaked against the smooth ground as I pushed myself harder, sprinting toward the exit ramp. My pulse roared in my ears, drowning out everything except the singular thought pulsing in my brain.

Get out. Get out. Get out.

I hit the downward slope too fast, my balance slipping for

half a second. My ankle twisted—just slightly—but I forced my legs to keep moving, barely catching myself before I went sprawling onto the rough concrete.

Where's Emma?

She was supposed to be nearby. She had been listening in, parked within sight. She should have seen me by now.

A fresh wave of panic surged through me.

Then—headlights.

A car whipped around the corner of the lower level, the tires screeching against the pavement, the high beams slicing through the shadows like a blade. The sudden burst of light stung my eyes, my body flinching on instinct—

Then I saw it.

Emma.

Relief punched through my chest, but I didn't slow down. She was already leaning across the seat, shoving the passenger door open before she even fully braked.

"GET IN!" she shouted, voice raw, desperate.

I didn't hesitate. I dove inside, my shoulder slamming against the seat as I yanked the door shut behind me.

Emma floored it.

The tires screamed as we shot forward, the car fishtailing slightly before she corrected it, sending us hurtling toward the garage exit.

I twisted in my seat, finally looking back.

Langley was still standing there. Calm. Still. Hands tucked into his pockets.

His head tilted slightly, like he was making a note of something. Like he wasn't worried. Like he had already won.

A cold shiver crawled down my spine, my stomach twisting violently.

Then we turned the corner, and he was gone.

For several long, suffocating moments, neither of us spoke.

The only sound was the dull roar of the engine and the rapid, uneven rhythm of my own breathing. I pressed a shaking hand against my chest, willing my heartbeat to slow down, to stop pounding so hard, but it wasn't working.

The freeway signs blurred past us, their green glow flickering against the windshield as we sped toward home. Emma's hands were clenched around the steering wheel so tightly her knuckles had gone stark white. Her foot pressed too hard on the gas, pushing well over the speed limit, but I didn't care.

I didn't tell her to slow down. I wasn't sure I could speak yet.

Finally, Emma broke the silence.

"V," she said, her voice trembling, "what happened back there? Our call got disconnected!"

I swallowed hard. My throat was dry, my lips even drier. "It's him."

Her grip on the wheel tightened. "The real killer?"

I nodded, jaw locked.

Emma exhaled sharply, a shaky breath that barely made it out. "Okay. Tell me everything."

So I did.

Every word Langley had said. Every step he'd taken. Every single thing he had made sure I understood.

By the time I was done, Emma's face had gone pale.

She was breathing too hard, her fingers flexing against the wheel like she needed something to punch.

Then she said, low and furious—"He threatened Scotty."

I nodded once, my teeth clenched so tight my skull ached.

Emma swore under her breath, then slammed her palm against the steering wheel, the sharp sound cracking through the tense silence.

"That's it," she said. "We're going to Lomeli. *Now.*"

I didn't argue.

42

NO LOOSE ENDS

"Your life was a blessing, your memory a treasure. You are loved
beyond words, and missed beyond measure."
–Unknown

Emma tore through the streets, weaving with reckless
precision fueled by pure adrenaline. The speedometer
climbed past numbers I should have cared about, but I
barely noticed.

My mind was still stuck in that parking garage.

Stuck on Langley's voice—calm, even, like he had all the
time in the world.

Stuck on his posture—still, controlled, not a single wasted
movement.

Stuck on the way he had *watched* me run—not with panic,
not with frustration. But with certainty.

He wasn't worried. He knew something I didn't. And he had
threatened Scotty.

A fresh wave of fury crashed over me, raw and blinding,

twisting tight in my chest. My hands curled into fists against my thighs, nails digging into my palms, but it wasn't enough. I wanted to hit something. *To hurt something.* To make Langley feel the kind of fear he had so effortlessly lodged in my ribs like a blade.

But all I could do was go to Lomeli.

This time, he had to listen.

The precinct was dimly lit, running on the low hum of late-night shifts, the air thick with stale coffee and exhaustion.

Martinez was mid-yawn when we shoved through the doors, his chair tipped back at a dangerous angle, his boots propped up on his desk.

He nearly choked on his own breath. "Son of a bitch, Jiménez," he sputtered, blinking blearily. "Do you ever sleep?"

"Do you?" I shot back. "Where's Lomeli?"

Martinez straightened, rubbing his eyes. "It's after midnight—"

"Where. Is. Lomeli?"

The sharpness in my voice snapped him fully awake. He studied me for half a second, then let out a heavy sigh. "Hang on."

He disappeared down the hall, and less than thirty seconds later, Lomeli emerged from his office, looking exhausted.

But the second he saw my face, something in his expression shifted. No exasperated sigh. No sarcasm. A single gesture toward his office door. "Inside. *Now.*"

Emma and I didn't hesitate.

The second the door clicked shut behind us, I spun to face him.

"It's Langley," I said, my voice flat. *Certain.*

Lomeli's eyes narrowed. "Langley," he repeated, like he was running the name through a mental database.

I nodded once. "Ian Langley. He's the one you're looking for."

Lomeli didn't react at first. His expression didn't change. But something in the room did.

A subtle, invisible shift, like the air pressure had dropped.

Emma perched on the edge of a chair, her arms folded so tightly across her chest that her nails dug into the sleeves of her hoodie. Her foot tapped a relentless rhythm against the floor, the only sound in the heavy silence.

"V met him tonight," she said, jaw clenched. "And he knew. He knew everything."

Lomeli's gaze flicked back to me, sharper now. "Where?"

"UCI parking garage. He told me to meet him there. Left a note at my house."

His jaw tightened. "And what, exactly, did he say?"

I exhaled slowly, steadying my voice. "That I needed to walk away."

Lomeli's eyes darkened. "And?"

I hesitated. "He threatened Scotty."

The temperature in the room dropped.

Emma sucked in a sharp breath beside me.

Lomeli went still. The kind of stillness that came before an earthquake. Before a gunshot.

Before violence.

His voice, when he finally spoke, was quiet. Low. Dangerous. "What else did he say?"

I swallowed. "He said he leaves no loose ends."

Lomeli's fingers curled into fists. He moved. *Fast.*

He grabbed his radio from the desk, pressing the button with a snap. "Martinez, get a unit to Jiménez's house. Now. Lock it down. No one in or out."

A brief crackle of static, then Martinez's voice came through, more alert than before. "Copy that, sir."

Emma and I exchanged glances, wide-eyed, tense.

Lomeli turned to me. "Your father and Scotty?"

"They're home," I said quickly. "They should be asleep."

He nodded once. "They'll be protected."

Something inside me loosened. But only a little. Because I wasn't the only one in danger.

Jillian. She was next.

My heart kicked hard against my ribs as I scrambled for my phone, my fingers shaking as I unlocked it. I had to call her. I had to—

Buzz.

A new text flashed across my screen.

UNKNOWN NUMBER

Too late

My blood turned to ice.

Emma saw the message over my shoulder. "Oh no—absolutely not."

Before I could react, Lomeli snatched the phone from my hands to scan the message.

His expression darkened.

Then—he grabbed his radio again, his voice like steel.

"Martinez, get a unit to Jillian Sosa's house. Now."

The response was immediate. "On it, sir."

But I barely heard it.

Because all I could hear was the pounding of my pulse, the sharp, shallow breaths rattling in my chest, and the words flashing across my screen.

Too late.

Jillian was already in trouble. And we were running out of time.

★ ★ ★ ★ ★

LOMELI DROVE LIKE A MAN POSSESSED, the engine growling as he pushed past the speed limit, the city blurring into streaks of yellow streetlights and empty intersections. Emma and I were crammed in the back seat of his unmarked car, gripping the seat as he took sharp turns without slowing down. Police sirens wailed ahead, flashing red and blue against the pavement, an electric storm of urgency.

My heart slammed against my ribs, fast and erratic, trying to outpace the sick, panicked loop playing in my head.

Too late.

No. *No, no, no.*

Emma's knee bounced uncontrollably beside me. She was gripping the hem of her hoodie so tightly it looked like she was trying to hold herself together by sheer force of will. Her voice was barely above a whisper when she said, "V, what if—"

"Don't," I cut in. I couldn't hear it. Couldn't let her say it.

Because if she did, it would become real. And I wasn't ready for that. Not yet.

The car jerked violently as Lomeli took the final turn onto Jillian's street, the tires screeching against the asphalt.

And the second I saw it, I knew. We were too late.

Jillian's front door hung open. A gaping, black void.

Cold rushed through me, numbing my limbs. My body knew before my brain did, understood in a way that made my stomach twist violently, like it was rejecting the truth before it could fully settle.

Lomeli barked out something—probably telling us to stay back—but I wasn't listening.

I was already shoving the door open. Already running.

Emma was right behind me.

The house smelled wrong. Not like blood, not like anything obvious. Just . . . *wrong.*

Too still. Too empty. Like whatever had happened here had sucked the air out of the room, leaving only silence in its wake.

Cops were already moving through the house, radios crackling, voices low and clipped as they checked each room. I barely heard them.

I didn't need to. I already knew. Jillian was gone.

Lomeli's voice was sharp behind me. "*Jiménez, stop!*"

I didn't listen. My feet carried me forward, into the living room—and I froze.

The furniture was overturned, a lamp shattered across the floor. The coffee table was shoved awkwardly against the couch, deep scratches gouged into its wooden surface—like someone had desperately grabbed on to it.

Like someone had fought.

Emma's breathing was uneven beside me. "*V...*"

I turned—and saw what she was staring at.

The wall. Or, more specifically—the message painted on it.

WALK AWAY

My stomach twisted violently.

It was written in red.

Emma let out a sharp breath. "Tell me that's paint."

I couldn't. I didn't want to know what it was.

A cop moved past us, sweeping his flashlight over the letters. The beam reflected wetly against the streaks.

"Smudges easily," he said. "It's fresh."

A chill shot through me, cold and electric, sinking into my bones.

Behind us, Lomeli stood with his arms crossed, his face unreadable, but his eyes—his eyes weren't.

I forced myself to meet his gaze. "Where is she?"

He didn't answer right away. And that silence—that hesitation—told me everything I needed to know.

"We're going to find out."

His voice was steady. Controlled. The way someone speaks when they need you to believe them.

But I wasn't stupid. He didn't know.

Neither did I.

The house was still humming with movement, cops talking into radios, cameras flashing as they documented everything— the wrecked furniture, the overturned coffee table, the streaked message on the wall.

But none of it told us where Jillian was. Langley hadn't left clues. Hadn't left fingerprints. Hadn't left anything.

Just a wrecked living room. A missing woman. And a message meant *for me.*

"WALK AWAY"

Emma stood rigid beside me, her arms wrapped so tightly around herself she looked like she was trying to hold herself together by sheer force of will. She wasn't doing a great job.

Neither was I.

Her voice came out small, controlled. "This is bad."

Duh.

Instead of answering her, I turned back to Lomeli. "What now?"

He ran a hand down his face, the tension rolling off him in waves. "We do our damn jobs," he muttered.

"We don't have time for that," I snapped.

His head whipped toward me, his gaze sharp. "She's been gone less than an hour," he said. "We'll issue a BOLO, check traffic cams near the neighborhood, pull surveillance from UCI—"

"That's not fast enough."

Lomeli exhaled hard, jaw clenching. "It's all we have right now, Jiménez."

It wasn't. This was happening too fast.

Doug's death had been a *warning*. Jillian's disappearance? That was something else.

I looked at the wall again. *"WALK AWAY."*

Langley wanted me to quit. He was expecting me to panic. To freeze up. To do exactly what Lomeli was doing—follow protocol. *Wait.*

But Langley had been steps ahead of us this whole time.

Which meant Jillian didn't have *days*.

She probably didn't even have *hours*.

I turned back to Lomeli, forcing the words out through gritted teeth. "He's not keeping her alive for long."

A flicker of something crossed his face. Just for a second.

Emma shifted beside me. "She's right. Doug was killed almost immediately. And if Langley thinks Jillian is a loose end—"

"Then we don't have time for a BOLO," I cut in. "We need to think like him."

Lomeli's jaw tightened.

I could see it—how much he hated that I was right.

But he didn't argue. Instead, he exhaled slowly. "Fine," he said. "Then tell me, Jiménez—where would he take her?"

The words slammed into me, hard and unforgiving. Because that was exactly the question I needed to be asking.

I yanked out my phone, my thumb flying across the screen.

Langley had worked at St. Lucia's. Riverside Serenity. Lakeview. UCI.

Each facility had one thing in common. Hospice care. Patients who were dying. People who were alone.

Where would someone like Langley take a person he didn't plan to let go?

Emma leaned in, her breath unsteady. "You're thinking what I'm thinking, aren't you?"

I met her eyes. "I think I am."

43

EVERGREEN PINES

"Tears shed for another person are not a sign of weakness.
They are a sign of a pure heart."
–José N. Harris

Emma stood beside me, her breaths fast and shallow. "V, come on. He's a planner, right? He doesn't do random."

"Right," I said, swiping through articles on my phone, my pulse hammering. "Which means this place—it's somewhere he's comfortable. Somewhere he knows."

Lomeli's sharp gaze locked on to me. "Are you about to suggest something reckless?"

I ignored him. The answer had to be here. Somewhere.

I pulled up one of the oldest articles I had on Langley—an old interview, barely a paragraph long, buried under years of reports. I skimmed the text, searching for anything that stood out.

Then—there it was.

"Langley started in hospice work back in the nineties," I said, my voice tight with focus. "But his first real job—the first place he worked long-term—was a nursing home."

Emma stiffened beside me. "A what?"

I turned the phone around so she could see the name on the screen.

Evergreen Pines Nursing Home, established 1993.

Her eyes widened. "V—"

Lomeli frowned. "That facility shut down over a decade ago."

I nodded. "And that's why it makes sense. It's abandoned. Isolated. No staff, no patients, no cameras."

Lomeli's jaw tightened. He hated that I had a point.

Emma was already pulling up a map on her phone. Her fingers flew over the screen. "Evergreen Pines is—only twenty minutes from here!"

The air in the room seemed to contract, tightening around us.

A slow, terrible realization settled in my gut.

If we were right—Jillian was there. Alone. Terrified. Running out of time.

If we were wrong—then she was already dead.

Lomeli hesitated for half a second. He turned, barking orders. "Martinez, get backup. We have a possible location."

The room snapped into motion. Radios crackled. Boots pounded against the floor. A rush of movement, of energy—controlled chaos, the kind that meant something.

I swallowed hard, forcing down the fear clawing up my throat.

We had one shot. One shot to be right. One shot to save her.

I gripped my phone so tightly my knuckles went white.

Hold on, Jillian. We're coming.

THE POLICE CONVOY tore through the empty streets, lights flashing, sirens silent. Lomeli had ordered them quiet. No warnings. No room for Langley to slip away.

Emma sat rigid beside me, her knee bouncing, eyes locked on the road. "We're gonna be too late," she growled.

"You don't know that," I shot back, forcing myself to believe it. But I did know it. Or at least, I feared it.

Jillian had already been missing for over an hour. Langley was careful. Precise. He didn't make mistakes.

So why take her? Why hold on to her at all?

Emma checked the map. "Two minutes out."

I looked ahead. The road stretched into a long expanse of nothing—dry grass, scattered trees, a looming skeleton of a building in the distance. Evergreen Pines.

It was massive, the kind of old nursing home that had once held hundreds of people, before it had rotted from the inside out.

The entire front wing was gutted. Windows shattered. Vines crawling up the brick like veins.

A place for the forgotten. A place no one came back from.

I swallowed hard.

Lomeli's voice instructed over the radio, "We go in quiet. No lights until I say. We need to catch him in the act."

I wasn't sure what "the act" was. But I knew I didn't want to see it.

Emma exhaled sharply. "This is it."

We pulled up behind the first squad car. Officers were already moving—silent shadows in the night.

I reached for my door.

"No." Lomeli's voice, sharp.

I froze.

He turned in his seat, pinning me with a look. "You stay here. Both of you."

Emma bristled. "Not happening—"

"You're civilians," he snapped. "This is police work. You do not go inside. You do not interfere. Are we clear?"

My fingers curled into fists. "Lomeli—"

"Are we clear?"

A muscle tensed in my jaw. I nodded. Because if I didn't, he'd make sure I stayed in this car.

Lomeli held my gaze a beat longer. "I mean it, Jiménez. Don't be stupid."

Then he was gone, gun drawn, moving with his officers toward the building.

Emma exhaled slowly.

We watched them go. Listened to the silence stretch—too long.

Something was wrong. I could feel it.

The air hung too still. No movement beyond the wind. No sounds from inside.

Emma's voice was quiet. "V."

I didn't answer. I'd already made up my mind. I wasn't staying in this car.

I stepped out, heart pounding.

Emma was right behind me. "V," she hissed. "This is such a bad idea."

I knew that. Didn't care.

Lomeli and his officers had already disappeared into the dark shell of Evergreen Pines, their movements swallowed by the crumbling hallways. The building loomed ahead of us, silent. Waiting.

If Jillian was still alive, she was inside. And if we waited out here, she might not be for long.

I turned to Emma. "We stick to the shadows. We stay out of sight."

Emma groaned but nodded. "*Fine.* But if we die, I'm haunting you first."

"Deal," I replied. We moved closer.

The air was thick with dust and decay.

The smell of mold, old medicine, something stale and rotting pressed into my lungs as we slipped through a side entrance, careful to avoid the main doors.

The dark hallway stretched in front of us—long, peeling walls, floor littered with debris. Wheelchairs rusted in corners.

We turned on the flashlights on our phones. It was all we had. I couldn't think about how ill-prepared we were for this.

An abandoned hospital bed sat in the middle of the hall, tipped on its side like someone had shoved it there in a hurry.

The silence was wrong.

I had expected noise—officers moving through rooms, orders being shouted, something. But there was nothing. Just the quiet hum of the wind slipping through broken windows.

Emma shifted beside me. "Where is everyone?" she whispered.

My stomach turned. "I don't know."

We kept moving. Every step echoed against the tiled floor, crunching against pieces of fallen ceiling, shattered glass.

A sound. A voice. Distant. Muffled. Female.

I froze.

Emma grabbed my arm. "V."

I yanked free, heart slamming against my ribs. Then we heard it again. A sharp, muffled cry, barely cutting through the silence.

We ran.

I didn't care if we were being reckless. Didn't care if we were making noise. Jillian was alive. She was alive, and she was terrified.

We rounded a corner into another hallway—darker, worse.

The walls here were smeared with something black, the light fixtures long dead.

Movement ahead. A shadow. Too far to make out.

But it was fast. Dragging. Heavy steps.

Jillian's moans cut through the air again.

My pulse spiked.

Emma gasped beside me. "She's down there!"

I bolted forward—but something slammed into me from the side. Hard.

I hit the ground, air ripping from my lungs.

Emma shouted.

Then hands—rough hands—grabbed my wrists. And a voice, too calm, too familiar, too close.

"You never listen, do you, V?"

Ian Langley.

Langley's grip was like iron.

I thrashed, kicking, trying to twist free, but his hands crushed around my wrists, pinning me against the cold, grimy floor.

Emma shouted my name, but my head was spinning, adrenaline surging too fast.

A smothered, panicked cry echoed down the hallway, cutting through my own panic.

I had to get up. Had to get to Jillian.

Langley's weight pressed harder, forcing me down, his fingers digging into my skin.

"Shhh," he murmured. "No one's coming."

Lomeli. The officers. Where were they?

I gritted my teeth, dug my heels into the floor—then

slammed my knee up as hard as I could. I hit something soft—flesh.

Langley grunted sharply, his grip loosening just enough.

I wrenched free, rolling fast, scrambling up just as Emma lunged.

She hit Langley full force, sending him stumbling back a step. "Run!" she shouted.

I didn't hesitate. I grabbed her hand, bolted forward—straight down the hall.

I tore through the darkness, Emma right beside me.

Jillian's cries were getting louder. Pain. Panic. Desperation.

"She's close," Emma panted.

We burst through a half-open door, practically falling into the room.

Jillian. She was tied to a chair. Duct tape over her mouth, wrists bound. Eyes wide, red-rimmed, panicked.

She thrashed, barely able to move.

A tray of medical instruments lay beside her. A syringe already prepped.

I froze.

Langley had been about to inject her.

Emma ripped the tape from Jillian's mouth.

Jillian gasped, choking out a sob. "Get me out!"

I fumbled for the knots around her wrists, my fingers shaking.

Emma was already working at her ankles.

A slow clap from the doorway.

I whipped around.

Langley stood there. Cool. Unbothered. Like we hadn't just escaped his grip minutes ago. Like he wasn't worried at all. "Impressive," he said.

My blood ran cold.

He wasn't angry. He was amused. Like he had planned this. Like he was still completely in control.

Jillian let out a shaky sob.

I grabbed the syringe from the tray, flipping it in my hand. "Stay back."

Langley smirked. "Or what? You gonna put me down, V?"

I gripped it tighter. I didn't get a chance to answer.

Because suddenly—

Gunfire.

Yelling.

And then—

Lomeli.

He appeared behind Langley, gun drawn, fury carved into every line of his face.

"Langley," he barked. "Don't move."

For the first time, Langley's smirk flickered. His hands twitched.

Lomeli's finger tensed over the trigger. "Try it," he said. Voice deadly.

Silence.

The air was razor-sharp.

Then—Langley dropped his hands. Surrendering. Just like that.

He didn't resist. Didn't lunge. Didn't fight. He just stood there, calm as ever, hands lifted slightly as Lomeli and two officers moved in.

A sharp click of cuffs.

Langley exhaled, slow and measured, like this was just another routine end to his shift. Like none of this was real.

My hands shook as I backed up, my body still thrumming with adrenaline.

Emma pulled Jillian into a tight hug, whispering something I couldn't hear.

I didn't move. Couldn't. Because Langley was looking at me.

Not at Lomeli, not at the officers forcing him to his knees.

Me.

His eyes were dark, sharp, knowing. Like he had already won.

Lomeli yanked him up. "Ian Langley, you're under arrest for the kidnapping of Jillian Sosa, the murder of Doug Holloway, and—"

Langley chuckled. *Chuckled.* "Detective," he murmured. "Don't insult me."

Lomeli's jaw clenched. "Shut up, Langley."

But Langley wasn't talking to him anymore. His eyes never left mine.

"You figured it out, didn't you?" Langley said, his voice almost conversational. "That's why you came here. That's why you came looking for me."

My breath hitched, but I didn't answer.

He smirked. "You really think this is over?"

A slow, sharp chill crawled up my spine.

Lomeli shoved him toward the officers. "Get him out of my sight."

Langley didn't resist. He let them lead him toward the door, but just before they reached it, he glanced back.

With one last, almost-smug look, he said, "Check your work, V."

The words hit like a slap.

By the time I found my voice, Langley was already gone.

44

IT'S DONE

"You've got to fully feel it to heal it."
–Griefshare.org

The cops were clearing out. Jillian had been loaded into an ambulance for evaluation, still shaky and barely speaking. The paramedics wrapped her in blankets, checked her vitals, murmured quiet reassurances. She barely reacted.

Emma stood beside me, arms crossed tight, her gaze flicking between me and the officers.

"You okay?" she asked.

I didn't answer. Because no. I wasn't.

Langley's words wouldn't stop replaying in my head.

"Check your work."

Not *"I give up."*

Not *"You won."*

Not even *"See you in court."*

Just *"Check your work."*

Like I'd missed something. Like I'd gotten something wrong.

Emma nudged me. "V, seriously, talk to me. You look like you're about to throw up."

I exhaled slowly, forcing the doubt aside.

That's what Langley wanted—to get inside my head, make me question everything, spin me in circles until I didn't know what was real. It was his specialty.

But not this time. Not anymore.

I glanced toward the nearest squad car, where Langley sat cuffed in the back seat, his face calm. Not angry. Not scared. Just watching me. Head tilted slightly, like I was still some unsolved puzzle he couldn't quite crack.

I held his gaze for a beat. Then I turned away.

Because he didn't matter anymore.

Whatever tricks he had left, whatever games he wanted to play—they didn't matter. The police had enough to bury him. His network was gone. His control was gone. He had lost.

We left Evergreen Pines in a daze.

Jillian had been taken to the hospital. Emma had called her mom. Lomeli had ordered his officers to secure the crime scene and start processing evidence that would take weeks to catalog.

Langley was in custody. It should have felt like a victory. But it didn't.

Emma drove me back to my car in the UCI parking garage. Neither of us spoke for a long time.

Finally, she exhaled sharply. "So, that's it?" she asked. "It's *really* over?"

I stared out the window. The dark landscape blurred past.

I nodded. This time, I believed it. The case was closed.

Langley was never going to hurt anyone again. Jillian was safe. We had won.

I felt the weight in my chest begin to lift. But why didn't I feel the victory?

Emma sighed. "V, say something."

I rubbed a hand over my face. "I don't know."

Emma glanced at me. "You don't know?"

I hesitated. "I mean, I know it's him. I know Langley's the real killer. But I don't know how to stop looking for something that's already been found."

Emma was quiet for a moment. "Yeah," she whispered. "I figured."

45

WAS IT ALL FOR NOTHING?

"When the magnitude of loss is so great, it can seem
impossible to articulate what you're feeling."
–Child Life Grief Notes

I didn't go to school Monday. After the night we'd had, neither did Emma.

Dad had been sick with worry when I got home around three in the morning. He didn't yell—just looked at me, tight-lipped, exhausted—before launching into a lecture about safety, responsibility, and how I was "lucky to be alive." I took it. I let him get it out. He deserved that much.

But I wasn't done yet. By 9:30, I was back at the police station.

Lomeli didn't look surprised when I walked in. Annoyed? Definitely. But not surprised.

"Jiménez," he muttered, rubbing his eyes. "You don't sleep, do you?"

I crossed my arms. "Did Langley talk?"

Lomeli leaned back in his chair, letting out a slow breath.

"Yeah. Didn't exactly confess, but we've got enough. And April?" He let out a short laugh. "She folded like a cheap lawn chair."

"She confessed?"

"To her four patients? Yeah," he said. "Claims she thought she was 'helping' them. Mercy kills, or whatever nonsense she's convinced herself of."

I swallowed. *Four?*

Lomeli rubbed his temples. "Fun fact? She really believes she's some kind of 'Angel of Mercy.' Turns out, her real name is Azriel—named after the Angel of Death in Jewish mysticism. Her family in Colombia was deeply spiritual, but both her parents died agonizing, painful deaths when she was just eight. Cancer. Six months apart. After that, she was sent to live with her father's sister, a strict woman in California who changed her name to April to make her more 'American.'"

I was distracted—my unanswered question still clawing for air.

"Four?" I asked. "Who were they? Who were the four she admitted to killing?"

Lomeli's expression stayed unreadable. "V, what you really want to know is if April killed your mom. Right?"

I swallowed hard and gave a small, almost imperceptible nod.

"I figured you'd ask." He reached for a folder on his desk, flipping it open. "I had someone pull her medical records." He paused, then said gently, "She wasn't murdered, V. At least, not by a person. She really did die from end-stage cancer."

The words hit harder than I expected. I stared at the floor.

"So I did all that for … nothing?" My voice came out quiet.

Lomeli sighed. "V, you helped put two killers behind bars. You saved lives. A lot of them. Don't call that nothing."

I shifted uneasily, unable to meet his eyes.

His voice softened. "And your mom? She hung on as long as she could."

Something in my throat tightened. I blinked fast, swallowing hard to keep the tears from breaking free. But there was still one more thing I had to know.

"What about the others?" I asked. "The other victims?"

"You mean the ones Langley tried to pin on April? She had no clue. Nearly fell apart when she found what he did."

I exhaled slowly. Somehow, that felt almost worse. April was guilty—but she'd been played too.

She wasn't innocent. Not even close. But Langley had moved her like a chess piece, setting her exactly where he needed, and she never saw it coming.

Lomeli watched me carefully. "So, is this the part where you finally let it go?"

I WASN'T sure why I went. Maybe I just needed to see her one last time.

The county jail smelled like bleach and stale air, the kind of place where time crawled, where everything felt stripped down and hollow. A guard led me through the maze of steel doors and linoleum floors until we reached the interview room.

April sat on the other side of the glass.

She looked smaller than I remembered. Paler. Hollowed out.

Gone was the bright-eyed hospice nurse who had sat in my living room two months ago, promising care and comfort, speaking in soft reassurances. That woman had been a lie. This one—this woman in the orange jumpsuit, hands cuffed loosely in her lap—was the truth. And the truth looked defeated.

She lifted her head when she saw me. Her eyes sharpened. "You got what you wanted," she murmured.

I didn't flinch. "Did I?"

April exhaled, shaking her head. "I never wanted to hurt anyone, V. Not like him."

I clenched my fists under the table. "You still did."

Her gaze dropped. Her fingers twisted together in her lap, pale against the rough fabric of her uniform. "I know."

Silence. The kind that stretches, that fills the space with things neither of us wanted to say.

Then I broke the silence, my voice soft and quiet. "You really didn't know? About Langley?"

April swallowed hard. "No," she whispered. "I swear, I had no idea. But when I found out—when I realized he'd been using me to cover his own kills—" She let out a shaky, bitter laugh. "You think I'm a monster, don't you?" Her eyes flicked back up to mine. "Langley is the real monster."

I didn't disagree. But that didn't excuse her. It didn't bring anyone back.

I stood up, the chair scraping against the floor.

April's fingers twitched.

"Do you think I deserve to be here?" she asked.

I didn't hesitate. "Yes."

Her breath caught. Just for a second.

Then I turned and walked away.

THE BULLETIN BOARD was the last thing to go. I stood in front of it, staring at the tangled web of red string and sticky notes that had consumed my life. Pinned at the center, April's photo still smiled back at me—serene, untouched. Almost like she had won.

But she hadn't. And it didn't feel as heavy anymore. This wasn't her story anymore. It was mine.

I reached up and pulled the photo down first. Then the strings. Then the notes. One by one, I dismantled the obsession, the late nights, the desperate need for answers. Until the board was bare.

Everything went into a box—the files, the notebooks, even the funeral lilies I'd pressed into my journal. A record of everything I had lost. Everything I had found.

I sealed the box with tape, pressing the label flat against the cardboard. A single word. DONE. I carried it downstairs to the garage.

Dad was at the stove when I walked in, flipping pancakes. The smell of butter and syrup wrapped around me, warm and familiar. Scotty sat at the table, humming to himself as he colored a worksheet.

"Hey, kiddo."

I stopped mid-step, turning toward him. "Kiddo? Wow, Dad, haven't heard that in years."

Dad smirked. "You don't like it?" He flipped a pancake, raising an eyebrow. "Perhaps I should say, 'Morning, detective,' instead?"

I shook my head, smiling. "Not anymore."

Dad set the spatula down. "What do you mean?"

I slid into a chair, running my fingers over the grain of the wooden table. "I mean I'm done. No more cases. No more investigations. It's over."

Dad leaned against the counter, arms crossed. "You sure about that? I thought you loved playing teen detective."

"I did, sort of," I admitted. I glanced at Scotty, who was still humming, still coloring, blissfully unaware of how much had changed. "But I think, I need to figure out how to be me for a while."

Dad watched me for a beat, then smiled. "You've always been you, V. Even when you were chasing bad guys and solving mysteries. But if you're ready for something new, I'm proud of you."

I exhaled, feeling lighter. "Thanks." Then, after a pause, "Oh, and, Dad?"

"Yeah?"

"Call me Violet. I'm retiring V, too."

Dad's smile widened. "Violet, huh?" He flipped the last pancake onto a plate and slid it in front of me. "Well then, Violet, eat up. You've got a whole life ahead of you."

I picked up the fork, the weight in my chest finally—finally—gone.

46

ONE LAST MEETING

"Grief never ends... but it changes. It's a passage, not a place to stay.
Grief is not a sign of weakness, nor a lack of faith...
It is the price of love."
–Anonymous

We'd met every Tuesday for six weeks. This was my last session at Waves of Hope. Zuri sat across from me, twisting a piece of yarn into small knots. Beside her, Caitlyn spoke about how hard this week had been—how her aunt was still riding her case about getting a job.

I listened. Sort of. I tried to.

The words floated around me, but my thoughts kept drifting —to everything that had led me here. The weight I'd carried. The weight I was finally starting to set down.

Then it was my turn.

I hesitated, staring down at my hands, the grooves in my

palms, the half-moon indents from where my nails had pressed too hard.

"I guess I'm learning how to let go," I said finally. My voice sounded steady, but it felt like a leap off a cliff. "Of my mom, of all the stuff I've been carrying since she died." I exhaled slowly, forcing the words into the open. "I've spent so much time trying to fix things, trying to make sense of it all. But some things can't be fixed. Sometimes all you can do is move forward."

Zuri pressed her lips together, and when she looked at me, her eyes were warm, understanding. "That's brave, V."

"Thanks. And please, call me Violet. It's the name my mom gave me, and I like it."

"Sure thing, Violet," Zuri said, her smile soft.

"But moving forward doesn't mean forgetting," Aiden said quietly.

I met his gaze.

He shrugged. "I used to think if I stopped hurting, it meant I stopped caring. Like if I wasn't sad all the time, I was letting my mom slip away. But I think . . ." He rubbed a hand over his jaw. "I think they stay with us, even when we start to heal."

His words settled deep.

I thought of my mom. Her corny jokes, her warm hugs, her voice in my head, reminding me to enjoy the sunshine.

She wasn't slipping away. She was with me.

I nodded, my throat thick. "Yeah, I think so, too."

Kal smiled. "Grief isn't about getting over it. It's about learning how to carry it differently."

She glanced around the circle. "And none of you have to carry it alone."

I took a deep breath and took the time to look at everyone in the circle, really look at them. This group had been good for me. Perhaps Dr. Sykes knew what she was doing, after all.

I sat on my bed, Lucky curled up against my side, his warm weight pressing into me with every slow breath he took. Outside, the late afternoon light slanted through my window, painting golden streaks across my floor.

My laptop balanced on my thighs, open to a college application website. A stack of brochures sat beside me—the same ones Dad had placed on the kitchen counter over a month ago. The ones I'd ignored.

Until now.

An open application stared back at me from the screen, the blank spaces daring me to start. A blinking cursor at the ready.

For weeks, I'd pushed this moment away. College. The future. The idea of moving forward when everything had felt stuck.

But now? Now, the future didn't feel so scary anymore.

I let out a slow breath and placed my hands on the keyboard. The keys clicked softly as I began filling in the form.

Name: Violet Jiménez

Date of Birth: June 24, 2001

Intended Major:

I hesitated, my fingers hovering over the keys.

Then I typed: Undecided.

And for the first time in a long time, undecided didn't feel like something to be afraid of.

It felt like possibility.

47

SCATTERED ASHES

*"Grief is the last act of love we can give to those we loved.
Where there is deep grief, there was great love."*
–Anonymous

Two months later.

The sun dipped below the horizon, casting a warm, golden glow across the vast stretch of black sand on the big island of Hawaii. I stood at the water's edge, my toes sinking into the soft, volcanic sand, the gentle waves lapping at the shore, creating a rhythmic, soothing sound. In my arms, I cradled a small wooden box adorned with intricate Hawaiian patterns—the box that now held Mom's ashes.

I clutched it close to my chest, feeling its weight, not just physically but in the way it pulled at my heart. I knew this moment was coming, but now that it was here, it felt heavier than I ever imagined. It was time to say goodbye.

Dad stood beside me, his face lined with the quiet sadness he never let show. He wasn't one for big gestures or long speeches, but I could feel the depth of his grief in the way his hand rested on my shoulder, firm but gentle. On the other side, Scotty held on to my waist, as if letting go of me might mean losing something else. I gave him a reassuring smile that we'd get through this together.

The breeze carried the scent of saltwater and plumeria blossoms, blending with the fading warmth of the day. It felt almost sacred, this place. Mom had always said Hawaii was where she felt most at peace, like the island itself held some kind of magic for her. And now, we were here to leave a part of her behind, to let her become a part of the place she loved so much.

I took a deep breath, feeling the gravity of the moment press down on me. The words I had prepared felt stuck in my throat, but I swallowed the knot and forced myself to speak, my voice quiet but steady. "Mom always loved this place. Hawaii was her sanctuary, her happy place. She told me stories about the adventures she had here. It always felt like this island was where she truly belonged."

Dad remained silent, his gaze fixed on the ocean. I could feel Scotty shifting next to me, uncertain, maybe not fully understanding, but he didn't say a word.

With trembling hands, I slowly opened the wooden box. The ashes inside were lighter than I expected, almost soft, and I scooped a small portion into my palm. My hand hovered over the jet-black sand for a moment before I let the ashes fall. They shimmered slightly in the fading light, settling into a delicate mound on the dark ground.

I cleared my throat, my voice catching as I whispered, "Mom, you may be gone, but your spirit will always be a part of this place. You'll dance with the waves, whisper in the wind, and feel the warmth of the sun. We love you to the stars and infinity—"

"Forever," Scotty finished, leaning into me.

I gave his shoulder a tight squeeze and added, "And we'll carry you with us, always."

I handed Scotty the box, and with Dad's gentle guidance, he poured a small handful of Mom's ashes onto the sand, his eyes wide but calm. He didn't speak, but I could see the quiet acceptance in his expression, even if he didn't fully understand what was happening.

Dad took his turn last. He didn't say anything. He took the box from Scotty, scooped up a handful of ashes, and let them fall silently onto the sand. His shoulders slumped slightly, as though he were carrying the weight of everything he hadn't said, everything he'd held inside. But then, after a long moment, he straightened, exhaling a deep breath as if something had finally been released.

We stood there together, the three of us, watching as the last of Mom's ashes became one with the sand, the ocean, the island. The sky had turned a deep indigo, and the stars began to peek out, one by one, their faint glow mirrored by the gentle waves.

For a while, none of us spoke. We just stood there, staring at the Pacific, its vastness stretching out in front of us, endless and eternal. It felt right, somehow—like Mom wasn't really gone, just somewhere else, part of something bigger.

Eventually, we sat down on the sand, our backs to the ocean. Scotty rested his head on my shoulder, and I wrapped an arm around him, holding him close. Dad sat beside us, his knees drawn up, staring at the horizon where the sun had set. We didn't need to say anything. There was nothing left to say.

As the stars fully emerged, twinkling in the clear Hawaiian sky, I found myself smiling—a small, quiet smile. Mom would've loved this moment. The simplicity of it. The peace. The connection between us, between the land and the sea, and everything in between.

She was here. She would always be here.

In the wind, in the waves, in the warmth of the sun and the cool night air—Mom had become part of the island she loved. And somehow, knowing that made everything feel a little more bearable.

We sat there in silence for a long time, the three of us, bound together by loss, by love, and by the memory of the woman we'd just laid to rest. I glanced over at Dad, his face softer than I'd seen in months, and at Scotty, his eyes wide with wonder as he gazed up at the stars.

48

FOREVER STARS

"Your grief is your own. No one else's will ever look the same. If anyone tells you how to grieve, trust you know better. Take as long as you need. There's a hole in your heart for the love you lost—and not everyone will understand that, because not everyone has known a love so profound. May you feel safe. May you find moments of peace."
–Tasche Laine

It was our last night in Hawaii. We'd spent Christmas here. We'd said bye to Mom here. We'd found peace here. It was a vacation with a purpose, and our first family vacation without Mom—but also, with her.

In the quiet stillness, Scotty and I sat side by side on the same beach where we had laid Mom to rest merely four days earlier. The gentle breeze played with our hair, and the scent of salt and sea filled the air, familiar and comforting. I looked up, my gaze drawn to the vast, twinkling sky—a sea of stars stretching endlessly above us. This was our moment, the one we had been waiting for. The moment when we could finally say goodbye.

I reached for Scotty's hand, squeezing it gently. His small

fingers curled around mine, holding on tight. When I glanced down, I saw his wide eyes reflecting the stars, a mix of wonder and sadness swirling in them. I gave him a soft smile, one that I hoped would tell him we were in this together, that no matter how hard it was, we would make it through.

"Mom's up there, right?" Scotty asked, his small voice barely above a whisper.

I swallowed hard, feeling the familiar ache of loss tightening in my chest, but I smiled for him. "Yes, Scotty. Mom's up there. She's one of the forever stars now, shining down on us. She's always with us, even if we can't see her. She's up there with Thunderbird."

Scotty shifted uneasily and whispered, "Violet, you know Thunderbird's not real, right?"

Speechless, I gazed at him, wondering when he'd figured it out about the bedtime story, the legend Mom used to tell him over and over since he was five. Thunderbird had been so real to him.

"It's okay, Violet. I had a good talk with Mom about it last summer. I used to believe he was real, but I'm not a little kid anymore. I just kept going along with it for you."

I chuckled at this and teased, "Nope, you're not a little kid anymore, squirt."

"Hey!"

"Gotcha." I winked, then sighed, knowing both of us had to grow up sooner than we'd wanted.

We lay back on the soft, cool sand, our hands still clasped, eyes fixed on the sky above. The stars twinkled and shimmered, each one a reminder of something bigger than us, something eternal. I traced the constellations with my finger, the same way Mom used to do, telling Scotty stories about the adventures she must be having up there, soaring among the stars. Somehow, it made the weight of her absence a little lighter. It was as if we could still feel her presence, watching over us.

Time passed slowly, the night deepening as we whispered our final goodbyes. I told Mom how much I loved her, how grateful I was for everything she'd done for us. Scotty, too, murmured his own words, his voice soft but steady. The ocean breeze carried our voices into the night, as though the universe itself was listening, embracing every word. I closed my eyes for a moment, and for the first time in a long while, I felt peace—not just for me, but for her, too.

As the sky began to lighten, the first rays of dawn creeping over the horizon, I sat up. Scotty followed, and we shared a glance that said more than words ever could. We had found our closure. We had found each other. And somehow, through all the grief and the tears, we had found strength.

We stood, brushing the sand from our clothes. I looked back one last time at the ocean, the waves lapping gently against the shore. Then I turned to Scotty, and together, we faced forward—toward the future, toward whatever came next.

The sun's warm light washed over us, casting long shadows behind us as we walked, hand in hand. And in that moment, I knew. I knew that Mom's love would always guide us, no matter where life took us. She was a part of us now, her light forever burning in our hearts.

The stars would fade with the dawn, but her memory, her love—that would remain, like the stars themselves, shining brightly in the dark, watching over us in our own sea of forever stars.

Dear Reader,

Thank you for being part of V's story.

It's hard to put into words how much it means to know you've walked alongside her—through the mysteries, the heartbreak, and the quiet moments of hope. Writing these books has been a journey filled with love, loss, and healing, and I'm so grateful to have shared it with you.

Stories like V's aren't always easy to tell, but they remind us that even in the darkest moments, we're never truly alone. I hope Violet's story brought you comfort, connection, or even just the feeling that someone understands.

If V's journey meant something to you, I'd be so grateful if you'd take a moment to leave a review on Goodreads or your favorite book review site. Your words help other readers discover this story, and they mean the world to authors like me.

If you'd like to stay in touch and hear what's next for me, and for the stories still to come—I'd love to invite you to join my newsletter. It's where I share updates, little extras, and personal notes along the way.

You can sign up here: taschelaine.com

For a personalized, signed copy of any of my books, visit our Lil Book Shop at lilpeterbooks.com.

Thank you for reading, for caring, and for being part of this journey.

With love and gratitude,

ACKNOWLEDGMENTS

Every book I write is a team effort, and *Forever Stars* wouldn't be what it is without the incredible people who helped bring it to life.

First, my deepest thanks to my amazing editor, Allison Rose Lutz at Wandering Words Media, for your sharp eye, thoughtful insights, and endless patience. Your guidance has made this story stronger in every way.

To my Beta readers—thank you for your honesty, encouragement, and for walking beside me (and V) through every twist and turn. Your feedback helped shape this story into something I'm proud to share.

To my mom, Kim Damato—thank you for always being my first reader, my sounding board, and my biggest cheerleader. Your love and support mean everything.

A special thank you to the talented team at **100 Covers** for designing book covers that perfectly capture the heart and mystery of this series. Your artistry brings these stories to life before a single word is read.

And most of all, thank you to my readers—for your curiosity, your kindness, and your love of story. Whether you've been here since the beginning or just found V's journey, I'm so grateful to have you along for the ride.

ALSO BY TASCHE LAINE

CLOSURE: Based On A True Story

CHAMELEON

CHRONICLES OF V

GLASS STARS

BRIGHT STARS

BROKEN STARS

FOREVER STARS

CHILDREN'S SERIES

Get Up, Lil Peter. Get Up!

You Can't Quit, Lil Peter, You Just Can't

Teamwork, Lil Peter, It Works

Pick Me, Lil Peter, Pick Me

Small Things, Lil Peter, Make A Big Difference

Smile Lil Peter, It's A Gift

Your Word, Lil Peter, Is Your Word

Be True, Lil Peter, Be You

Hold On, Lil Peter, Or Let It Go

What If, Lil Peter, What If?

ABOUT THE AUTHOR

Tasche Laine is a storyteller at heart, weaving tales across genres for readers of all ages. From her award-winning novels *Closure* and *Chameleon*, to the heartfelt mysteries of her young adult series, *Chronicles of V*, and the charming adventures of *Lil Peter*, co-written with her husband, Peter Valdez, Tasche's writing is as versatile as it is captivating.

With a background in journalism, teaching, and editing, Tasche brings a keen eye and a compassionate touch to every story she tells. Now happily nestled in the Pacific Northwest with her husband and their two mischievous pups, Story and Page, she draws inspiration from misty mornings and towering trees.

Want to know what she's writing next? Visit taschelaine.com to stay connected.

tiktok.com/@taschelaine

instagram.com/tasches

facebook.com/TascheLaine

goodreads.com/tasche_laine

amazon.com/author/taschelaine

bookbub.com/authors/tasche-laine